Giveadamn Brown

GIVEADAMN BROWN

ROBERT DEANE PHARR

This edition first published in 1997 by
Payback Press, an imprint of Canongate Books Ltd,
14 High Street, Edinburgh EH1 1TE

British Library Cataloguing-in-Publication Data

A catalogue record for this book is available upon request
from the British Library

ISBN 0 86241 691 4

Typeset in Minion and Serif Modular by
Palimpsest Book Production Limited,
Polmont, Stirlingshire
Print and bound in Scotland by
Caledonian International Book Manufacturing, Bishopbriggs

Introduction

For some novelists, success almost feels like a preordained right. Get yourself a liberal arts degree, go to a graduate writing program. Wham, you have agents beating down your door, bam, now the publishers are in a feeding frenzy. Goodbye school loans, hello best-seller lists. Okay, so maybe it isn't quite that easy, but when you consider the travails of one Robert Deane Pharr, it sure feels that way.

The son of a minister father and a school-teacher mother, Robert Deane Pharr was born in Richmond, Virginia, in 1916. Soon after graduating from Virginia Union College in 1937, Pharr set course on a career that would occupy his entire adult life. For twenty-two years, he traveled along the eastern seaboard, waiting tables at pricey resort hotels and exclusive private clubs.

It was a grueling, grinding existence, but literature helped see him through it. A voracious reader, Pharr read Tom Swift, Dick Prescott, and Horatio Alger as an adolescent, of which he would later remark: 'It was the worst reading regime a young black child could have. It totally unprepared me for the life I had to live.' It was only upon reading Sinclair Lewis' *Babbitt* that Pharr found a writer to whom he could relate. 'By the time I was seventeen, I had already made up my mind to do as Mr. Lewis had done, only I would let white people look at the black man as he lives when the white man isn't looking or listening.'

It wouldn't be until Pharr turned fifty-three that the world would enjoy the fruits of his labors. While working at the Columbia University faculty club, Pharr summoned up the courage to ask an English professor to read a 750-page manuscript on which he'd been working. The professor did, and was totally blown away. Released by Doubleday in 1969, *The Book of Numbers* was a great success.

Detailing the bloody rise of a small-town gambling kingpin, *The Book of Numbers* raised an important issue: How does a smart and ambitious black man achieve the American dream when all options are foreclosed to him? But sociological questions alone aren't what make this work resonate. Characteristic of all of Pharr's best writings, *The Book of Numbers* simmers with wicked irony and crackles with twisted humor.

A play-it-safe-writer would've gone for the easy score when dreaming up a follow-up. Pharr's next novel was *S.R.O.*, a 600-page monster which follows the lives of various drunks, junkies, and prostitutes, all stuck in a flea-bitten Harlem single-room occupancy hotel. 'His description of narrator Sid Bailey's alcoholic fantasies,' *New York Times* book reviewer Jan Carew wrote, 'is so vivid that one is almost forced to look away from the page to avoid the smell of his putrid breath and the bite of his terror.' While some (like your editors) view this as a glowing recommendation, the public didn't bite, and the work quickly faded into the past.

Still, Pharr refused to turn away from the dark side of life, and his next two novels, *The Welfare Bitch* and *The Soul Murder Case* fared even worse. The latter, a paperback original, quickly fell out of print; the former might as well never have been released. Its title alone ensured it would never make it onto library shelves; its grim story scared off all but Pharr's most diehard fans.

Finally, we come to a different animal altogether, *Giveadamn Brown*. Published in 1978, the serio-comic adventure tells the seemingly familiar story of a young southern boy who travels up to Harlem, and quickly becomes the kingpin of a powerful drug empire. Been there, done it? You haven't. Skewed and surreal as a funhouse mirror, reading *Giveadamn Brown* is like reading Donald Goines on acid.

With that little goodbye kiss, Pharr quietly retreated to upstate New York where he died eleven years later.

Success must have been sweet after fifty-three years of struggle, but Pharr wasn't so intoxicated by it that he caved into the pressures of the game. For that reason alone, you gotta give him his respect. But the legacy of this ultimate iconoclast lies not just in his unwavering biography, but in his renegade fiction, which given half a chance, will finally be seen for the masterpieces they always were.

Marc Gerald and Samuel Blumenfeld

1

Perhaps it's best to explain the man's name. He was christened Lawrence Brown. But the day Lawrence made eighteen, he got drunk and was arrested. The next morning the judge droned, 'Five days.'

'I don't give a damn,' Lawrence laughed.

'Well, let's make it ten and see if you do.'

'I still don't give a damn.'

After the judge got up to fifteen and Lawrence still didn't give a damn, the judge decided the boy hadn't sobered up. Since the judge secretly and hopelessly lusted for Lawrence's sixteen-year-old cousin who cleaned his law office, the man sighed and motioned for the sheriff to take the boy back to his cell until he *was* sober.

But from that day on, Lawrence Brown became a famous man in the town of Wiggins, Florida. At first all the townspeople – black, that is – called him I-Don't-Give-A-Damn Brown. Then it was shortened to Giveadamn. Few people called him anything else as long as he lived.

His disposition rode up with him to New York. When he opened his tiny fix-it shop on Lenox Avenue in Harlem and was immediately robbed into financial disaster, he said cheerfully, 'I don't give a damn.'

He knew how to wait on tables. His father was the headwaiter in the only hotel in Wiggins ... as well as being a preacher. Giveadamn could always find a job, so he went out to Sheepshead Bay to the great Lundy's Restaurant and got himself hired as a waiter. He labored and prospered enough to reopen his shop, and this time named it Brown's Shop of the Second Coming, because he said he gave new life to long-dead appliances.

Giveadamn was almost six feet tall but weighed only one hundred and fifty pounds. He was more the color of asbestos than just plain black. His mouth was an open book. His lips were much too large to be puckered or sucked in. There was nothing to do but let them hang natural, like the truth.

He had been in New York a little over a year when he sat on a bench one morning in a neighborhood playground in Harlem and watched twelve Mercedes and Lincoln Continentals and Jaguars pull up and park. He saw a black teen-age boy emerge from each one and head out on the playground's basketball court. There he watched them lay down bets on the shots they tossed up to the basket from the foul line. The odds ranged anywhere from five-to-one to eight-to-one.

He could see they weren't betting with dimes and quarters. He thought, those could even be ten-dollar bills changing hands, and he went away from the playground in wonder. His new girl friend, Margo, who had grown up wild on the streets of Harlem, was no help when he told her what he'd seen, not any help in the kind of way he wanted.

'They're the kids,' Margo said. 'The kids the pushers began to use a few years ago. You know. Things got real tough back there for a time. The fuzz was shaking down every man and woman who walked along Eighth Avenue and everywhere else. So the smart pushers started using seven-, eight-, nine-year-old boys to deliver. They were good. They began to let the kids sell.

'Shit, Giveadamn. Those kids became couriers for the big boys. Like the cops were looking for some real smooth dude in a big shiny hog to be making the five- and six-kilo deliveries. But it was children on bicycles making them million-dollar connections. More likely they was shooting hundred-dollar baskets.'

'Margo, those boys are all over sixteen. You mean they been dealing in heroin in one way or another for as much as eight years?'

She nodded. 'A lot got hooked. A lot died. But the cool ones got so much money and connections now you can't guess them at all.' She paused and grew solemn, righteous. 'But they need money! You realize how much money a fourteen-year-old black boy got to pay some adult to go downtown and buy him a ten-, twelve-thousand-dollar automobile! Thousands! How much you think them kids have to spread around before they can get themselves a boss apartment down on the East Side?'

Giveadamn swore he would never return to watch those children again, but he did, seven more times, seven days running.

The first time he'd seen it he hadn't believed it. Nothing about it made sense. Every morning Giveadamn returned to the scene of the impossible to watch the impossible. As always, it was a little after six o'clock. All the muggers had made their pocket money and were off the scene. It was the safest time of day in Harlem, the police all drunk by then, sleeping it off somewhere until time to go in and check out. Anyone could step into the middle of the street and shoot around for fifteen minutes with a machine gun, and nobody would even know it, much less care.

Sometimes he'd watch as many as twenty boys. They always came singly on their own wheels. Always in the big, new, gleaming cars. They double-parked them on the street and got out and walked onto the basketball court. They were like children with too much money, too worldly to spend it on candy or skateboards. Smart enough to know they had too much money, but not smart enough to know what to do with it. Nobody, Giveadamn decided, is that smart.

But these boys were not arrogant. They were thoughtful if not kind; if one of them stumbled and fell, another rushed over to the fallen boy with real concern. And they were soft-spoken. Not profane, at least not unduly so. Especially when they missed a basket.

As he watched, he realized he longed for something missing in his own life, perhaps being a winner, yet remaining quiet and soft-spoken and decent to everyone around him. With a few thousand dollars in his pocket, he might just do the same thing these kids did every morning soon after sunrise. But he'd never had more money than he needed, so he didn't know what he'd do.

On the sixth morning he sat watching as the last of the

youths drove up and parked. The boy got out, went to the trunk of his long white Continental and got out basketball shoes and a basketball. After putting on his sneakers, he dropped his dress shoes in the trunk and made sure it was locked.

The boy then dribbled the ball all the way across the court to where the others were waiting. Once at the foul line, he began practising free throws.

'Okay,' he said, 'are we all ready?'

Giveadamn could hear him clearly.

'You ready? I got my eye. Who's in on this first one?'

All of the boys threw bills down on a pile and the boy at the foul line went over, knelt, and from a roll of bills in his pocket covered all their bets. Only one of the boys didn't bet. He said, 'Junior, you're warmed up, right? Since you already got your eye, how about betting me three?'

The boy called Junior smiled. It was a very pleasant smile. He might have been the best-looking of all the boys, but it was a pretty close thing to judge. 'You put them down. I'll cover them.' It was done.

He went back to the foul line, studied the basket and from a one-handed push, the ball arced up and swished through the net.

The group jeered, groaned and applauded in a kind of chorus. Junior picked up the money. And then it was the next boy's turn to stand at the foul line.

The next morning an older boy, a young man of Giveadamn's age, joined them and Giveadamn could sense bad vibrations. Nothing evident. It was more that the thing was no longer just a game.

When the time came for the newcomer to shoot, he didn't want money left on the ground and didn't want any of them to hold it. He'd pay up later, he said. The kids all seemed to start walking in circles, then one of them, Junior, went over to Giveadamn and asked would he hold the money. Giveadamn took it. It was no big thing. If the shooter made his shot, he took all. If he didn't, Giveadamn knew these kids well enough by now to know they'd divide their winnings fairly.

It was as the boys walked away and back onto the court that Giveadamn glanced down at the money in his hand. He began to tremble. They were all old one-thousand-dollar bills. He thought about dropping the money and hauling ass, but he wasn't that good a runner. So he sat and trembled while the new boy on the court put six straight shots through the basket.

Then he walked over to Giveadamn, took the money from his hand, counted it carefully and shoved one of the bills into Giveadamn's shirt pocket. 'Buy yourself a drink,' he said.

Before noon, Giveadamn, riding a hunch, bought himself one thousand dollars' worth of lottery tickets. He had the feeling it was another big day in his life, like the day he'd earned his nickname and made every man, woman and child in Wiggins an admirer and friend.

Margo thought differently. She smiled brokenly. 'So you think you seen money used like toilet paper. Listen, you ever hear of the C.C. Riders? You ever hear of the Cocaine Club? Well, it's all the same dudes. And what dudes! They took the shabbiest tenement in 115th Street and gutted it. I mean they tore out everything except the dirty old stinking front of the building, and inside they got the finest club money can buy.

'It costs ten thousand to join. The dues is maybe a thousand a month, and for your one lousy grand all you get is a key to the front door. And one hell of a wake and funeral when you get wasted.' She paused. 'Or maybe a nice little taste every week . . . if you go to prison.'

'I don't believe it,' Giveadamn said softly. 'I don't want to believe no more about this so-called ghetto called Harlem.'

'Maybe you shouldn't. Like the truth is that the C.C. Riders are only punks for real. They're dealers. But they are only the middlemen. Like the last guys the narco goes through before it hits the street. They're big, but nothing like the Doll Baby or Studs Thompson or Jimmy Adams.

'But the C.C. Riders are freaky studs for power. They're mean as hell. Crazy, too. They mostly ride motorcycles. Like one time one got killed on his bike. The crazy mother-fuckers tried to bury his motorcycle with him, and when the under-taker started a hassle they kicked the living shit outa him and threw him in the hole on top of the coffin. It was damned near a riot out there on Staten Island. The Cocaine Club is big, rich and crazy as well, Giveadamn. You want to know how crazy this world can get, you go join 'em. After all, you got a hundred grand coming from them tickets you bought . . . you hope.'

She paused and her lips curled even more. 'I forgot,' she said apologetically, 'you can't join. Everybody who's eligible has first got to do time in Attica.'

It took Margo a while to forgive Giveadamn for putting all that money on a bunch of lottery tickets, as long as it took to learn two of his tickets were going to be in the final drawing. Maybe, she decided, he was a walking miracle.

We all hear stories of the gigantic bail set for heroin bigshots. A half million dollars is the usual, not the unusual bail, for those big black boys – sums no judge would ever think of setting for the white Mafia. But black pushers raise enormous amounts of cash, and then the D.A.s and the judges refuse to accept it. They refuse on the grounds they don't know where the cash came from and maybe it's illegal gains – from somebody like the legendary Harry Brown. Such bills (produced as if Harry Brown stamped them out himself) come from the depths of Harlem's hell.

Dope is a dream of wealth, and sometimes the only dream for the black ghetto youth. To set up a great dope empire is a dream, the very same kind of dream that Wall Street and the exploits of Robert Vesco offer to slum (and upper-class, too) white boys. All Harlem aspired to Harry Brown's empire – though his empire was only a figment of their own imaginations. But people are fighting and dying for dreams every day all over Harlem, all the time.

The black man's life in white America is only a dream, and this is the story of some of those black dreamers. It is the story of one Giveadamn Brown, the all-but-forgotten nephew – some say son – of Harry Brown. Giveadamn, as he knew, was born to become a legend – though he was more or less an empty-headed fellow in spite of the high regard he had for his own intellect. He had come up alone from that small town in the South. He came riding a bus into a tiny nation called Harlem, which was addicted to the quest for the finest golden fleece the world shall ever know, and he lived a clean life to the very end, an easygoing young man who feared God and hated violence.

It's also the story of Studs and Doll Baby, both crazy. Blood crazy. And Sonny Roberts. And Margo. And Connie, the hawk. And a lot of others who, for a while, had the golden fleece in their hands and could almost swear it was real.

Giveadamn got out of the bed, stretched and yawned. Then he gazed with a kind but jaundiced eye at the rackety little refrigerator crowded into one corner next to the hotel's excuse for a washbowl. He had told the manager he would not want the box. It was too small and too damned noisy. But he had finally come to like the manic little contraption. And if he was honest about it, the darned thing was a lot less noisy than the million and one crickets that sounded off all around Wiggins, Florida.

He put on his bathrobe and began to gather his shaving stuff and toothbrush. The sink in the room would never give up any of its water at this time of the morning. But he didn't give a damn about that now, not this morning. He even began to whistle as he lathered his face, then he remembered Margo and glanced back at the bed.

Foxy Cool Momma was awake, sitting upright and solemnly staring at him. Like she always did. He grinned at her. His lips in that dark and strictly unhandsome face were boundless. They really seemed everywhere at once. But when he smiled, everyone immediately knew just how wonderfully kind Giveadamn Brown really was.

Nobody disliked Giveadamn. It was his kindness and the thoughts behind his ugly face that counted. Like he was ugly ... with a weird sense of humor, but none of this was a burden on anyone. When the man grinned, you did not notice his ugliness, or suffer it or even have to make believe you did not see it.

'Foxy Cool Momma,' he said, and went into a country preacher stance and tone, 'you have never spent the night here, you haven't sat in bed the next morning and looked at me like you don't know whether to bite me or sell me as I is to the devil in hell.'

Foxy remained silent and deadpan. She seldom smiled. A serious little doll, but a perfect little doll just the same.

Giveadamn got down in a preacher crouch and waddled toward her, one finger upraised in holy adjuration. 'Mene, Mene, Tekel Upharsin!' he intoned.

Foxy's sherry-brown features shifted from solemnity to rage. 'What the hell you talking now?'

Giveadamn stood up. 'In my native tongue, that means somebody been weighed in the balance and found wanting. So after a couple of months I got the right to ask why. Why? I ain't mad. I just wants to know why you sits there in my best shirt with nothing on underneath and looks at me so stern.'

She shook her head. 'The man sleeps. Gawd! Can he sleep! And he grins all over the place like nothin's happening. Like nothin's ever happening. He's crazy.'

'A crazy nigger is the most entertaining kind of nigger.' He went to the bed and brushed back her unbuttoned shirt to kiss her tiny nipples.

For a moment Foxy let him. Then she slowly moved his soapy cheek away with two of her fingers. Getting out of bed, she started to rummage in the top drawer of his dresser.

Giveadamn continued shaving. After a while he said, 'I bought none, so there is none.'

'There better be.'

It was funny how she said it. Not a threat. Not really. She had only to forbid the ocean to move and it would stand still.

As he finished shaving, she found what she was looking for, a small bottle of terpin hydrate and codeine. She opened the bottle and began to sip at it. She moved one hand behind her back and waved it at him. A cute and feminine gesture of distress; also an imperious gesture.

Giveadamn shrugged and sighed. He carefully rehung his towel and went to the refrigerator. He got out the water bottle and poured her a glassful. Then he stood patiently until Foxy finished off the cough medicine and tossed the empty bottle into the trash basket. She took the glass of water, gulped some, then blew out her breath contentedly. 'Wow, I needed that.'

'Like a silver-plated dum-dum bullet in your left breast.'

She snapped her fingers and did a short wicked grind with her hips. 'Babee, you know I am at all times an angel of death. Which makes it very important for you not to ever sell me no new ideas. Dig? Like if I didn't have this crazy thing for you, I would begin right now making you stay home from work, and I would lay you back down in that bed and stone-fuck you to a thousand deaths. Then I could keep me all of your one hundred thousand dollars.' She stopped and stared deadpan. 'You think maybe, then, if I put on some real heavy black clothes and went down to that lottery office, them shlumps might just listen to me whooping and hollering about my poor dead common-law husband and hand over all that fine bread?'

'Foxy, I have not won a hundred thousand dollars . . . yet. I might never win. And I have told you and begged you not to bring it up any more. Whenever anybody has bad luck, it's because they talked it up on themselves.'

She did not bother to hide her exasperation. 'All life is the fun of expecting, Giveadamn. Hell. You know damned well yourself that what you get is not half as much fun as what you expect. Like, you know, the greatest speech in the world is *I Have a Dream.*'

'That's exactly what I'm talking about. Niggers don't seem to be able to remember that Junior ended up with a hole in his head, in the same spot he stored his dream.'

She took a deep breath, the better to express her fury, but she was thinking about what he'd said, and then she nodded. Giveadamn said things like he was some kind of comedian, but he was right most of the time. He was kinky and correct. That was probably why she had this kinky kind of temporary thing for him. She came running every time he called and sometimes stayed for three or four days. Not once had she asked him to pay her; and when a city chick on the hustle don't bother to ask a country boy for her bread, there's got to be some strange shit in the air.

She began to feel mad again. The whole damned business was getting out of hand. She began to pace about. She had a high-stepping gait. More like a prance than a walk.

Giveadamn watched her and figured pretty much what was going on in Margo's head. And if she was mad, the best thing to do was to make her even madder and get her over it. He said softly, 'But if I did get my hands on a hundred grand, I wouldn't spend it like you'd want it. Like if there was a bigtime shrink who could turn you off narco for the rest of your life, I'd turn all that bread over to him without even bothering to count it. Or without bothering asking you about it either.'

She stopped and glared at him with a look that was part love and part hate, all pure. 'I told you in front I been hooked one way or the other since I was fifteen.' She raised one hand and began to count off her fingers. 'Cocaine. I started at the top with king of them all. Then I got demoted to wine. But it was good wine. Not the pee the winos guzzle. Then I stepped back up and went for some grass and even some hash. Then I was suddenly on heroin without being able to remember where or when.

'And if you got any brains and imagination at all, heroin is going to send you to prison. So while I was in the joint, they put me in the kitchen for a while and there I got promptly introduced to nutmeg. And babee, when you run up against nutmeg, you have had it for real. You're crazy hooked when you're on that stuff.'

Giveadamn let her run on just as if he had not heard it all before.

She smiled bitterly. 'Maybe whiteys call whores "hookers" because there's lots of women gotta be hooked on something or else they don't function at all. So don't talk to me about some shrink. You know what I mean. Like I been clean lots of times – from narco. But every time I promptly got myself hooked on something just as crazy. Like one time I was so clean I wouldn't even touch a cigarette, but I was dice crazy.

All I did was roam around looking for a game. In the street, in an alley. Anywhere they'd let me in the game. I lost more weight shooting crap than on any kind of narco. And one time I even got me some religion. Wow!'

Giveadamn grinned. 'Me too. Girl, I come from a gospel-crazy family. My father was a deacon and all of his sisters were sister deaconesses. Hell. My pop used to go over to the jailhouse every Sunday morning at six o'clock sharp and hold a prayer meeting. My father was the original jailhouse rocker. Elvis Presley don't know a damn thing about Jailhouse Rock. But I never got me hooked on it.'

He had just said 'hooked' when they both heard the first of three light raps on the door. When Giveadamn opened the door, the short, slim man who stood outside was about to knock again. He looked like a little Puerto Rican lost in the smallest hotel on the upper West Side. Maybe even in the wrong hotel. And pretty high too.

The man smiled politely and suavely. He was really a handsome little dude. 'I came to get my wife,' he said. He had no Spanish accent.

'Sorry, my man,' Giveadamn said cheerfully, 'you got the wrong room. Don't go knocking at wrong doors for your wife. You just might find her.'

'No. I got the right room.' He was still polite, but his vocal cords sounded tight, as if he had just met up with some dynamite heroin. He pointed into the room. 'Margo there is my woman. I came to get her.'

Giveadamn had only known Margo for the past month and a half and during that time she had only stayed over four times, each time for three or four days. Was this little junkie standing there her pimp?

He turned to see how Margo was reacting. She was sitting on the side of the bed sedately, her face without expression. She could have been watching two strangers.

'To set the record straight,' he said, 'you know him?'

'That's Kiki. And I never married that man in my life. I ain't even seen him in two years. He's high, Giveadamn. Shut the door in his face.'

But Kiki had stepped into the room.

'You're a swell guy, Giveadamn,' he said smoothly. He was smiling with admonition but kindly. 'I just don't want you two to get too sweet. I mean, like say you get hold of this hundred grand, you're going to go for Margo in a big way. And I can't have you wanting to hurt my wife after she takes your bread and leaves you broke. I got to take care of Margo, see? You understand my position?'

Margo was the only person in the world who knew Giveadamn was holding two tickets in the final drawing for the big payoff. But he smiled cheerfully as he said to Margo, 'I guess it's about time you take him home with you.' Then he swiftly turned and cuffed the tiny junkie up the side of his head. He swung hard with the back of his hand, but Kiki tilted his head and shed the blow like so much idle conversation. The next moment a stiletto was in his small hand, and the thing was sticking up to the hilt in Giveadamn's belly.

Giveadamn looked down at the hilt of the knife and tried to convince himself it was really there. The junkie was gone. Margo came off the bed with a shriek and rushed at Giveadamn with a dagger like the one already stuck in his gut. She was coming right at him, her eyes so insane she did not even seem to see. On she came. And he rode a crazy elevator to the floor, wondering all the time how two niggers could do such a dumb thing for one hundred thousand dollars he didn't even have.

But Foxy went by Giveadamn and out the door and she saw Kiki just as he took the steps. She shrieked again and hurled her blade at him.

When she got back to Giveadamn, his eyes were shut, his face placid. Two old black men who lived down the hall came to the door and peered in as she threw back her head and howled. They nodded as if they knew doll-faced little hep chicks like Margo always killed the men they loved and they had no intention of interfering. She had stabbed her man, and it was her problem, not theirs.

Margo got to her feet and went out into the hall to sob into the extension phone for help – and the two old men nodded again.

2

Gracie was now a frowning Buddha. Every freckle on her face oozed condemnation. 'But how could you? How in the world could anyone give Kiki that boy's address?'

Foxy shrugged and then shivered her shoulders in anger. 'When I saw that blade sticking out of Giveadamn, I got this feeling of everything being over. Doom, I guess. Not death. Like death was going to take its damned good time to get around.'

'Shee-it!'

Gracie tried her best to understand. She never would, because Gracie believed all decent women picked out one man to love and made do with him in spite of hell. 'I think God would have made it all right for you and Giveadamn,' she said.

'But I don't want him, Gracie. I don't want any man like him. It's something you can't explain. I'm no good for him. I'm bad luck. Like when Kiki made the scene, all that should have happened was for Giveadamn to have taken one look at him and told me to get my hat and coat. That's all. But Giveadamn almost died. That knife went clear through his pancreas or damned near. And to make it real good – although I know you'll never believe it – I never told Kiki Giveadamn's address. I only told him Giveadamn had my nose open and it wasn't a comfortable feeling. Kiki must have followed me. He could even have seen me on Broadway shopping or something and shadowed me. But you'll never believe that.'

Gracie stared, silent.

The doorbell rang and Gracie sighed and then went to answer. She came back in the living room with a changeling straight out of hell. The Korean hell. He was tall and walked handsome, but Lobo Turner had got half his face blown away in Korea.

The right side of Lobo's face, seen in profile, was so handsome in a fine noble way that he looked like a storybook prince, but his profile from the left was all horror, a mouth twisted and bubbling with white spots, a withered ear and cheek, a slit of an eye.

Margo got up to greet him. 'Lobo. How's my ace boon coon?'

His smile made him more grotesque. 'Fine. Fine, Margo. Just saw you come in here, so I thought I'd drop by and say a word. How's tricks?'

'Not bad considering my man's in the hospital. But he might be coming home any day now.'

'I heard.'

Margo stiffened. 'Heard? Heard what?'

His voice was smooth and pimpish. 'Now, who the hell don't know fine brown Margo Hilliard? Of course, nobody could ever see you going around with that little spic, but that's your business. Out on the turf folks are wondering who it was got the spic jealous enough to try offing a dude, you know how it is.'

'My business is nobody's but Margo's. Dig?'

Lobo nodded, but then said curiously, 'Well, who is the stud? I mean, you ain't ashamed of him. I know damned well you ain't coming like that.'

Foxy Cool Momma cooled it like she was supposed to. 'A country boy, Lobo. Just an innocent country boy. He works. Real square. Gets drunk maybe once a month, but even when he's drunk, he's no big deal. We're just friends. You know me, Lobo. What the hell would I be doing with a country boy who still goes to church on Sunday?'

Lobo was instantly bored. He turned to Gracie. 'How's that sweet kid of yours, Gracie?'

Gracie beamed. 'Toni's getting sweeter every day, Lobo. Looks like sometimes that child can actually scare you. I mean she's so very good. And isn't she pretty?'

'A doll. A perfect doll. I like it when she stops by the house and she and my boy look at TV together.'

'Like sister and brother,' Gracie said firmly, like it better be. But she said no more as she continued to nod her head.

'And the babies?' Lobo asked with a slight tone of derision. But Gracie didn't notice. 'Fine. You want to see 'em?'

'Not today. Not today. I just dropped in to see how you and Margo were doing.'

'I saw Ranger coming out of your house the last time I was by,' Margo said suddenly. 'Everybody talks about Toni, and I love her too. But that boy of yours is getting more like you every day, Lobo.'

'He is that,' Gracie said. 'That little boy is actually pretty, Lobo. And he's no little boy any more. He's seventeen and I see old women stopping him on the street. And you know what that means, Lobo. You're going to have to quarantine that Ranger of yours.'

'He's been schooled,' Lobo said easily. 'I schooled him well from the git go. Up from scratch.'

'He'll never be the player you were, Lobo,' Margo said. 'You had 'em all. I guess you could have been the best if you wanted.'

'Wanted? I was!'

She laughed. 'They were pimps in those days and not players. You hustled, Lobo, but you never laid back and waited for some dizzy 'ho' to bring you your bread.'

Lobo decided if that was the way she wanted to picture it, let her. Margo had never been his type of chick anyhow. From the moment she hit the streets, Margo had been both headstrong and cocky – and a killer. A stone killer, a knife-happy little midget.

It was an apartment house on the East River, famous for its wealthy white tenants. Harry Brown, its only black tenant, owned the building. Harry and Ossie Winbush left the white brick building with the blue canopy that ran to the curb. They walked to Harry's parked Mercedes.

They were impressive-looking men. Harry Brown was perhaps sixty. Ossie Winbush could not have been over thirty-six or -seven, maybe even younger, but neither of the two, since reaching his majority, had ever entered a scene without causing talk.

One look at Ossie and you heard questions like, if Sidney Poitier made it, why hadn't this beautiful black stud? After that, one wondered how mean Ossie was.

There was no doubt about Harry's meanness. You only wondered if he planned to kill you now or later.

Harry had a nose like a crazy cucumber. His skin was fairly light, but he gave the impression he used a black India-ink-base after-shave lotion. His shoulders were gigantic and in the classical V-shape of the ring slugger. He was known to have broken the necks of two men.

Ossie went around the car to the driver's seat. They both got in. When they entered Central Park, Ossie said, 'I'm not going in with you, Harry.'

'That figures.' It was all Harry said.

'I don't like to be around when you put your good left foot in your mouth.'

'The boy is trifling. He has to be. I'm just going to keep my conscience clear.'

Ossie laughed but said nothing.

Harry suddenly straightened up. 'What's that?'

'Huh?'

'In back of us, fool.'

Ossie softly but steadily applied the brakes. The police car rolled nearer and then up beside them. The officer in the seat nearest to Ossie motioned with his hand he would like them to pull over to the side of the roadway.

'I've seen that rookie before,' Harry said.

Ossie pulled over and stopped. He and Harry watched the two cops confer for a moment before the one Harry said he had seen got out of the car. He came over to Harry's side. He tipped his cap. He spoke softly for a few minutes.

'Follow them,' Harry said to Ossie.

The rookie trotted back and got in the squad car. The car pulled away, but without sirens going. It was a brisk pace, though not an eye-catching one.

'Some highjacked shit?' Ossie asked quizzically.

'Better not be. And if there was, I don't think any rookies would be in on it. But the action is getting more exotic every day. I'm beginning to think I won't get to visit that boy today.' As if to right his last doubts, he said vehemently, 'Hell, I don't even know that boy!'

Ossie said nothing. The police led them out of the park to 110th Street and then over to Eighth Avenue. As they rode up Eighth Avenue against one-way traffic, both men noted along their way the deterioration, even the carnage, heroin had caused. They passed the corner of 112th Street and were now in the official heroin center of the world. But all the neighborhood looked like to an inexperienced eye was death and unpaid taxes.

The squad car slowed to a stop in front of a decrepit tenement, like dozens of others in the neighborhood.

'Now, who is silly enough to believe the top commissioner is waiting within?' Ossie murmured.

'Don't worry about it,' Harry said. He nodded at a black detective walking toward them. 'That's Freddy Morris. He's young and not too eager, which means he is not any more greedy than the others. I've never been able to make up my mind about how stupid he is. Nice boy, though.'

'Um.' It was all Ossie intended to say.

It might have been Harry's grim grin that told Freddy to bring it all down in front. 'They've fucked over Francis Williams, Harry.'

Harry exploded a short laugh. 'What the hell are you talking about?' he asked.

'All Francis will say is we got to come up with his stash or we gonna have three cops lynched on TV.'

'Start from the beginning,' Harry said.

'Some men in uniform broke in on Francis uptown and confiscated every gram he was holding. They put him in a car for the ride to the precinct; but all of a sudden they stop and push him out of the police car and tell Francis to get lost. No arrest. See?'

Harry whistled.

'Francis gave us an hour to return those fifteen kilos, and

thirty minutes gone by already. Then he's gonna throw down his statement to Melba Tolliver and while the cameras are turning he's gonna lynch our men.'

Harry reached over, turned the key, and the motor hummed softly. 'So give him back his fifteen kilos.'

'But we don't know who's got them!'

'Well, go find him fifteen kilos. Buy 'em. Think of it this way: Maybe you don't owe Francis, but you do owe your men.'

'It would cost millions!'

'I mean Francis has been *wronged.* You are the criminals, and it just don't sound like Francis to let you guys off so easy.'

'We'll kill him when it's all over,' Freddy said.

Harry's eyes widened.

Freddy made an effort not to whine. 'You're respected, Harry. We know Francis worships you. We figured you could talk to him. Make a deal. Anything . . .'

'You figger to sucker me in on the kill?'

'For God's sake, Harry! We can't have no execution of three cops on TV. What the hell you think this is anyhow?'

'I think it's a damned good show.'

Freddy wiped his face. 'You're talking shit when I sent for brains!' he yelled.

Harry smiled. 'This situation is fraught with danger for New York's Finest. The cops Francis got up there are white, aren't they? Shit! That makes it okay to call in the FBI. But only your little black ass is in charge, as you say.' Harry pointed his finger at Freddy's chest. 'Trouble with niggers is they don't ever want to act like niggers when they get put in a nigger position. However, the main thing I got to know now is, Do you still want me to go talk to that boy?'

'Yes. And whatever Francis wants, you can promise. But about his heroin I just don't know. Make a deal. What you promise the brass will have to agree to . . . for the time being. And you know yourself you can promise that there's never going to be any charges.'

Harry nodded thoughtfully. He could settle this thing for Francis in five minutes, but he didn't think Francis would go for it.

Harry left his car and stood on the sidewalk. If Francis had been holding Shirley Chisholm hostage instead of white cops, the whole street would be flooded with white cops armed to the teeth, ready to shoot everybody, including Shirley. But now when the pictures of the lynching were flashed on the screen, the police would immediately apologize for their lack of discretion for having put a 'potentially great' lieutenant in charge. They wouldn't mention his color, but Freddy's photo would be in all the papers.

'Where's he at in the building?'

'I don't know. Just go on in. He got eyes and ears all over this block. It's his block. You can see for yourself nobody stops and stares.'

As he entered the building, Harry allowed himself a laugh. The kid he had all but suckled had grown up to be the first black man on the face of the earth to give the establishment an offer they couldn't refuse.

After the first flight of stairs, his footsteps told him the building was empty. Francis had deliberately cleaned house. There weren't a million welfare bitches and their little bastards swarming around. The average punk would have figured them in for protection.

On the third-floor landing he spotted a body and was about to nudge it with his foot when the body rolled over and grinned. An old woman. Maybe sixty. He saw she had only one leg. He glanced around for her crutches. He saw none.

'I gave 'em to Francis, Mr Brown,' the crone said. She had a fresh and breathless quality in her voice.

'Your crutches? Why?'

'So's he would know I'm staying right here. I ain't moving from this spot until somebody comes along and moves me. And when they does, I'm screaming.' She acted like she sort of regretted Harry wasn't going to make her yell.

Harry laughed. 'You don't weigh a hundred pounds,' he said indulgently. 'How much screaming you expect to get heard?'

'You'll be glad I'm a featherweight after you carry me up to the next floor.'

Harry knew her voice did not sound breathlessly girlish

just because she was happy, but it seemed to. 'That's the story, eh?'

'Francis will never open up unless I give him the word.'

Harry bent and scooped up the little woman in his arms.

'Which door?' he asked when they reached the top floor.

The woman pointed. Harry went to the door and kicked gently with the toe of his shoe.

'The gang's all here,' the woman called out distinctly. Almost at once the door opened.

Harry refused to glance at Francis' face. He went across the room and deposited the woman in an easy chair. Then he turned to face Francis. And as he looked at the young man, he had a bad feeling. Just that. Premonition. No clues. Something bad was going to happen.

Francis had closed the door. He motioned with his head for Harry to follow him into the next room.

And there they were. Three of them. Two white, one black. The men were seated on the floor in a tight little circle. Manacled to each other with what Harry knew had to be their own handcuffs. The place stank. But the weirdest part of all was that Francis had those three men sitting there naked as jellyfish.

Harry stared and his face went through a dozen changes. Black men simply do not do this kind of thing to cops of any color. He mourned for Francis but a minute. Then he snarled, 'This is a bag of the worst shit a snotnosed, black-assed bastard could ever think up! But just because it's your shit, I'm gonna help you.'

Francis smiled. 'Bingo,' he said lightly.

His airiness infuriated Harry.

Francis went to a table and picked up a bowl. Like some kind of crazy black faggot, he got down on his knees and began to spoonfeed each of the officers in turn.

'What the hell is that?' Harry shouted.

Francis looked up like a choirboy from his work. 'Farina and Pepto-Bismol.'

Harry considered the stench that hovered over the room. At least one of New York's Finest had shit on himself.

'I'm in,' Harry gritted. 'I don't know why, but I'm in. And your only out is . . . Costa Rica maybe. You ready to go?' He turned and said the last part over his shoulder.

'Thanks again, Harry. But I don't speak Spanish.'

Harry whirled. 'You got the nerve to be talking about "speaking"? Don't you know the man's gonna cut your tongue out before they even start to look for your balls? They'll never let you live. But if they did let you live, you'd still never be able to tell it.'

'Now, that's not fair at all, Harry. You know me. I never blow my own horn. Now have I?' First he looked sad, then that smile came across his handsome black face. 'Every time a cop hears my name from now on, he's gonna grit his teeth.' He raised one arm dramatically. 'But that whitey is gonna *think*, too. He ain't just gonna act out his rage no more. He's gonna stop and wonder if maybe he ain't fucking over another Francis Williams.'

The woman laughed. Harry spun around to glare at her.

'You and I are getting old, Harry Brown,' she said. 'Even Shaft is old today. You could never dream of all the things that boy's got in his head.'

Harry blew breath out between his lips and looked around the room. It was a neat and orderly place. Very well furnished. He supposed it was one of several places Francis worked out of. But at the moment its very neatness added a note of fatality to this thing that was happening. The first thing anybody realized about Francis after they got over his handsomeness and gaiety was that he was one competent sonofabitch.

'How'd you get these men up here?'

'I invited them. Me and the hostess with the mostest.'

It figured. Francis had the women.

'What the hell you planning to do anyhow?'

'I thought the Finest were my friends,' Francis said.

'You come on like you know it all,' Harry said.

'I know it was the fuzz.'

'Jimmy Adams, Doll Baby, Studs Thompson, Sonny Roberts are all dead? Or maybe you scared 'em into playing dead?'

Francis thought that over for only a moment. 'They wouldn't

trust white boys to steal the stuff. Like what's to stop them from keeping on with the stuff? You know Studs, Jimmy, Sonny and Doll Baby are not that dumb.'

Harry took his time. 'Why didn't you call the dealers together and tell 'em what happened? Why didn't you tell 'em what was going to go down if your stuff wasn't repaid? Get it?'

'It wasn't none of them. I could handle them. It was five of the Finest,' Francis said almost dreamily. 'Three were even in uniform. Tommy Dorlon was one of them. He didn't even bother to try to hide his face.'

'Nobody in the know knows who took you off. How many guns you got anyhow?'

'Sorry,' Francis said pleasantly. 'I've already said this ain't your race today, Harry. Maybe tomorrow when the track is dry we'll give you a workout. But right now you go back and . . .'

'Shut up!'

Francis stopped grinning.

'Boy, don't you know you're like my other skin? I don't usually go around collecting debts, because the people I let owe me come to me when they're ready and pay. But you're fucking up. You owe me. You owe me to tell me what your plans are. You owe me to ask me if I got a better plan than you got.'

'I only owe you a promise that I'll be smart. Smarter than whitey. That's all I owe and that's all I'm going to pay.' Francis snapped his mouth shut then and went over to the phone, which was on the table with the bowl of Farina and Pepto-Bismol. He dialed a number he had memorized. When someone answered on the other end, he spoke crisply. 'My name is Francis Williams. I am a black man who has been robbed by the police of this city. At the moment I am at home with three hostages who also happen to be members of New York's Finest. In exactly thirty minutes I am going to hang my hostages by the neck from my fourth-floor apartment window until they are dead. Nothing will change my plans unless the police return that which they have unlawfully taken from me.

'If you will send Melba Tolliver and camera men up here to this address, I will tape a statement, giving you the name of one of the five police officers who robbed me. You have thirty minutes to get here.'

He hung up and turned to face Harry.

'Fuck you,' was all Harry managed to say.

Francis started to say something else, but didn't.

'The only thing that really bugs me is that you don't trust me. I *know* you have no intention of giving yourself up . . . or getting blasted out of here.'

Francis seemed to be far away. 'There's a camp meeting going on in every little nigger man's soul, Harry. Real camp. And nigger camp ain't never for sale. Not for real it ain't. After this, people are going to remember me. I been working from a black handicap . . .'

'Cut it!' Harry said. 'All the papers is gonna print is that an unidentified black madman was slain in a running gun battle with a whole slew of heroic cops. Then they print the cops' names. Get it?'

Francis grinned. 'No way. No way . . . I ain't got long to live anyway.'

The sound of many sirens wafted up to them. Harry began to swear softly.

'Okay, Harry,' Francis said coldly. 'Now get the hell outa here and outa my way.'

Harry sighed. He turned to leave. It made no sense to stay. He turned back to shake Francis' hand.

But Francis was no more! Francis stood there with a gun in his hand pointed toward the men on the floor who had been watching without a word, their hopes obviously riding on Harry. Sweat came out of Francis in short quarts, and the fingers of his shaking hand were too weak to pull any trigger. A baby girl could snatch that rod from him.

Harry's stomach spun. It was so goddamn unreal. It was like Harry could hear every pore in the kid's body crying for a fix, and he had never known Francis was a junkie. Was that what Francis had started to tell him a minute ago? Francis was devastated. Harry was, too, with rage and disappointment.

Harry wondered how his love for this animal had blinded him to Francis' habit. There was nothing now he could or wanted to do for Francis. Francis knew – shit, everyone knew – how he felt about junkies.

He heard the old woman make a sound like a cry. He turned to see her down on the floor, inching her way to her crutches over against the wall. She had to be a part of the whole bullshit Francis had lived, and so he did not help her.

When the woman got up on her crutches, she swung her way to Francis, took his hand and led him out of the room.

Once more Harry considered Francis' captives. They were lower animals than the punk kid. They had heard every word they'd said. They had seen it all happen too. They knew Francis was helpless, yet none of them had made a move. Only their wrists were handcuffed. They could have risen in a body and crab-walked out of the room and down the stairs. They hadn't.

He went to the door through which the woman had taken Francis. He saw she had Francis on the bed and he still seemed in bad shape. He wondered why she was taking so long to give him a fix. Maybe she already had, but it sure didn't look like it unless Francis was dying from an overdose.

He turned to the old woman. Her one leg was ulcerated, the giveaway sign of the farthest-out junkie of them all. Her leg looked like she had been skin-popping for years. It wouldn't be long before this bitch had no legs.

To his amazement the damned-fool woman grinned. 'Me and Francis are blood kin. And we gonna make it. In a couple of minutes he's gonna be all right.'

He stalked out of the apartment and down the stairs to the street. At the front door he met Freddy Morris. 'Francis is dead,' he said and kept on toward his car.

Freddy caught up with him. 'Dead? Real dead?'

'Your men are dead, too.' Harry stopped and stared flat-eyed at him. 'So why don't you clean all this shit up at one time, once and for all? You fill the front of that apartment on the top floor with tear gas. Then accidentally on purpose, one of your men fires a tracer bullet up there. There won't ever be no real questions asked.'

Freddy jutted his lip thoughtfully. 'I don't like to think of that.'

'Well, you have to now.'

'Anybody else up there?'

'No.' Harry walked over and got in his car, but did not drive away.

Ossie knew Harry was uptight. He said not a word. He saw the pellets of tear gas arc up and into the apartment but not who fired them. Harry searched among the crowd of swarming cops now on hand. He wanted to see which one heisted the rifle. He wanted to know if he was a white or a black man.

It was a whitey who shot the tracers up. The blast was louder and more violent than Harry expected. Flames billowed from the windows. He imagined he could feel their searing heat. After five minutes Harry told Ossie to start the car and they slowly drove uptown.

As Harry drove uptown with Ossie, he felt blameless about Francis. Yet something still moved him he did not understand, because it was nothing like he had ever felt before – a deep feeling of loss. Not a feeling of loss for Francis exactly, but a kind of loss of what to him Francis had always stood for – the Harlem of years ago. Francis had looked like things past in so many different ways, like the Harlem that had already begun to hit the skids the day Francis was born. But he grew up with the big body and plain damned good looks that were what it was all about back then – back when there were fifty nightclubs running from Minton's to 135th Street.

Francis had stood for Clarence Muse, who insisted on hiring a white chauffeur so folks would know who was who. And Siki with a monkey on his shoulder instead of on his back. And little Florence Mills. And all the people like that.

Francis had looked like times way back when a colored kid could stand on the corner of 135th Street and watch all the goddamn black headlines walk by: Marcus Garvey, W. E. B. DuBois, Booker T. Washington. They were all supposed to have once passed each other on that corner without so much as batting an eyelash.

And Bessie and her gin bottles. And the Johnson Brothers. And Jimmy Weldon had written the Negro National Anthem, which everybody laughed at because how in hell can a goddamn nigger have a national anthem? It was guys like that made Harlem Home to Heaven.

Now as Harry stared out the window of the car, all he and Ossie seemed to be driving past were loitering junkies. All triflers. All as worthless as Francis. It had ended as it should. There should be nothing left to bury because the devil in hell couldn't dig a grave deep enough to hide the stink from junkie shit like Francis Williams.

That boy at the hospital was clean. Cleaner than the Virgin Mary – a fool, but he was clean. He turned his head and snapped at Ossie, 'I'm going to see that fool boy.'

Ossie, who had not said a word since Harry's return from the apartment building, said nothing now.

'... and the devil in hell can't say a word to me. You hear?'

'Now?' said Ossie.

'No. Not now. When I'm ready. First that fool has got to have more bread. I want you to take care of that.'

3

The jive was humming.

As the word got around that Francis Williams had been offed by the cops and Harry Brown, that fifteen kilos of heroin were still missing, there was lots of speculation. Who had those fifteen kilos? What was going to happen to them? The man at the center of the speculation was Harry Brown, because wasn't he supposed to have some secret formula for making heroin five times as pure as what was put in, yet with the same amount coming out? Maybe even five times as much came out.

Sonny Roberts and Doll Baby and Studs Thompson and Jimmy Adams, New York's biggest black dealers, were all thinking about Harry and his secret formula. It was a fantasy they shared. Each one pictured Harry in some laboratory full of test tubes, hovering over a strange fluorescent, quaking machine. They wanted that machine. In their saner moments they knew it couldn't exist, but they were men with imaginations that drove them to the sides and ends of madness. And Freddy Morris was out and around stirring that madness up with questions.

History is not the story of man's inhumanity to man. It is more an account of the sequence of events which we like to call human affairs, caused by the decisions or acts of a few men. History is a few men coping with their insanity.

Giveadamn Brown was insane. So was Doll Baby, who was crazier than Harry Brown, who was not quite as crazy as Sonny Roberts, but who was more of a megalomaniac than Jimmy Adams. Of course, none of these were as mad as Studs Thompson. But Studs was a female, which accounts for that.

Sonny Roberts was the biggest dope kingpin in the Bronx and also parts of Harlem in which Doll Baby was not strong. He was forty-three, the first and oldest of the young turks who slaughtered their way to the top of the heroin racket in the many ghettos of New York and Queens.

Sonny was handsome, masculine, suave, intelligent, and proud. He was also very polite . . . a kind of deadly politeness. He gave every man a chance not to get wasted, but some fools were always taking advantage of Sonny's good manners. Like that goddamn Harry Brown. It was like it was a greater honor to be killed by Sonny Roberts than to live, and he was ready to take on Harry himself and do him the honor.

Sonny sat alone in the main room of his ten-room apartment and pondered and brooded. Sonny believed in all sincerity that, more than Francis Williams, he was the one and only man in the rackets who was a kindred spirit of Harry Brown's, and he had thought Harry always understood so. Who else on the scene could approach Harry? Now Francis was gone? Then how come Harry gave him the snotnosed kid treatment? He was Harry's rightful heir.

True, Sonny was now out on bail because Harry had put up a million dollars, but it was *how* Harry had put up the money that made Sonny so unforgiving and resentful. Sonny had first put up the million himself – out of the cash fund he was saving for Hollywood – but the square-assed judge wouldn't take it, just because it was Sonny's. So, naturally, Sonny sent for Harry Brown and Harry put up his bread.

The judge wasn't going to take that either. When the judge asked Harry how he happened to be holding a million bucks in cold cash, Harry had snarled, 'That's what the Internal Revenue people are for. Go ask them.'

And Harry had walked out of court. The judge opened his mouth to call Harry back and sock him one hell of a contempt of court, but the D.A. rushed up and grabbed the judge's gavel. Grabbed the sonofabitch and wouldn't let him bang it. And all the time he was rapping hard to that square-assed judge.

So Harry had walked out of court without one damned word to Sonny, like Sonny wasn't important enough to bother with. Then later Harry sent around his main man, Ossie, to tell Sonny Harry's fee for putting up the million was two million. Shee-it!

Ossie got his two million right on the spot, and Ossie turned and split without 'thanks' or any other sound. Harry hadn't even called Sonny to say he got the money.

Nobody could get away with that, not with Sonny Roberts. Sonny picked up the phone and dialed Jimmy Adams' number. He heard the phone on the other end ring three times and then hung up. He didn't want to call Jimmy anyhow: Jimmy was not his friend and never would be. On top of that, Jimmy had a little sense. It would be hard to use him.

On the other hand, Studs Thompson and Doll Baby were stupid. If he was going to do business with anyone, it would be best to first psych those two up and see about making them allies, even if it was just for a little while.

The doorbell rang. When he went to answer it, Freddy Morris was standing there alone.

'Good afternoon.' It was all he said to the detective and all he intended to say. Freddy was a black cop who got used and abused by the whiteys on the force. He had a reputation for being honest, but Sonny figured that was because black cops simply weren't allowed to put their sticky fingers into the dope take.

'I came to talk to you about Francis Williams,' Freddy said.

Sonny shrugged and stepped back so the young black detective could enter. Freddy walked in through the big foyer into Sonny's lavish living room. He gazed around, not with a look of admiration, then he turned to inspect Sonny.

'Somebody lifted all of Francis Williams' holdings before he died. I want to know what you know.'

Sonny said, 'I deal only with the men stationed in the Bronx. If you want a payoff, go see them. I'm not getting up any more than my usual weekly nut.'

'You know what happened to Rap Brown,' Freddy said slowly, feeling his way.

Sonny laughed. 'That was the CIA set him up. They couldn't have done it if Rap was smart.'

'Rap was smart.'

'He's in jail, ain't he? A twelve-year-old kid could have told him he could have knocked off Chase Manhattan a damned sight easier than that dealership.'

'The police weren't guarding the place,' Freddy said sharply, then realized he was a fool. Sonny was right. The police had been hired to ride shotgun on that joint twenty-four hours a day. So why lie? 'I want to know what happened to all those kilos.'

'Why come here?'

'I could make you tell me.'

'You could make me tell you a damned lie to make you stop leaning on me.'

'Does Studs Thompson ever come to Manhattan?'

Sonny smiled and relaxed. 'How would I know? I hear she keeps a harem out there on Staten Island; what's to bring her to town?'

'What's with this CIA bit everybody in Harlem likes to dig?'

Sonny shrugged. 'Maybe it takes a thief to know a thief. Maybe it's just as simple as that.'

'What do you *know?*'

'What does anybody know?'

'I'm asking you, Sonny. You think the CIA got those fifteen kilos?'

Sonny shrugged. 'Ask them.'

'Just who do you think I should ask?'

Sonny thought about it. He reviewed the little facts and bits of innuendo he had that argued the guilt and chicanery of the CIA. It all added up to just about the same kind of shit he had to tot up to prove something about Harry Brown. His face changed expression. 'Shee-it!' he said. He looked at Freddy with astonishment. 'There's only one answer. Harry Brown!'

Freddy walked out to the foyer. 'I'm not stupid,' he said as he put his hand on the doorknob. 'I wish I were, for your sake.' Then he was gone.

In the street Freddy decided to go down in the One Hundred Twenties and see what was happening. Perhaps one of his informants would have something to tell him that would give him some ideas.

At the corner of 135th Street and Seventh Avenue, he saw a huge green Mercedes go through a red light. Because there were three pretty black boys in the front seat of the big car, Freddy decided to pull them over to see what was happening. He did. And it was not until he got out and was walking back to the Mercedes that he saw the big black bulk of Doll Baby sitting in the back seat.

No one inside the car made a move, so Freddy opened the rear door of the limo. Doll Baby, deep inside a mink coat, stared at him. He said, 'Your boy needs driving lessons, Doll Baby.'

'I told him to run that light,' Doll Baby said severely, indignantly. 'I'm on my way to prayer.'

'You is what?'

'If you had all the sinful crooks and liars and con men messing over you all the time that I got, you would learn to do some praying, too.' He had spoken in aggrieved tones, but suddenly his voice was all deep and hard, 'What you stop me for anyhow? You *know* who I am.'

Freddy grimly nodded. These dealers and whoever was in back of them ruled this man's town. But he still said, 'You know the law.' Sonny's crack about coming around for a payoff had him in a rage he hadn't been able to work off. He said, 'Open up your trunk.'

Doll Baby turned in fury to the handsome youth sitting in front of him. 'Give that mother-fucker some bread!' He bellowed it out as if the boy should have done it long ago.

'You open the trunk,' Freddy said tightly and pulled his service revolver at the same time. 'Doll Baby,' he said, 'the next time you call me a mother-fucker I'm going to put the hottest piece of lead up your funky pussy you ever enjoyed. You're gonna still be coming when the undertaker is doing the best he can for you.' Then he pointed the gun at the boy behind the wheel. 'Let's take a look in the trunk.'

The boy sighed, got out and went to open the trunk. There was nothing inside, not even a toolcase. A squad car with two white patrolmen drove up. They recognized Freddy and the occupants of the Mercedes. They got out and joined Freddy. They were grinning companionably.

But Freddy wasn't. He was having no luck at all.

Doll Baby was a church fanatic. Not a religious fanatic; Doll Baby had built unto himself a church and he worshiped *it*.

The building was not much of a church to look at. Not on the outside anyhow. It had once been a store. A store that specialized in new and used furniture. The new furniture had been highjacked. The used furniture was formerly highjacked furniture that had been repossessed.

But the interior of Doll Baby's church was quite all right. It was together. It had padded seats, nice wide seats. There were exactly ninety-eight of these seats. Doll Baby knew the count because they were all his boys had been able to steal and put into the truck at one time. And he had not deemed it wise to send the boys back to the plush little East Side moviehouse again that night. Ninety-eight was enough seats anyhow.

The altar and all the main decorations, candlesticks and such, had been unknowingly donated by various Catholic churches in and around the Harlem area of Manhattan. They were nice, considering.

No woman ever attended Doll Baby's church on order. It wasn't necessary. Some of the sharpest and richest young cats in Manhattan, Brooklyn and Queens attended regularly. And sometimes as many as forty-five lush black teen-age girls attended services at a time. All knowledgeable, and it was a damned sight more than carnal knowledge they knew.

Doll Baby was modest to a fault, especially since he was a three-hundred-pounder who did not waddle. He had a light, firm step with a hint of the *joie de vivre* a fat woman puts on after a risqué compliment from a handsome dude. Maybe that was because handsome young dudes were always complimenting Doll Baby. They had to – if they wanted to stay young, black and handsome for long.

*   *   *

Freddy sighed disconsolately as he drove around 116th Street and Eighth Avenue.

It did not take him long to spot Deep Freeze. As soon as he had the smalltime rat in his car, Freddy headed for Central Park. Then, cruising slowly through the park, he said, 'Did you tell one of my men to keep an eye out for what Doll Baby might be carrying today, Deep Freeze?'

'Whaa—?' It was all Deep Freeze could get out. 'What happened?'

'Some of my men just nailed Doll Baby with maybe two, three hundred thousand dollars in the trunk of his car. What he ever do to you to make you do that, Deep Freeze?'

The mind of the petty criminal can grasp truth. It's the baseless lie he can't handle. He can meet the truth with logic and alibis. Deep Freeze, feeling he was already dead, was determined to take some bodies with him. 'Studs Thompson!' His voice was cool.

'You sure?' Freddy felt as if he was beginning to believe in the trunk money himself. 'You got that from somebody, didn't you? You were in on it. Let's have it all, Deep Freeze.'

Deep Freeze moved his bottom to get more comfortable. 'Figures,' he said. He smiled now, smugly. 'The story's out that Studs is coming to Harlem. She's going to take over Eighth Avenue. It sounded crazy as hell the first time I heard it, but what the hell, Studs *is* crazy.'

'I been hearing that too,' Freddy murmured. 'Wonder what Harry Brown is going to do about it?'

'Dunno,' Deep Freeze said honestly. 'But things are happening. Like, did you know that Harry Brown got a nephew just showed on the scene, and the nephew's got hisself a woman I used to deal with?'

Freddy shook his head to signify it was all news to him.

'I hear Harry's put out a contract on his broad, this Margo. The way it goes is Harry hates all junkies, even ex-junkies, and I ain't sure she ain't still using. But that ain't got to be the way it is at all. See? The thing I begin to think is Studs is using this Margo to get inside Harry's operation. You know. Find out how he cuts his heroin. And where. Harry knows what this Margo's up to, but this Margo stallion has laid some fine trim on this nephew, see? And so the nephew won't give her up. She's a constant danger to Harry and everybody else. And so he's having her wasted. You keep your eyes open and see if that ain't so.'

Doll Baby's long green Mercedes rolled up in front of the Church of Better Harlem. Three handsome black young dudes got out and opened the doors of the edifice. After they entered, scouted around and returned, Doll Baby stepped forth. It was warm, so his lush mink coat hung loosely from his shoulders. But once on the street, Doll Baby shrugged off the coat and carried it with one hand, very carelessly, so it dragged the sidewalk. Just like the rich white bitches in the movies.

He entered the church quickly and went to his favorite pew. He knelt, bowed his head and sighed deeply, sorrowfully. Tears began to flow. They blended nicely with the sweat that ran from his smooth black brow. Then he lifted his head and said aloud, 'Gawd, let me tell you what the mother-fuckers done did now . . .'

4

Giveadamn, still in the hospital, lay and counted his blessings.
Two weeks had passed since he'd been stabbed. He had the
damndest hole in his gut. It did not want to heal. But he had
a woman. And he had himself one great big one hundred
thousand dollars. He ought to stop brooding.

'Mr Brown, what in the world are you thinking about?' She'd
heard he'd won, too. Everybody in St Luke's knew it.

He looked up at the student nurse, Miss Howard. 'I was
thinking about how gloomy I'm getting,' he admitted.

She smiled, a nice smile. 'I like you, and one reason I
do is because you're always so cheerful, Mr Brown.' She
was a girl of about nineteen with long blond hair and gray
eyes.

'I came to tell you I heard you were going home tomorrow,
so cheer up.'

'What day is it?' he asked.

'Tuesday, July the first. Why? Something important?'

He let out a sigh. 'No. Only, it seems like in three weeks I
wouldn't still be so banged up.'

'I think it's mental. Once you're out in the fresh air . . .'

Then he heard the neat clip-clopping of heels in the corridor.
It was Foxy Cool Momma with her high-stepping walk coming
to see him.

When Margo came in, she spoke first to Miss Howard, then
she turned to Giveadamn with a big smile. It was a smile that
almost turned Giveadamn off the first time she favored him
with it. She had the phoniest-seeming smile God ever gave a
woman. It was perfect. Too damned perfect. It was just like
she was posing for a toothpaste ad.

But Giveadamn had come to know the smile came only
under perfect conditions. Unlike most people, Foxy did not
believe in smiling just to be nice. So when she smiled, it was

because she could not keep from smiling, so the smile came to him now like a sort of glory.

Miss Howard disappeared. Margo said, 'Babee, I think I have given you enough time to decide what we're going to do with all that bread. I don't care what you do as long as you don't ask me to play chump with you.'

When Giveadamn looked inquiringly at her, she said, 'I don't mind walking down the street and people saying a lot of things behind my back. But one thing they'll never say is, "There goes the stupid bitch who had a man with a hundred grand and she let him blow it all." Dig what I'm saying, Giveadamn?'

He nodded thoughtfully. 'I been thinking, Margo,' he said. 'I was lying here thinking … it's like this, Margo: I don't know shit. I really don't. I'm sitting here now with a hole in my belly just because I didn't know Kiki was a chump who came by to see for himself his woman was gone forever.'

She nodded.

'All I had to do was shut up and smile.'

'You don't slap grown men, Giveadamn. And once you do, you should come within an inch of jail before you stop killing them.'

He shook his head almost sadly. 'Why was I so dumb as to get stuck in the gut? How come I don't ever tell you what's happening instead of you always telling me? I used to think I was pretty smart.'

'Goddammit! I'm older than you are.'

'No, you're not.'

She suddenly stared at him. 'How old you think I am, Giveadamn?'

'Same as me about.'

'I'm thirty-eight.'

'No, you're not.'

'Don't tell me, Giveadamn. I ought to know.'

'You look younger than me.' It was all he could say for the time being.

'All rotten people are baby-faced, Giveadamn.'

When Margo left, she passed Miss Howard in the hall.

Something alerted the little nurse to trouble, and the one thing she did not want was for Mr Brown to be upset.

Miss Howard put her head in the door. He seemed to be sleeping. She stepped in and moved the visitor's chair quietly back against the wall before she saw Mr Brown had opened his eyes.

'What's wrong, Mr Brown. What is it?'

And then the room sort of caved in with what it could not really hold. It was like somebody had rocked hell. It was evil. Mean. Above all else, this thing was mean.

Both Giveadamn and Miss Howard looked to see who it was and what the intruder wanted. They saw a man, an ugly man wearing a soft tailored suit that still was not able to correct the sloping V of the shoulders.

The man came in and picked up the chair and moved it. Then he sat on it and fixed his gaze on Miss Howard. Miss Howard fled.

'I know you,' Giveadamn said. 'I'd know who you were even if I never saw you before.'

Harry Brown said, 'I read in the papers you won, so I looked around for you. I was told you was here.' He lit a cigar. Its rich aroma went well with his suit. 'I wrote and told your dad to come up here and help me over twenty years ago almost. But he didn't even answer my letter.'

'He thinks selling dope is a sin.'

Dark and ugly as he was, the man still managed to exude a healthy and righteous prosperity. The eyes that should have been shifty and piggish were clear and bold and appraising. 'Let me explain something, Lawrence – I hate junkies! A junkie is an animal who is best killed on sight. When a junkie takes some heroin into his body, he takes his best shot. When a junkie is full of heroin, he is the best he can ever be. Take heroin away from him and he is lower than he ever was while he had junk in him. A cured addict is nothing. Less than nothing. He is a thief, murderer and child molester. He's better than that when he's full of heroin. He don't hate the human race when he's high. That's why a junkie needs junk. I've sold them their junk. And the grocer on the corner will sell you what you got the money to pay for, but that don't convince him you got a right to eat it.'

Giveadamn stared at him in amazement. 'Is that what you came to see me for?' He was suddenly too weak to feel either rage or fear.

Harry said, 'A junkie is born with a broken life. Selling an addict something he was born to use is no sin in my book. You think whiskey-store dealers go out and pay for the funeral of the guy's wife they sold the whiskey to? All junkies are homos and thieves. I tell you, they are freaks. If they didn't steal for heroin, they would be stealing to satisfy their freakish lovers. The men and women both. And don't you forget it! But, no, that's not what I came up here to talk to you about, Lawrence.'

The room again clamped down on Giveadamn.

Harry talked on in a hypnotic monotone. '. . . but I'll never have anyone around me who is afraid of prison,' Harry was saying. 'A man who is afraid of prison cannot be trusted.'

'I don't want to hear any more,' Giveadamn said weakly.

Harry moved his chair even closer to the bed and said, 'Junkies are dogs . . .'

'I don't want to hear this,' Giveadamn said weakly. 'I don't want to hear no more.'

'They never kick! A junkie is nothing but a raving package of frantic yens.'

'I tell you I can't stand any more!'

'The reason you are here is because you let a junkie whore fuck you,' Harry said bitterly. He got up and strode out of the room. But he was back in the doorway in a moment. He stood there, huge, waiting.

Giveadamn gazed at him a long time. 'You want me to sell my soul to the devil, don't you?'

'The devil owns you already. I'm trying to buy you back from the devil!' He sat down again.

5

'We got ourselves enough bad habits already without going and getting hooked on four walls,' Foxy said. Her shoulders quivered.

Giveadamn grunted. For once he was as poker-faced as Foxy. Ten days had passed since he left the hospital, but nothing was back to normal. He couldn't seem to get with it. Something had hold of him and wouldn't let go. He was weak and sore, sluggish.

'Yeah,' he said. 'These walls are getting next to me, too. But I thought as long as you had your blessed TV, you were satisfied.'

Foxy shook her head. 'No way. No way. Got hustling in my blood, I guess. Like you got to get out and dig the action even if you don't do anything about it. If you don't, you might just as well be in the joint.'

They got dressed and went out.

Had it been up to Giveadamn, they would simply have strolled Broadway and window-shopped. But as soon as she reached the first corner, Foxy hailed a cab and gave the driver a 137th Street address.

The cab pulled over in the middle of a block of rather modest but very neat and well-kept brownstones. She paid the driver, then led the way up the steps of one of the better-looking houses. She rang the bell and turned to Giveadamn and said querulously, 'We'll stop here a minute. I got to pee.'

Foxy heaved a sigh of exasperation and began to fumble in her purse. Then she pulled out a key and opened the door of the house herself. As soon as they entered, she shoved Giveadamn toward what could be called a parlor and said, 'Sit.' Then she was gone, evidently to the bathroom.

Giveadamn sat. It was a nice and friendly old kind of room. It sort of had a natural right to be musty, but it wasn't. He decided it had been very well-abused. Nothing was exactly in tatters, but children had been allowed to romp here. And grown-ups had enjoyed a few drinks. It was a nice room.

Margo had come out of the bathroom and was now yelling for someone named Gracie.

The voice that answered Margo and began a lively conversation was young and vital. It was a sexier voice than Foxy's. It was a sure bet that she was years younger than Foxy. Giveadamn slumped in the easy chair and waited.

But Foxy came back alone. And immediately went to the stereo and started some records playing. Then she went into a new dance step.

A teen-age girl came through the front door and slowly walked into the room. She was a little black button of fifteen or sixteen, and she was of the same beautiful black stuff the unseen voice was made of, but it couldn't have been her voice he'd heard.

Foxy gave a little scream of joy and ran to snatch the child's schoolbooks. The two of them began to work out. And the kid really could dance. It was evident Foxy had schooled her. And then it hit Giveadamn the kid and Foxy were related.

When the music stopped, the girl came to Giveadamn and put out her hand. 'I'm Toni,' she said.

Before Giveadamn could rise and introduce himself, a total catastrophe waddled into the room, stared at Giveadamn for a moment, then began to make happy noises as she came close. She grabbed his hand.

Nothing like this had ever appeared before his eyes. The woman was some kind of midget; she seemed to have no definite age. She was shorter than Foxy, but she had to weigh in at well over one hundred and sixty pounds. One third of that great weight was in her massive breasts. All the rest appeared to be in her hips. She had a powerful butt, a true masterpiece.

Suddenly the massive midget smiled and became an instant beauty. All woman and all right. 'Such a tender little lamb chop,' she murmured in the sexy voice Giveadamn had heard before and wondered about. She turned to glare at Foxy. 'Maggie,' she said, 'you don't have as much sense as an elephant. You don't even have as much sense as the peanuts they eat. How in the world could you let a tender little lamb chop like this get involved with something like Kiki?'

She turned back to look up at Giveadamn. 'I almost died with you,' she said with a little moan. 'And I'd never even seen you. But Maggie told us all about you from the very beginning. You're beautiful and I only hope you have brains enough for the two of you. Do you?' But she did not stop for an answer.

'Are you hungry? There's always food enough to feed three armies in this house. I have a man who weighs two hundred and fifty pounds plus eight other mouths to feed. And he lays bricks all day, so you know when he comes home he's hungry from way back. But me? I hardly have time to stop cooking to eat. So what do you want? A drink? Don't you want a drink first? Drink anything you like. And if you're church folks, we got tomato juice. How about tomato juice?'

She turned to Toni. 'Toni, fix Giveadamn some tomato juice.' Her eyes inspected Giveadamn again. 'You lost weight, didn't you? I can tell.' She turned back to Toni, 'Make him eggnog instead. And use the black rum. It's got iron.'

The doorbell rang and Foxy went to answer it. She was back in a moment with a tall handsome girl. The latter was not exactly beautiful, yet there was something unusually attractive about her. Perhaps it was the snow-white suit she was wearing. Slacks and Eisenhower jacket to match. She was tall, fairly light-skinned with a close-cropped head of fine hair. As soon as she was in the room, she bowed in an oriental sort of way. Then she broke into a delicate waterfall of Spanish.

But it was the glint of comedy in her eyes that surprised Giveadamn and made him aware this chick was one of his kind of people. For the first time since he had got out of bed, he was feeling all right. He slumped back again in the chair and listened to the women chattering. Toni brought him his eggnog.

The tall girl kicked a hassock toward Giveadamn and sat on it. 'You're Giveadamn. I'm Stella. We're all one happy family,' she went on in that lovely voice.

Gracie waddled over and imperiously motioned for him to

get up and follow her. He obeyed and Gracie led him up the stairs of the four-story house.

When they reached the top floor, Gracie was gasping but she waved with pride. The entire floor was one big room, and the room was literally one huge playpen. In the pen were six infants ranging in age from about five months to fifteen months.

'Where?' It was all Giveadamn could think to say. And he repeated it. 'Where?'

'Foster homes,' Gracie said proudly. Suddenly she was very serious. 'I got my own particular thing,' she said. 'And my thing is this. Did you know that if a baby doesn't get the right food in its first two years, it affects the brain and he'll never have good sense? Like you can't cheat on a child's food and then later expect him to grow up and have good sense. And I know I'm right. They did it to Maggie,' she ended softly.

'Maggie? Why do you always call her Maggie? And who is "they"?'

'Maggie is her name. I don't blame the poor thing for choosing Margo. It's cute and nice, but I learned to call her Maggie. I didn't know how ugly a name it was until after.'

'Who is "they"?'

'My mother.' Gracie looked at him as brutally frank as Foxy, her sister, could look. 'Our mother was a 'ho', Giveadamn. Only my aunt, her sister, took me the day I was born. She was a church woman and wouldn't even let my mother come near me until I was a pretty big girl. My aunt was good to me. Better than any mother could be in the whole wide world. But Maggie had to live with my mother, and she starved until she ran away from home when she was fourteen.'

He heard again Foxy's voice in the night. There had been so much compacted loneliness in it: 'Spaghetti, Giveadamn. That's all there was. Not even butter. Just spaghetti. Spaghetti.'

When they went back downstairs, Foxy, Stella and Toni had disappeared into the back of the house somewhere, but he could hear their laughter.

Gracie followed the laughter, but he took his seat in the same old chair and picked up his eggnog. He closed his eyes and thought, Margo simply could not have starved. Yet he knew she had.

But Margo was not a runt. She was tiny, but perfect — tiny. And in some miraculous way she was a rangy little woman. Rangy, neat, compact. A miniature Juno. Her legs were perfectly shaped. From the very beginning he got a kick out of watching her step into her panties and seeing the muscles play in her thighs as she lifted her leg.

At thirty-eight, she could stand up in beauty with any girl anywhere who was not even twenty-eight. Margo had beat all the odds. By rights she shouldn't even be living. He grinned suddenly. There was only one answer to the whole goddamn thing: *a nigger ain't nothing but a goddamn miracle!*

They had not been back at Giveadamn's room long when the newly installed phone rang. It was his Uncle Harry. 'Boy, have you been thinking over what I said to you?'

Foxy was listening hard. 'There's nothing to think about.'

'Are you really afraid?' There was no emotion in the voice. Harry was merely seeking the truth.

Giveadamn grinned into the receiver. 'I wish me a long life.'

'Why don't you come by for some more talk even if you don't want to take me up on what I got to offer?'

'I need bread. I'll pay you back.'

'Goddamn!' his uncle exploded. 'Now, why the hell couldn't I have realized that you might be jacked up? Why haven't you been down to the lottery people?'

'I don't know. I just can't seem to get my motor started.'

'I'm going to come by and get you in the morning.'

Giveadamn hung up. He went over to Foxy. She was lying on the bed watching TV and pretending she hadn't heard a word. He sat on the edge of the bed and tentatively put his hand on her waist.

'Turn it off first,' she said. 'It's a lousy program anyhow.'

He was not tired any more. He felt so good now he wondered if he had imagined all the weakness he had suffered. He felt in great shape. Such great shape he wanted to take his time and enjoy the night.

He kissed her lightly. She sighed and snuggled her body totally into the curves of his own. He burst out laughing. Foxy came up to a sitting position and looked down on him. Her expression was the same, but her eyes glared with outrage.

'What's so funny?' she snapped.

He laughed even more, but finally he said, 'It is funny. I mean, it's funny how I feel so damned funny about you. Like I love your body almost as much as I love you. I mean, I appreciate it. I really do. I mean, I think I would have to offer my regrets if you had any other body. Your body is my security blanket. Dig it?'

The next morning Giveadamn was feeling so well he took his first constitutional alone. When he returned, Margo was sitting up in bed, and she regarded him with a grave visage as usual.

For openers he said, 'You don't dig me, do you?'

'I guess it's that I just can't get over you.' She stared at him for a moment. 'That night I let you come up and start hitting on me in that bar, I said to myself, "Be cool. Cool, babee. You don't want to go throwing no drink in this goofy dude's eye."' She laughed bitterly.

'You're still kind of ashamed of me, aren't you?' he said. 'You've done all them big things and heard you some small talk. You been to the well a million times and never got your pitcher broke. I mean, you rate a more hip kind of cat. It's more like you don't know what to do with me, isn't it?'

She came off the bed in a sort of leaping glide and was holding him tight the next moment. Her mouth was against his chest so that her words were muffled. 'I don't know what I want. I guess I want to turn you on is all.' She clung now.

He began to massage her back. She started to rise gently against him. And then he had her in the bed. Or perhaps it was that she had him in the bed.

An hour later they were still lying in bed, talking lazily.

'Damn!' he said softly. 'I forgot all about Uncle Harry coming.'

'Uncle Harry? What Uncle Harry? You got a uncle in New York? Giveadamn, you act like your family is the biggest secret you got.'

He had been afraid to tell Foxy Cool Momma about Harry Brown's offer. Now he faced it. 'My uncle's name is Harry Brown. He's supposed to be big in dope around town.'

Foxy gasped. 'He – he's coming here?' She looked around distractedly. 'Here? You said here?'

'Cool it, babee. He might not come.'

Once more she looked around the room. Her tiny shoulders were no longer straight. 'I'll come back for my things. You mind bringing me my things?'

'Now sit still and tell me what's eating you.'

'Harry Brown kicks junkies' asses.'

'Meaning?'

'Just what I said: Harry Brown kicks junkies' asses. Why didn't you tell me about him before?'

'Tell you what? What the hell you think ass-kicking's got to do with you and me?'

'I'm getting out of here. Forget the clothes.' She got up and began to dress rapidly.

'Margo, you're really scared.'

'Why shouldn't I be, you dirty mother-fucking sonofabitch!'

'You aren't on parole any more now, are you?'

She didn't even hear him. She put out one hand. 'I loved you, Giveadamn . . .' She let her words hang.

'What did you do to make him want revenge?'

'I used his shit,' Foxy said bitterly. 'I used his shit.'

An hour passed. At half-past eleven the phone rang; it was his uncle. 'I got a man who went and got himself in a hassle,' Harry said. 'I don't know how long I'm gonna be tied up, but I'm sending a messenger over with five hundred dollars. He should be there in a few minutes. I'll call you first thing tomorrow if I don't get back to you today.'

Giveadamn got dressed and waited.

Cohen called from downstairs. A guest was on the way up. The young man Harry sent was twenty-three or four.

He was well-dressed and might have been a young lawyer or law student.

He entered with a kind of ceremonial politeness. 'Mr Lawrence Brown?' he asked. And when Giveadamn said yes, the fellow extracted a sheaf of twenty-dollar bills and counted them twice in rapid succession. Then he handed the money over. 'It's a pleasure to meet you, Mr Brown.' He was gone before Giveadamn could start a conversation.

Giveadamn left almost as quickly as the messenger. Ten minutes later he was ringing Gracie's doorbell.

'Hi, Giveadamn. Come on in.' Gracie extended her hand as if to pull him into the house. 'Where's Maggie?'

'Isn't she here?'

Gracie read his worry. 'You two have a go at each other?' she asked gently.

When they were inside, she sat beside him on the divan and said, 'I'm glad you came alone, Giveadamn. Maggie told me like how it was when Kiki stabbed you,' she said.

'How was it?'

'She was petrified, Giveadamn. She couldn't move or speak. I mean, you'll never understand all the guilt she feels inside. Maggie lives by a different code than you and me. She thought one look at Kiki and you'd never speak to her again.'

'Has Margo been here today?'

She did not answer and he saw she was not going to.

'Where can I find her?'

'Don't worry about your Foxy. She's yours, Giveadamn. So you can afford to walk slow.'

'I'm afraid she'll go back on that stuff, Gracie.'

Her face was still. 'I told her I would kill her if she ever did again. And she knows I will. I almost killed her once before.'

'When?'

Her face was iron, not flesh and bone; she would not speak.

'Toni is Margo's daughter,' Giveadamn said slowly.

'Are you telling me or asking me?'

'Neither.'

'You're damned near screwy as Maggie,' Grace mumbled.

A few minutes later Giveadamn left. He decided to go by his shop. He had not been there since he'd left the hospital. It had been locked since Kiki stabbed him. All the way down to 118th and Lenox he kept his eye out for Margo, but he did not see her.

He got out of the cab in front of his shop. He could tell nothing had been disturbed by the condition of the grating in front of the place. He stood in front of the store and studied the street scene. It was the same. Always the same. He did not know any of the junkies, although he ran his shop in the midst of them. But there was no reason for them to come into his store. If a broken appliance was stolen, it was sold in that condition.

Now he wished he could go down to the corner and start a conversation with at least one of the fifty addicts who congregated there. He could ask questions. In fact, he would buy an addict a dozen bags of heroin if only that addict could tell him about Harry Brown or where a scared junkie girl runs to hide from Harry Brown.

6

At 110th Margo boarded the bus to Eighth Avenue, and at Eighth got off and started uptown.

Near the corner of 112th she met the Uglies, Joan and Edna. The two women had always been a mystery to Foxy. They were about thirty years old now and had been strung out since high school, where they had met and become lovers. But the mystery to Foxy was, Were they born queer or had they become lovers simply because each was too ugly to ever make it with a man?

'I'm selling,' Edna said. Drunk as she was, she sounded cool and businesslike.

Foxy did not smile, but her voice was pleasant enough.

'You two 'ho's still pushing your meth?' she said conversationally. Then she said wonderingly, 'Everybody talks about how meth is killing more and more people every day, but nobody realizes how many of you 'ho's die from the wine you buy with the bread you get from selling your damn meth. Shit. That damned wine will kill a damned sight quicker than either meth or narco.'

The Uglies laughed. They pounded Foxy and each other on the back.

'Hell, nothing's that funny,' Foxy said deadpan. 'If I described you two's funeral, you'd still crack up.'

Just as quickly the two ugly lovers stopped laughing and assumed a serious attitude. 'What the hell,' Joan said. 'You walk with the undertaker every goddamn minute of the day on this avenue now. You hear about Francis Williams?'

'Francis used to be my main man a long time ago,' Foxy said offhandedly. 'I heard he died in a fire.'

'Harry Brown had him offed. Damned pigs did it for him.'

Foxy turned slowly, stepped into a vacant storefront and

started puking. The two women, who thought she needed a fix, bobbed their heads in commiseration.

'You jacked up, honey?' It was Edna. She had come and put her arm around Foxy's shoulder.

'Naw. Pregnant,' Foxy said crisply.

'Shee-it!' Joan exclaimed.

'How old are you, Margo?' Edna asked.

Foxy stared down her. 'How old you think?'

'Older than us. Older than water.'

'Fuck you two bitches,' Foxy said carelessly and started walking up the avenue again.

On the corner of 114th she met Deep Freeze. 'What say, man?' she said. 'What's happening?'

'Something new every day, Margo,' Deep Freeze said. He was the oldest pusher on Eighth Avenue by virtue of either death or all the other pushers having worked their way up to dealerships by now.

'So what's new?'

'There's more money today in kidnapping than narco, Margo. You ever stop to realize that?'

'So what else is new?'

'Of course you heard about Francis, Gawd rest his soul.'

'Yeah. But what he do to Harry Brown?'

'Nobody's talking. When it comes to that goddamn Harry Brown, everybody gets a tight lip. Usually anything I wants to know, I can go to my man on the beat, but even the fuzz ain't talking.' He drew himself up and his eyes widened expressively, 'You ever see or hear of anything like that Harry Brown?'

In the middle of the block between 111th and 112th, Margo stopped in front of a worn tenement. She climbed the stairs to the top floor. She went to the last door on the right and knocked.

Kiki opened the door, saw who it was and jumped back. She raised her hands almost imperceptibly to show they were empty. He relaxed and stepped back farther so she could come in.

She wiped her eyes. She saw he was not sick. He was not high either. Maybe he had a couple of hours before he needed a fix.

'I knew you would come,' he said.

She said nothing, but walked over and stared down at the bare and dirty mattress. It looked like a typical shooting-gallery mattress. Bloody, dirty and puke-stained, too. Only it wasn't. Kiki did not have sense enough even to run a shooting gallery. Just one more dumb spic with a cute face and some dynamite head. If it wasn't for her, he would have starved to death long ago.

'I knew you would come,' Kiki repeated. 'That's why it don't make no sense for you to keep going away. You always come back.'

Her eyes took him in just as if she was not there, only her eyes. 'It's been three years since we lived together.'

'What difference that make? You come where I am. You stay as long as you want. What difference it make?'

'I don't know.'

'Why you crying? I never saw you cry before.'

'I'm high.'

'Narco?' He said it eagerly.

She shot him a glance of contempt.

'I could get a job, Margo. I can shoot pool, Margo. You know I can shoot pool, Margo.'

'You can shoot pool,' she said wearily.

'You got terp?'

'I quit.'

'Giveadamn won't let you do nothing. What's he anyhow, some kind of nut for real?'

'He's Harry Brown's nephew.'

Kiki stepped back.

She watched his reaction and wanted to look away. 'If they wanted your ass,' she said, 'they would have had it by now.'

He grinned. 'You told him that you wouldn't stay if they wasted me, didn't you? I know you did. You don't have to tell me. I can look in your eyes and see.' He touched her tentatively.

She let him. Suddenly her knife was in her hand. 'I'm going to kill you, Kiki.'

He cowered back into a corner.

She had hoped he would make a wild attack and then it would have been over for her, but Kiki was as scared of her as she was of Harry Brown. She thought maybe Kiki was too jacked up to buy another knife. He had left the one he had still hanging in Giveadamn. She tossed her knife on the bed and then stared at it, a stiletto she had carried for years.

Kiki made no move to come out of the corner. She sighed and went to the bed and lay down beside the knife. She thought how nice it would be if she could just lie still until she somehow outwitted the unlisted sonofabitch. She closed her eyes and woke up with Kiki's head moving between her legs. His tongue was teasing her clit. At least he was putting out his best. Kiki had some real dynamite head. The best head on Eighth Avenue.

She began to move in acknowledgment of Kiki's tongue. The sounds that came from his mouth soothed her. It was like a promise that she was going to die in beauty.

But when the true ecstasy of the thing began, she saw only the face of Giveadamn. No use to lie. She'd rather be lying beside a dead duck Giveadamn Brown than enjoying the most dynamite head in the world. As orgasm came, Foxy dwelt with death once more. Like everybody has to die. And if your ass is tough enough, you choose your spot. Sudden death don't count.

She would never again lie on a filthy mattress. When they came for her, she could be stretched out on her man's clean sheets.

She reached down and hit Kiki upside the head. 'You've had it, mother-fucker. I'm going home.'

7

The taxi had gone only two blocks when Giveadamn had the driver stop at a bar so he could make a phone call. Ten minutes later, he was under the blue canopy in front of his uncle's address. It was one of those buildings that announce all guests, but it was no hassle for Giveadamn. The lobby attendant had been alerted. He was taken up in the elevator, and two minutes later was following his uncle through the huge apartment. He saw all the white and gold. White rugs, white furniture. Gold lamps. Gold bowls. White tables and stands. They passed a book-lined room and Giveadamn almost whistled.

What was not white was trimmed in gold. Every room he passed, as Harry led him to what evidently was the rear of the apartment, seemed to be laden with golden objects. There were so many things made of yellow metal that Giveadamn began to realize, some, perhaps most, of them were not gold for real. But they all gleamed.

They came to a wide and handsome living room. It was at the rear, yet it faced a big terrace. But the damndest thing about the room was a hole in the floor.

It was really a hole. A hole that Harry must have had cut there so a winding staircase could be built to the room below. Harry led him down the twisting stairway. Giveadamn followed his uncle's massive back, feeling small, and as though he was in the care of a grown-up.

And then they were in a vast playroom. Or maybe it was a barroom because it had two bars, one at each end. Between the two bars were scattered thousands of dollars' worth of red, green and black plastic furniture molded in exotic modern designs. But Giveadamn picked out a soft armchair while Harry went behind the nearer bar. He had the feeling the chair was spreading its arms and enfolding him like a baby. He had never known about such furniture.

He studied Harry's ugly face. He wanted to see if he could find any degree of pride of possession, but Harry did not show any. Harry seemed at ease. 'I've come here to make a deal with you,' he said before Harry finished making the two Bourbon and waters.

Harry gave him a hard, angry look, as if the man was not used to getting offers, then he smiled. 'Eh?'

'I come in with you. I do everything you say. I give you my ass. But . . .' He paused because the dice were going down for real now. 'You have to leave my woman alone.'

'What's wrong with her?'

'You know.'

'Oh. That one.'

'There might never be any other than "*that one.*"'

'I see.'

'A deal?'

'I want to get this thing straight about the girl first. Why you bargaining her?'

'The story goes that you would not like a favorite nephew keeping company with an ex-junkie.'

'And?'

'You might kill the girl.'

'Your woman told you this? That I would kill her?'

'Yes . . . have her killed . . . if it makes any difference.'

Harry came up to him from the bar. Harry's finger, one inch from his nose, looked like a piece of knockwurst. 'You see what makes a junkie tick,' he said tightly. 'You see? Now here's a junkie bitch thinking all of a sudden she's so important in the scheme of things I'm going to off her. You understand how that goes? Why isn't she afraid I might come and give her ten thousand dollars and tell her to get lost? If she's a junkie, she'll take the ten. It's a sure bet. And why isn't she afraid I will come to her and tell her she gets all the heroin she needs for her personal use the rest of her life if she stays away from you? Why? Why does she have to consider herself so important?'

'Because you're not exactly an unknown soldier!' Giveadamn said. He didn't know why he put it that way.

Harry's rage increased. 'There was a time when a man could

control what was said about him. But no more. A man's name is what the public's imagination says it is.' He seemed to be boring in now. 'What is this girl's reputation?'

Giveadamn shrugged and refused to say more. Harry stared. Just stared. They stayed that way for a long time.

It got on Giveadamn's nerves first. 'What is it I have to do?'

Harry went back to the bar, brought their drinks, and as he began to talk, Giveadamn had the impression his uncle was thinking hard and slowly. 'There's been hassles,' Harry said. 'Big hassles. I own the Harlem police, but the feds are another matter. Like tonight there is going to be a connection. I need a new face, a clean face. Somebody like you . . .' He paused.

'Go ahead.'

'It is not a hard thing to carry out, but you must do it exactly like I tell you. I never allow anyone to improvise on a job.' Harry frowned.

Giveadamn nodded. Something was wrong, but he did not know what.

'All I want is a guarantee my woman is left completely and totally alone.'

'How good are you with a pistol?'

'Real good. I'm a country boy. I killed rabbits on the run.'

Harry studied him for a long time. 'You really going to risk prison for this – this dope fiend?'

He couldn't tell if Harry was impressed, disappointed, or what.

Giveadamn had been home about thirty minutes when Foxy knocked. He opened the door. She had on her best smile. 'I'm not scared any more, Giveadamn.'

He put his arm around her as she came in. 'Don't need to be scared, kid. I went over and talked to my uncle today.'

Her look was unbelieving. 'You did. What did he say?'

'He promised to let you alone.'

Foxy twisted her body so that Giveadamn's arm was no longer around her shoulders. 'He did? Why?'

'Sit down. Cool off. Come over here and sit down.' He patted the bed where he was now sitting.

She would not come.

'How much dealings you ever have with your uncle anyhow?'

'I never really saw him until he came to visit me in the hospital.'

'I'm scared you might have promised him something to get him to raise up off my back.'

'I promised nothing.'

She came over and lay down beside him. It had grown dark in the room. They were silent. At one point Giveadamn raised up and bent over her, then bent to kiss one of her tiny breasts that still seemed as young and firm as a girl's.

'You and these goddamn titties. Here I got to go stuff old stockings in my bra to begin to even look like a woman, and you keep trying to wear what I got away. But go to it, babee. Your dues are paid up at all times.'

'You got the weirdest sense of humor,' he said.

'What you like you're always gonna get, Giveadamn. Like it's a pleasure to serve you.' Then she put her arms around his neck and kissed him a long time. Then she got up and began taking things out of the closet and laying them on the bed.

'You act like you're getting ready to cut out.'

'I am. So are you. You went by Gracie's, didn't you?'

'Yeah. Looking for you.'

'So we got to go by and tell her not to worry no more.'

'Can't you call?'

'If I called, it would only upset her more. She would think whatever was wrong is still wrong and I'm lying. We have to go by and let her see us for herself.'

'I don't think I'll go,' Giveadamn said slowly, tentatively.

She looked at him coldly. 'Put your clothes on.'

He had lied to Foxy. He'd had a right to because there was no way of knowing how big a liar his uncle was.

'I said, put your clothes on.'

'I'm waiting for my uncle to phone.'

'Fuck your funky uncle.'

So he began to put his clothes on. That was all she'd asked of him. He put them on silently while she dressed just as silently.

When she was ready to leave, she characteristically shivered her shoulders. 'Well?'

He decided he would walk her to the corner and put her in a taxi. They went down to the street.

At the corner he hailed a cab. He opened the door. But Foxy stood looking at him. He sighed. He would ride over to Gracie's with her, let her out and take the cab back. If he wasn't home, his uncle would call again. It would be no big sweat.

As they got out of the cab in front of Gracie's, Giveadamn noticed a man come down the steps of the brownstone next to hers. There was a good-looking boy walking beside him, and the man was more than good-looking; he was handsome and debonair until they got close enough to see him clearly. Almost half the man's face looked as if it had been boiled in a cauldron. Giveadamn looked away. He looked back just in time to see Foxy give the man a kind of salute. If he saw what he thought he had, Foxy'd clenched her fist and snapped it to her breast. And – the oddest part of all – if he had seen what he thought he had, he wasn't at all sure Foxy knew she'd given the man a salute.

The boy beside the man was, he now saw, pretty. In Giveadamn's book there was no other word for him. And he had to be the man's son. The build was the same, and except for the mangled half of the man's face, so was the hair and skin. Giveadamn could believe that before his accident, the man must have been the handsomest stud in Harlem.

Margo had already begun to exclaim over the boy. She turned to Giveadamn. 'And he was just a little child yesterday. Giveadamn, this is Ranger. He's Lobo here's son.'

Lobo grinned casually.

'Goddamn, Lobo, you're breaking this kid in to be a real heartbreaker, aren't you?'

'He's cool,' Lobo admitted. 'I tell him there's no use ever playing chump in this world. No excuse whatever.'

Giveadamn had the uneasy feeling Lobo, though not looking at him, was telling him something. He didn't like the man.

When he and Margo got to the top of the steps, he said, 'What happened to his face?'

'The war. He came back with it. Lives next door here with the boy. The boy's mother is dead, been dead since he was a little kid. Lobo's brought him up.'

'How'd she die?' Giveadamn asked curiously.

'Jumped out a window, dead drunk. But I sometimes think Lobo threw her through the window because he told me once she'd been taking that boy, when he was little, into bed with her.'

'She was his mother.'

Margo rang the bell again. 'Yeah, but they was both naked.'

'He seems very polite,' Giveadamn said lamely.

Gracie answered the door, and she grabbed Foxy in her relief to see her with Giveadamn. Foxy had been right as usual. Giveadamn could see her sister had been a lot more worried than she'd shown that afternoon. And then it came to Giveadamn he was less worried about Margo than Gracie or anyone else.

When they were in a taxi again, heading home, Margo frowned and said, 'Maybe you don't really understand what I'm all about, Giveadamn. It's like this: life is nothing but a case of giving and taking. You take what you want and give it to who you want. Understand?'

He understood that.

His hand wandered over her body. He did it sort of furtively. He did it very often now because he wanted to find out exactly where she carried her stiletto. There were only five feet one inch of her and less than a hundred and ten pounds. So where the hell did she carry the damned thing? He swore he was going to find it without asking.

The phone rang. He made a leap for it before Foxy could think of answering. 'Hello,' he said.

And then Foxy hit him with a Georgia Tech block. His body did not stop moving until his head hit the opposite wall.

He saw her take the phone. 'Harry Brown?' she said tightly. 'Listen, Harry, I'm scared of you . . .' A real deep pause. '. . .

personally. But my man is not getting into any shit with you. Not now. Not never. And I don't give a damn what you do to me. You are not going to get him fucked up in no narco racket. You can fuck over me but not him. So take your best shot, bastard, mother-fucker!' She slammed the phone down and turned to him. 'I've politely waited long enough for you to get your ass in shape. First thing tomorrow morning we go down and collect.'

The only thing wrong – it was Friday night.

8

Toni had been in sweet turmoil all the time she had wanted Ranger's love and he had denied it . . . sexually. On the other hand, he had increased that sweet turmoil when he not only put down sex in the same words her mother so often used, but gave her a mission. Really a holy mission to go out and *enjoy*. She was doing it for Ranger and that made all the difference.

She gazed around the room. Everybody here looked all right. It was a crowd like everybody belonged. There were not any old people. Maybe some of the basketball players were kind of olden but not too much. Like being here made them young enough.

One. The one who was the star ever since she could remember was kind of old. Maybe even older than her father, but then he couldn't be. Basketball was rough, a game for young men.

She began to wonder why she was so calm and realized it was because she did not want to go through with it. Not really. Not for real. It was easy to think of doing it, but when the time came for the man . . . whoever he was . . . to put his hands on her, to open her blouse . . . yes . . . she would let him do that. But nothing else. Lots of girls in school said it was all right as long as you don't go chump and take off your 'drawers.'

Ranger had got up from the arm of her chair and wandered off. She imagined he was going into the next room to cop a smoke. In the next room they were smoking. She wondered why all the big deal about that. Like why didn't they smoke right here? The smell of pot was all through the apartment, so what difference did it make?

The dude who was giving this little get-together came and sat on the arm Ranger had used. He looked at her and smiled. It was a nice smile. Cool, not frantic or whatever you wanted to call it. 'Ranger is always talking about you.'

Those six words warmed her and made everything all right. The man knew she was Ranger's woman. And the man knew that no one could really have her but Ranger. She relaxed.

The small lie came easily, 'Ranger is always talking about you, too.'

He looked at her quizzically.

'Ranger told me that you know how to win. Smart,' he said.

She had no intention of saying Ranger was a liar. And he wasn't. She was smart enough and if she needed more smarts, Ranger would most certainly give them to her.

Then, all at once, she knew this was the man Ranger had picked for her to trick. Ranger did everything smart without even trying. There were lots of girls right here now who would be glad to go with this star for free. Maybe even give him money so they could boast he had done it to them. She turned her head so she could inspect this dude.

He was all right. He was dressed down. He was cool. Like if she didn't have this thing only for Ranger, she wouldn't mind talking to this dude for real.

She began to wonder what made this dude uptight ... have what Ranger called a 'cunt collar.' Like here was a superstar who was supposed to have everything, yet here he was getting ready to lay out good bread for the stupidest kind of nothingness in the world. She was so glad and thankful that Ranger had put her head on straight about that. Suddenly she was impatient. Like why didn't this dude go right ahead and get it on?

'Want to see the rest of the house?'

So he was going to get it on. She sighed with relief.

'I want to show you a kitchen that is a kitchen.'

To her surprise, he led her from the room and then downstairs. It was exactly like her house, her parents' house. The kitchen was on the street floor. In fact, now she thought about it, there couldn't have been much difference: a brownstone is a brownstone.

But where her mother had a huge pantry, this dude had a little restroom. There was no other word for it. Not a bathroom, but a restroom. Like if you suddenly got tired cooking or got faint from the heat, you could go in this neat little cubbyhole and flop right across the tiny bed. It was sort of way out, weird even. She began to giggle.

And it was like the giggle turned him on.

'Ranger said you didn't smoke.'

She wasn't prepared for that. Now who in the whole wide world has not smoked at least one time? It was like taking a bath, or going to the A&P. You had to do it at least one time in your life, or you were not exactly in this world. Everybody smoked occasionally. After all, Margo and Gracie used to smoke it openly when she was little. It was only since she grew up that they had stopped it in front of her. They went upstairs, but the smell came into whatever room she was in while they were upstairs.

She giggled again.

He smiled broadly. 'All you little girls are the same. I don't know why. Give you a couple of puffs and the whole world seems funny to you. I had a girl once, she smoked a whole joint first thing in the morning and giggled for the rest of the day. S'funny, huh?'

He lit a joint. She gave out with a happy little laugh. Ranger must have said that this was going to be her first time . . .

She took the smoke when he handed it to her, and as she took a drag, he began to unbutton her blouse. She was sorry she had decided to go bra-less. It would have prolonged the thing.

The smoke was really great. She relaxed and seemed to step out of her skin so that she could sort of go over in a corner of the room and watch this bigtime star get real frantic with the girl who stood before him.

He wasn't cool now at all. But what was to be expected anyhow? Like if he wasn't frantic, he wouldn't be a john. He was on his knees before her. She had not even realized he had finished sucking her nipples a long time ago.

The thing she had fretted most about was not yet even in the act. She wondered vaguely when he was going to take it out of his pants. It seemed like he would have done that already. She wondered if he was a freak. She had heard a hell of a lot about freaks . . . all of it bad. In fact, all the girls talked about was what freaks did and how it was important to stay away from them. One freak could ruin a woman for life.

She reached out and touched his cheek, like an act of self-preservation. His tongue was toying with her navel now. Her panties were coming down in his grasp. It did not matter.

And now he was doing like faggots were supposed to do it to men. She was not exactly horrified. It was just that she had not expected this. She looked around her because it seemed necessary to take stock of things.

She was looking at the door when it slowly, silently began to open. It was not exactly a thing to get scared about, but she was . . . a little. And as she thought about that, it seemed like she was more scared of what she might submit to. Like the big idea of the whole thing was not to enjoy it.

But it was Ranger coming through the door. She trembled. At the last minute he had changed his mind and was coming to save her. Only she was already beyond saving because the dude's tongue was way up now. It felt good to her, so it must feel good to him. And Ranger was too late. She wondered if Ranger would want her now.

She was unable to remember it was Ranger put her up to this. She only worried Ranger would no longer want her. She began to cry. And then the tears washed her away. They washed her way over to the same corner of the room it had seemed like she was standing in when the dude first started into his thing.

And she was not there. Not really, although she could feel Ranger pick her up and lay her on the tiny bed. It was good that the bed was so tiny. It was only large enough for one person. She could not be molested on the bed. Not really. But Ranger was atop her. He was humping her like crazy. Only his thing was nowhere in the act. His pants were open. She knew because she could feel the skin of his body. He was soft. She guessed no one else could tell. She began to giggle again.

Ranger's breath was going faster. His body went through convulsive humps, but it was like nothing. She opened her eyes. The dude was now in the corner of the room and he was humping his rod with his hand. He was humping a damned sight faster than Ranger was atop her.

And the dude's eyes were so crazy. Crazy as hell. The dude moaned. She had never seen or heard of a man get off like that, but she knew he had shot his load. Ranger must have known, too, because he stopped and got off her.

The dude looked sick and wilted. Ranger went to him and held out his hand. The dude put something in Ranger's hand, and Toni knew it was not money.

The dude went out of the room. Ranger hugged and kissed her. But not for long. He took a packet from his pocket. It must have been what the man handed to him. She knew what it was.

But she did not exactly fight. She knew she would not have to fight. She could say she was going to tell her mother. She could even say she was going to tell her father. Why, she could even say that she was going to tell *his* father!

But Ranger said in a voice as kind and gentle as any baby doctor's, 'This is not what you think it is. This is a shot for your health, Toni. No shit. This is what all the smart girls use to avoid V.D.'

He did not give her too much that first time. Toni did not get ill. She went up on the finest high she would ever have in her life. All other shots that followed in the next three weeks did not nearly approach that beautiful high with its truly orgasmic explosion in her vitals. She was one of those who took off beautifully the first time, and for the rest of their dope-leadened lives seek just one more wonderful fix like the first.

9

Even though he had gone to bed in a rage, Harry awoke on Saturday morning from a sound and dreamless sleep. His bedroom, on top of the duplex, was directly above Ossie's and he grunted as he heard the water flush in the bathroom below. Ossie was up and about.

He decided he did not need Ossie to accompany him anywhere today. Ossie would be a drag; already Ossie had shown signs of liking this whore who went by the name of Foxy Cool Momma. And anyone with a name like that was more or less a pile of zilch in any field.

He silently ate the breakfast Ossie had prepared and brought. Country ham in its own gravy, grits and eggs. It was better than just good. And the big stiff had never been south of Baltimore, even when he was playing with a pretty bigtime college basketball team.

Thinking about Ossie's culinary skills brought on memories of Ossie's mother. A rather good woman. Rather good. Not the best because of the simple fact both her children broke her heart: the girl dying from an OD and the son getting asked to leave college.

He put down his napkin and rose from the table saying, 'That was good, Ossie.'

'At least that's more than you'll say to the rest of us underlings you meet today.'

Harry glowered. 'What's that mean?'

'It means you're still uptight for having visited that boy like you was Gawd, instead of acting like you know damned well the kid and his woman don't need anything you got.'

Harry stalked out.

He drove directly to Eighth Avenue below 116th Street, parked and waited. The slag, the driftwood, the grifters, and the scum would all come by to grin, bow, shuffle their feet and try to find out what tune Harry was willing to pay money to hear today.

From where he was parked, he could see the burned-out hulk of the building that was Francis Williams' bier. He felt nothing. Not even a cold satisfaction. He did not even bother to wonder why he had not been told through the grapevine that Francis had turned junkie.

A flashy Lincoln Continental passed from the opposite direction. The driver recognized him, slowed, made a U-turn to come park behind him, then got out to come to Harry's car.

The tall young man smiled easily, openly. 'What's happening, Harry?'

Harry said, 'Hello Manning. Up and out kind of early?'

'You're slipping, Harry,' Manning said. 'You know I take care of all details before eleven in the morning. The other dudes think different, but from what I can see, the damned plainclothes don't get outa bed till then. What's happening, I said.'

'What's the story on a junkie named Margo?'

Manning reflected, 'She's never had much class. Cute as hell. Still is, with a fine shape and a wicked-looking little ass on her. That girl could have made the top ten songs with lots of dudes I know. But she always sort of went for the sorriest assholes obtainable. Born losers. Real slobs. She even had a greasy spic onetime. Still might.

'All I know is, you can forget her. There's nothing she got to offer could do you the least bit of good,' Manning said. 'Unless maybe you want her for some kind of hit girl. She has killed, but not for money, far as I know. Margo Hilliard is a professional killer, Harry. Even if she does it for free. Years ago when she first hit the streets they used to call her "The Electric Knife." You know,' Manning nodded sagely. 'The Electric Knife they called her, and electric knives hadn't even been invented back then.'

Harry lapsed into thought. Heavy thought. This Margo was exactly what he knew she had to be: the last word in nothing, a stone dummy. Suddenly he was sorry he had gone to St Luke's Hospital to visit some boy he knew nothing about. Finally he said, 'I want that bitch in prison and I don't give a damn how she gets there. Only get her there.'

Manning grinned. 'Not me. Not me, Harry. I'm superstitious like that. My mother made me go to Sunday school.'

'You owe me.'

'And I pay. I pay good, Harry.'

'Like now?'

'I'm not a hit man, Harry.'

'Who said to hit her? I want her unhappy.'

'Why not try some roots?'

Harry glared.

'I got this big Haitian nurse in my back pocket. She's a nurse for real in a hospital in Queens, but she is also a voodoo dame when she gets home from work. Now this bitch can make this broad of yours sick as hell. You know.'

'Margo is no broad of mine.'

Curiosity got the best of Manning. 'What the hell she do anyhow, Harry?'

'She's still alive and breathing and walking around. And she has made herself an offer she can't refuse. However, I refuse to let her accept it.'

'Oh. I dig it. She ripped you off?'

'Never mind. The point to remember is, I don't like her.' Then – 'Who ripped off Francis Williams?'

Manning took a long, hard look at Harry. 'You don't know? Or you don't know if I know?'

'I know what Francis said, but I don't believe it any more.'

'Francis said it was the fuzz,' Manning said heavily. 'And it was the fuzz. Harry, you know good and well that the cops in Harlem are the only ones dumb enough to do a thing like that to a man like Francis. You forgetting that Francis was cool? That dude was like dry ice. He was so damned cold he could burn the shit outa you and not even know he was doing it. Harry, Francis was an ace. A real ace of spades. The tops.'

'No he wasn't. How long had he been using?'

'Francis never used.' Again Manning was puzzled at Harry's odd attitude. 'What made you ask?'

'He used. I saw him go into withdrawal.'

'No you didn't!' It was not until long after that Manning realized he had called Harry a liar. But even when he did, he decided that he was not going to play too much pussy for this new Harry Brown. 'The devil in hell couldn't make Francis take a snort, Harry,' he said evenly. 'Not even coke, and coke is like ice cream around town. He did not use, Harry. But Francis played hard. He really did. I've seen him in what you might call a state of utter exhaustion.'

Harry started the motor. Manning took the act for exactly what it was, opened the car door and stepped out in the street.

But since he had called Harry a liar, he decided to get involved in some crap he did not approve of.

'I'm going to tell this voodoo broad about Margo for you.' He touched his hat then and quickly walked away. Harry guided the big car away from the curb.

10

The following Monday Giveadamn got up late. It was almost eleven o'clock when he finished his walk. When he got to the front of the hotel he saw the Rolls-Royce parked in front. There was a big handsome black dude behind the wheel and a smart-looking white guy beside him. It was not until he saw the car had a third passenger that he got worried. Harry Brown was in the back seat.

He gave a kind of cheerily appreciative look at the big car and then bounded up the stairs into the hotel.

In the room he said, 'Your golden chariot waits without.'

'Without what?' She was deadpan, sitting on the bed.

'It's a Rolls-Royce.'

'I'm going someplace in it?'

'Yeah.'

'Yeah?' She shrugged into the bright-orange jacket of flimsy stuff that matched her slacks.

'We get to ride in a big hog when we go to collect a hundred grand. Besides, if Harry's out front and you're no longer afraid of him, we don't got too much choice, do we?'

Her face was truly beautiful. She came down the steps beside Giveadamn and came directly to the car. She did not wait for Giveadamn to open the door. And when she got in, she merely said, 'Hi,' then froze into an erect statuette of dark-cherry red-and-brown stone.

Harry stared. The more he stared, the chillier she got. She did not move an eyelid, although Harry could see she was breathing hard. He had never seen a woman sit so erect and yet somehow at ease.

Giveadamn had gotten in. Harry continued to stare, but the little junkie whore looked straight ahead of her like she owned the damned car and everything in it. He quietly told Ossie to head downtown to the lottery offices.

'This is Joe Glass,' Harry said to Giveadamn. 'He's a lawyer. A money man. I want him to go in with you.'

Giveadamn nodded.

No more words were said until after Giveadamn and Joe Glass had entered the New York State Lottery building. Then Harry said, 'What's your name?'

'Margo.'

'I'm Harry Brown and this is Ossie Winbush. Glad to meet you.'

She coolly turned her head to look him over. Finally she said, 'You'll have to kill me to change what I said Friday night.'

He nodded thoughtfully; he was still considering precisely that. But he said, 'I got no argument with you, Margo. In fact, I like your stance.'

That was all Harry said. But about three minutes later, he murmured, 'Madame X.' Then he said bitterly, 'Ex-whore, ex-addict, ex-con, ex-lesbo . . .'

Foxy flinched but said nothing.

So Harry said, 'I don't know as I would like to see that boy keeping company with an angel, but maybe you happen to be a little too much on the other side, what do you think?'

His tone was so conversational that it took her unawares. 'Harry,' she said, 'Giveadamn Brown happens to be twenty-six years old. He is not stupid. In fact, he is very intelligent. You are not a judge. At least not the kind of judge I'm used to, so I don't have to plead any case. Get what I mean? I already pleaded my case with Giveadamn and he liked what I had to offer.' She turned to stare straight ahead again. 'Case closed!' she snapped.

He laughed. 'You are a contradiction of everything I ever believed in, but I got to go with you.' His look told her he was being strictly on the level. 'I got to go with you.'

Her eyes widened.

'Lawrence told me what you think of me and what you think I will do to you. You are wrong, but that is not the point. The point is that after the way you cussed me out on the phone, you intend to take his money and run. You can't do that.'

She asked a question with her eyes.

'I believe in that boy,' Harry said heavily. 'He came to me and just about offered his soul in exchange for your health.'

Now her eyes held hatred, but he went on: 'You and I got workhorse minds. Stallions, but workhorses just the same. Lawrence thinks kind of dainty. He got a dainty mind, but it's good. I know it is. I'm taking that boy under my wing.'

She blinked.

'I have not been in narco for almost three years now. Do you believe that?'

'No.'

'Why?'

'I would have heard.'

'And if you had heard, what then?'

She looked askance. Then she said, 'There would have been a lot of . . . well . . . jockeying. Everybody would have been out to take over your share of the market. You know.' She thought about that. 'Shee-it! With what you're supposed to have, the dudes would be machine-gunning it all over town.'

'Do you doubt that I am the shrewdest man who ever dealt in New York City?'

She turned to study him in amazement. She had never thought about it before, but with Studs Thompson, Jimmy Adams, Sonny Roberts, and Doll Baby having everything locked up, there was nothing for Harry Brown to be holding and dealing. The part of the action that Francis Williams held had been swallowed up in a bloody skirmish.

'Talk ain't shit,' she said. 'I hear you got a way to make five ounces of heroin out of one.'

He shook his head. 'You just cannot stop the Harlem rumor mill. It's because I still pay off the police. I'm not about to let those greedy sonsofbitches suddenly realize I'm expendable. They just might plant some narco someplace and send me away.'

'They would kill you,' Ossie said flatly. 'There's nothing else to do when the goose stops laying.'

'I don't want that boy to know yet. I just might change my mind. Almost did, but I don't think I will. But I got to tell you because I don't want you to run. Just keep him happy.'

She took his hand. She wasn't used to guys like this.

Giveadamn and Joe Glass came out of the building. As soon as he got in the car, Giveadamn handed the check to Margo. She smiled and kissed it. Then Harry took it out of her hand and gave it back to Giveadamn. 'Sign it,' he said.

'Why?'

'That's the second reason I got my man Joe here along today. He's going to buy you a bond. One bond. One hundred thousand dollars.'

'But . . .'

'I'll loan you living expenses for the time being. Anyway, I want you and Margo here to come live with me. I been doing a lot of thinking over the weekend.'

'I can't. I mean, I don't want to get any further than walking distance from St Luke's.' And then Giveadamn said, 'This hole is not acting right. I don't know what's wrong. I feel great, but if anything, this darned hole is getting worse.'

'Okay,' Harry said. Then he told Ossie to drive to Saks. When they were in front of Saks, he handed Margo a pile of hundred-dollar bills. 'Get lost,' was all he said.

After that, Giveadamn signed the check and they dropped Joe Glass off on Forty-second Street near his offices. Then Harry said they would go home.

When they were in the playroom or barroom – Giveadamn could never make up his mind what to call it – Harry said, 'Take it off!'

'What?'

'Your shirt, boy. Pull it off.'

Giveadamn did, and then Harry attacked the bandages over the unhealed wound. It was then Giveadamn discovered what Margo knew before – this big, mean man thought a lot of him.

With tight lips Harry examined the wound. The edges of the hole were a grayish color and were puckered like a cauliflower. 'Ossie!' he said quietly. 'Get Sammy on the phone. Have him set up everything necessary for this boy to get into Mayo Brothers.'

'I don't need all that,' Giveadamn protested.

'A lead-pipe hole can do better than this thing's doing,' Harry said to him. 'I never saw a wound exactly like this before. I don't know what's happening, but I want a *team* of doctors to check you over. How long's it been?'

'Since I got stabbed? About a month.'

'Naw.' It was a very definite statement, that one word. And it meant that this wound had not only Giveadamn Brown to contend with, but it also had one Harry Brown as its enemy.

After Harry brought new bandages and bound the wound, they sat and talked. That is, Giveadamn and Ossie did most of the talking. Harry sat and brooded more than anything.

'In view of the fact you are my nephew, I don't like the idea of you two living alone. There's a lot of shit in the air. There's a man named Sonny Roberts who acts like he's lost his mind. Every time I look up, he's sniffing around, seems like.'

'Yesterday,' Ossie said to him, 'I heard Studs Thompson sent word to Eighth Avenue she is coming to town, and if she decides somebody got to go as an example to the rest – why not you?'

Harry blew out his breath. 'After you leave Mayo Brothers, maybe I should take you down to Bimini for a spell. How much you weigh anyhow?'

'About the same. One fifty. I never weighed more than that.'

Harry seemed to be wrestling with some inner problem. 'I knew your mother before she married your father. She was older than your father . . . and beautiful. That was twenty-three years ago,' Harry said quietly, savagely. 'The last time I saw her you was only three.'

'I remember she died of a fatty heart.'

Harry snorted. 'In a town like Wiggins, the GP makes up illnesses to fit the purse. If you ask me, your mother had something else – maybe asthma. Maybe she was allergic to Morris Brown.'

Giveadamn seemed to remember his mother taking him for a walk in the woods. Suddenly, without warning, she'd had an attack. That's all he could remember: her fighting for breath.

'It could have been asthma,' he agreed. 'After all, I got it, too. At least I used to have it, not any more.'

'Asthma, rheumatic fever, they're all a part of growing up. But you don't have that any more, eh?'

'Sometimes I have a hard time breathing, but I just take it easy and it goes away. I take cold tablets.'

Harry snorted. 'Well, we'll get it all cleared up.'

'Foxy sure is going to enjoy this trip,' Giveadamn said. 'She's got a good sister. Her sister keeps six babies at all times.'

'How the hell can a woman have six babies at one time?'

'You're not listening. I said she keeps six in her home at all times. She gets them from the foster-homes people.'

'What's this?'

'She has this theory that malnutrition is the root of black stupidity. And so to do her share, she takes in these infants and makes sure they get the correct diet. It's a wonderful idea. You've got to meet her.'

'I plan to. What's her name?'

'Gracie.'

Foxy had bought almost eight hundred dollars' worth of clothes and shoes and was back wondering where Giveadamn was when he called.

'Hell, no. I'm not going to *meet* you at my sister's. I want to arrive in front of Gracie's house in that helluva hog of a Rolls-Royce just like you.'

'Stand by then.'

It seemed Ossie had a date, so Giveadamn and Harry left together about five minutes after Ossie. Ten minutes later Harry was in a shootout. According to Giveadamn, that is.

They had left the building and got into the Rolls. Harry paused to adjust the rearview mirror. He saw something in the mirror that made him curse. He reached in the unlocked glove compartment and took out an automatic German pistol.

Then Harry got out of the car and went to a big Mercedes parked farther down the street. Giveadamn did not get out of the car. Instead he watched the action through the rearview window. He watched Harry point the gun at the Mercedes' front tires and shoot. Then Harry calmly walked back, got into the Rolls and drove off.

'What was that all about?'

'Sonny Roberts. The faggot's been following me now for over a month.'

'Just because he's a faggot? Isn't he a Harlem businessman?'

'Yes, to all your fool questions. I believe he's lost his mind. Can't be any other reason. He ain't mad at me, I don't think.'

'You shot his tires out and you don't think he's mad? But you must have an inkling of what he wants.'

'Lawrence,' Harry said heavily as they entered Central Park, 'the people in narco nowadays simply do not have good sense. They are smart . . . crafty is a better word . . . but they are crazy. Now the logical thing to guess would be that Sonny wants to feel my ass. That's logical. But I'm willing to bet that's not it.'

Foxy was waiting in front of the hotel. She got into the car, quivering with anticipation. Going downtown in a Rolls was no big thing, but driving up in front of Gracie's in this dreamboat was something else.

'Drive real slow,' she ordered Harry. 'I don't want nobody to make no mistake about who's in the back seat.'

She set the mood, and it was a pleasant, if short, drive to Gracie's. But Harry hardly acknowledged the introduction to Gracie. 'I want to see these babies of yours and hear what you got to say about feeding them regular.'

Gracie beamed. 'You bet.' Then she and Harry disappeared upstairs.

When he came down in an hour, Harry said he was ready to leave. But the doorbell rang. Gracie went to answer it. It was Stella, and she was stunning in a sky-blue safari suit.

Harry sat down and took her in. Stella had eyes of obsidian black and the devil was hiding in them.

Harry sat and looked at those eyes. And then he looked into them. And she came over to him as if she had no choice, as if she had been summoned. She was trembling.

Harry said slowly, without a smile, 'I don't know who you are, but you are going to have to reckon with me.'

She smiled.

He grunted. 'You know already, eh?'

She nodded.

'I'm Harry Brown.'

'You got a black name like I got a Spanish name. You and I are common. I'm Stella Rodriguez.'

'You married?'

'Sort of.'

'You sort of don't like your husband, though?'

'I married when I was thirteen.'

'How come? Pregnant?'

She shook her head. 'In love. His hair is what you call nappy. He's been on heroin for years.'

'Get rid of him!'

She stared her astonishment. 'You don't walk away from a good man.'

Harry looked as though he was about to slap her. 'They never come back. No addict ever . . .'

'*I* kicked.'

He got to his feet. He looked around as though dazed. Quietly, he strode out of the room and out of the house. Stella's eyes followed him. No one seemed to have noticed, but Foxy had watched it all. Stella was hurt; Foxy got up and came to her. 'That's Harry Brown,' she said grimly. '*The* Harry Brown. You got to've heard of him.'

Stella looked at her. Then she came out of it and said tightly, 'Margo, I don't give a good goddamn who that man is.' And she broke down and cried.

Giveadamn was watching now. He said, 'Did you tell Harry you were once on the stuff?'

Stella nodded.

'How can a sonofabitch sell narco and hate junkies like that man does?' Foxy was angry.

Stella straightened up a little. 'Margo, he can't hurt me. I'm smarter than this.'

Margo put her arm around Stella. 'You touched that rough sonofabitch. I was watching. He flipped. He flipped, Stella. He's coming back, and he'll tell you he's sorry.'

Stella shook her head.

Gracie came in and said, 'What's the matter, Stella? Where's Harry?'

'She's raving,' Foxy said offhandedly. 'She flipped over Harry Brown.'

Margo walked to the door. 'Come on, let's go,' she said, looking at Giveadamn. 'I'm sick in the stomach from this shit.'

Giveadamn came, but all the while he was looking at Stella, worried.

Foxy rapidly led him out of the house, down the front steps. In the taxi, riding back to the hotel, Giveadamn was disturbed and silent. He liked Harry better all the time, and the more he learned about him, the more he understood him. But it was upsetting the way he'd left Gracie's without a word to anyone; embarrassing and upsetting. After all, he'd brought Harry there as a guest, and it was as if Harry didn't think enough of them to bother to behave – or think enough of him. Then why was Harry trying so hard to help him, caring enough about getting him cured to fly him around all over the place? Did Harry think he owned him just because he was his nephew? That made no sense.

And another thing: Harry hadn't brought up that errand thing again; he had a hunch Harry never would. What was that all-important errand and why was it forgotten?

At the hotel, Margo's heels clicked up the stairs ahead of him. In the room he said, 'I got to talk to Harry. I'm bothered.'

'You ought to be. But don't have no more to do with him is what I say.'

Harry was already back at his apartment. When he answered the phone, Giveadamn said, 'I want to come up. You going to be home awhile?' He was, so Giveadamn left at once.

Over at Harry's, he went in past the man in uniform at the big double glass doors and across the marble floor to the elevator in the far corner and up to Harry's private entrance. The elevator man waited until Ossie came to the door. Harry was in the living room, his stocking feet up on a glass cocktail table.

He had his tie loose, his collar open, a big glass of Bourbon on the rocks in one hand. He looked disturbed, too.

He glared at Giveadamn, but his voice was calm when he said, 'Sit down. But don't expect me to say I'm sorry about anything.'

Giveadamn sat down. Ossie sat down, too.

'Look. I got to say I don't like the way you acted, you know, at Gracie's, because I like Gracie and Stella. Like they're my friends and all. But I know how you felt. I really do. What I can't understand is why you care about me. I guess you do. I know you do. But I don't know why. You talk to me about the Mayo Clinic and about taking me to Bimini. You worry about Margo being bad for me. It's like I was your son, not your nephew. And I'm not your son. I definitely am *not!*'

Harry nodded at Ossie. Ossie got up and left the room. While they waited, Harry said nothing and never took his hard eyes off Giveadamn. Then Ossie was back with a piece of paper in his hand. He laid it on the low glass table beside Harry's feet and in front of Giveadamn. A birth certificate.

'That me?'

'That's you, Lawrence. And from now on, you ain't going to forget it. I won't let you.'

Ossie was staring at Giveadamn sadly, as if Harry had just broken him some bad news. Giveadamn stared back at Ossie, his big lips hanging open in amazement. Ossie nodded.

Things seemed to be happening too fast for Giveadamn. He didn't remember anything about the ride back to his hotel in Harry's limousine, but when he got upstairs and started to pack, it was clear his life was going to be different from now on. It scared him.

Margo was scared too. She said, 'That sonofabitch has ignored you all your life, and now when he's old enough to die off any minute he all of a sudden comes around and wants to lay claim on you. He's a shit, Giveadamn.'

'No, Margo. He's deeper than that. He's got a lot of real principle.'

'Shee-it. Like what he did to Stella?'

Giveadamn paused in his packing. Foxy was leaning against the doorway, arms folded, watching him. 'His principles are kinda strange. I got to admit that. But I trust him.'

'How the hell you know he's your father? He say so?'

'He showed me a copy of my birth certificate. His name was on it, clear. I saw it.'

'If he's going to leave you anything, you get him to sign some papers, Giveadamn.' She sighed. 'I just hope you don't get it in your head you're going to be some kind of bigshot wheeler-dealer, because, Giveadamn, I'm telling you right now, you ain't cut out for it. Unless Harry trots you on a leash down 125th Street, you wouldn't last ten minutes out there. Some of the people I know, if they want what he says he's going to give you, would cut your hip pocket out and your ass with it.'

And that was how Giveadamn and Margo came to move into the apartment house on the East River near Sutton Place. There were two weeks of celebration, and though nobody who came to the parties had ever heard of Giveadamn Brown, they found him introduced to them by Harry Brown, no less, as Harry Brown's son.

And that was when Harry Brown's son began to think he might like living up to his father's expectations – as long as there was no violence.

One thing about Margo, she knew the street. She knew whereof she spoke.

Sonny Roberts, for one, when he heard that Harry had revealed to the world a son and heir, accepted the story in a more or less casual manner. This was an insane world. Anyone who wanted to survive and be on top of the pile had better hurry up and get as crazy as everyone else. Hadn't both Nixon and Agnew proved it? *Almost*, anyway. Maybe they weren't quite crazy enough.

Well, he was going to be, Sonny decided. What he better

do, and not waste any more time, was get Harry knocked off before he got that simple-assed Giveadamn broken in. Then he could wait and watch and see how things went as the killings got started. If he moved at the right time, he could clean up, sell out and take off for Hollywood and spend the rest of his life producing black movies.

He'd knocked off fifteen kilos of the finest from Francis Williams and nobody knew it. Not even now. He could handle Harry Brown just like he'd fucked over Francis and got away with it. And there was no time to lose. Not if he wanted to be America's black Sam Goldwyn when he got to the Coast with five million bucks the IRS officially declared sanitary.

Sonny picked up the phone and in his excitement dialed too fast and messed up. He hung up and dialed again, calling Norman Russell, known as Sparks. Sparks was in most ways a stupid man, except around an automobile; then he became a genius. He couldn't pass the test to get a driver's license in the State of New York, but Sparks could fix cars. He could even make them.

The police had been saying a lot of hold-ups had been pulled off in stolen cars they were not even sure were stolen – or could even, by rights, be called cars.

Sparks and his son rode the city's streets in search of wrecks and abandoned vehicles. They stripped them at curbside, and then Sparks put together new machines the cops called stolen because they didn't know what else to call them.

When Sonny got Sparks on the phone and told him his problem, Sparks asked, 'How does this dude drive?'

'What do you mean? What kind of car, or how does he drive it? Anyhow, he drives like everybody else. I don't see no difference.'

'What I mean is,' Sparks said, 'you give me a quick-tempered driver, a dude who suddenly steps on the gas to cut in and out real fast to pass some stupid dude or dame, and I'll show you a mother that can get hisself killed in no time flat. It's real easy, Sonny. You give me a wrench and ten minutes under his car and he's dead.'

That was all Sonny wanted to hear. He said he'd meet Sparks in an hour.

Sonny handed Sparks five one-hundred-dollar bills. 'Now, this man has a bunch of cars. More than me. But I only want you to fix up one of 'em. I don't want some smart-assed fuzz fucking around after the accident and finding out that every single one of this man's cars is fucked up. You know. Like once is an accident. More is on purpose.'

Sparks nodded and got in his truck with no more ado. As far as he was concerned, this unknown dude was dead.

11

In the days that followed, Harry's apartment was from time to time inundated with women with asses. At least, that is the only way Giveadamn could think of the suave and svelte girls who came to the house. All were not good-looking. Some were ugly. But as Giveadamn was the first to point out, they all had wonderful asses.

All of these young women wore slacks. And their sexy rumps filled and stretched every millimeter of the expensive pants. Giveadamn had never met girls in their late twenties exactly like them. They were from the same mold. They all entered the premises and kissed Ossie. Tongues doing most of the work, Giveadamn saw. All wore Afros. Most had tiny waists and big tits. Most were brown-skinned, ranging from Foxy's reddish mahogany to ebony.

In every way they were very cool and, although they were usually accompanied by men, they were women without men.

Giveadamn finally had to ask, 'Margo, who and what the devil are all these chicks with asses? How come their slacks fit over their rears so perfectly? Always perfectly?'

'Bodysuits and pantyhose, Giveadamn. You know. But most of those chicks don't have to worry. They got the butts that naturally were made for slacks.'

'But how do these girls live? I mean their lifestyle. They all seem to go out of their way to mention *jobs*, but they never mention what they do.'

Foxy realized that Giveadamn had never had a chance to meet any of Harlem's female fugitives before.

'These are practically all Harlem-born broads, Giveadamn,' she said. 'Maybe a few come from South Carolina or Florida, but they got to Harlem before they started to menstruate. It's a pretty sure bet some of these kids were 'ho's before they were in junior high, but for some very weird reason they suddenly took their asses downtown and got a job.

'A ghetto chick used to have three choices. Now she got four, with college. But when these kids first started making it, there was only three. They could get knocked up by the dude they loved and get their asses put on welfare. They could be a junkie "ho". Or they could go downtown and get a job.

'Those that go downtown are roughly divided into two parts,' Margo went on. 'Some go down there to pick fights with the whiteys all day long. The others go down there to get their asses felt.'

'Huh?'

Foxy's eyes widened at Giveadamn's lack of knowledge. 'You can do a lot with a man if you let him pat your ass,' she said. 'Especially if you slap another guy in front of the guy you let pat, for doing the same thing. The guy you let pat goes right out and starts to boast that you can't be touched by nobody but him. You don't even have to screw him after that, especially if he's married. So the girls who know how to get patted and when not to get patted get promoted. The so-called militant bitches get flat feet and almost always pregnant in the end and on welfare – the same as those who never bothered to look for a job at all.

'But these chicks got promoted. And suddenly they is ambitious. They go to night school, computer school, even college at night. Pretty soon they are taking vacations in the Caribbean and all that way-out *Jet* magazine shit. You know. They're good kids. I like 'em, but damned if I understand them.'

'I do already. They simply make the best of their opportunities.'

'That's the way it is. These chicks went downtown and got on the fast track. They outran the black men . . . what there is left that ain't on narco. Lots of these dumb bitches have bought houses out in the woods somewhere. They're up to their pretty assholes in debt. And no smart black dude is going to marry a mortgage. You know. So you got to figure that black dudes got to offer only what Ossie got to offer. Not one thing more, and at least Ossie is cold. They can be seen with him, and everyone knows they ain't putting out hard cash for his company.'

'If that's their game, I don't see where Ossie has that much to offer. Not really. You realize Ossie is a disgraced Olympic star? He has no visible means of support. I know he really has, but damned if it's visible. So what the heck he got that these would-be high-society chicks want?'

'Nothing,' Foxy said wearily. 'Nothing at all. But that fits the bill exactly. These bitches don't want nothing from a black dude, because a nigger wants to get repaid for everything he gives up. I guess I ought to say that Ossie offers them equality. I mean like Ossie can be screwed and that's it. They get to exercise with an equal and it don't cost nothing.' She reflected a moment. 'All these chicks want to know is, Can a dude afford 'em? But that don't mean they got any intention of charging 'em.'

They stopped talking because Giveadamn was about to meet one of the girls he was asking about. The truly dark and handsome beauty had strolled over and flopped down on the lounge beside Margo. There was plenty of room, but Margo moved a little closer to Giveadamn in a gesture of welcome. 'My man has been measuring your ass for size,' she said to the girl, whose name was Boots.

'Better now than later,' Boots said. She sighed and lounged back comfortably. 'How my hips got anything to do with you and your man?'

'Oh, raise up, bitch,' Margo said genially. 'It's all wrapped up in the fact that this dude of mine is at a party with some of the really smart black women Harlem got to offer, and all he thinks about is their drawers don't show.'

'The man just might be for real. Like you ever stop to think how boring it can get for a working girl to meet up with nothing but nothing dudes who come on with how much they appreciate your brains? Hell, it's been a long time since a black dude came up and said something about how he got the works that can lay more on my fine black frame than all the goddamn computers down on Wall Street.'

'Once a 'ho', always a 'ho',' Margo said.

Boots slumped and stretched herself. Every curve of her fine body strove for attention. 'I got the mind of one,' she said most agreeably, 'but nobody ever gave me a chance to be.'

Harry came down the winding stairs and beckoned for Giveadamn. When Giveadamn came over to him, he said, 'You realize there's not a single woman in this house right now that woman of yours can hold a decent conversation with?'

'What you think she's doing over there on the couch with that kid named Boots?' Giveadamn asked. 'We're having a very philosophical conversation.'

'C'mon upstairs,' Harry said gruffly. 'I want you to meet people who amount to something.'

Boots and Foxy sat side by side and watched Giveadamn and Harry ascend the stairs. Boots said reflectively, 'Come to think of it, how the hell you manage to even be present here? I don't dig it at all. Not at all. By rights you're supposed to be dead. You know that, don't you? You're an ex-junkie.'

It was a cold, hard jewel inside her that made Foxy refuse to answer.

'Well, you know it,' Boots insisted. 'The man had Francis wasted because Francis had begun to use the stuff.'

Margo spoke out of a deep study. 'How you able to prove Francis was a user? He never did as long as I knew him.'

'I'm going to pull your coat on something nobody knows much, Margo. Francis had sickle-cell anemia. In fact, I'm going to also let you in on something I found out when I was dealing: damned near every addict I knew well had sickle cell. Notice I said *had*. They was dying anyhow. It's like everybody has it. Maybe Francis . . .' Boots' spoken thoughts died away in their own doubts.

When Giveadamn edged away from Harry and went back downstairs to the lounge, Margo was not around, so he went to the bar for a drink. A pretty chick was tending bar with gusto.

'What you having, babee?' she asked.

'I ought to have you with two cherries, but it'd probably be too rich for my blood,' Giveadamn murmured. It was not until the girl's eyes began to sparkle that he realized he had said it aloud. 'I didn't really exactly mean that,' he said. 'Sometimes things sort of pop out of me.'

She looked ferocious. 'You make with apologies and I'll knock the livin' hell outa you!' She filled a glass with ice and waited for him to tell her what to pour. 'Aren't you the lucky son of Harry,' she asked.

'The *only* son of Harry.'

'I like you.' She looked at him inquisitively. 'Don't you feel like a sheep in wolf's clothing?'

As usual, he grinned.

When Boots got up and strolled away, Margo went out the door that led around an ell to the bathroom that was more or less a public lavatory in the household scheme at Harry's.

She shut the door and was about to twist the latch to lock it when the door was pushed back and a big dark woman shoved her way into the small room.

The woman was not only an alien in this home of Harry's, but she wasn't a denizen of Harlem either. Foxy went for her knife.

The woman smiled, if a little tight-lipped.

'Not to worry.' There was an unmistakable accent.

It was the accent that infuriated Margo the most. She feinted with her knife toward the woman's eyes. The woman swayed away from Margo.

She looked at the woman's hands for the first time. There was a Syrette in her left hand. It made Margo grin. 'From Harry, bitch?'

She was at ease now. This stupid bitch was one of those musclewomen who work in nursing homes and the like, a female gorilla used to overpowering nuts and sedating them.

'Not to worry,' the woman said again as she inched a little closer.

As her knife found its home in the woman's heart, Margo felt the first waves of confusion. Whoever had sent the woman had not told her there was always a knife on the person of her intended victim. Harry Brown would not have been that thoughtless. Or would he?

Harry Brown could have set this up with the idea that she would now face a murder rap. But if he thought so, Harry had another think coming. When you were up against a sharpie, you got sharp yourself. Like any other time, she would have left this room, cursing and demanding to know who the hell this dead bitch was. But not now.

Margo stepped to the washbowl and rinsed her blade. She put the blade away and reached down for the woman's legs. She pulled on the body so that the woman's rump almost touched the door while she held the woman's legs high, being careful to avoid the seeping blood. She squeezed out, letting the woman's legs drop against the door. Anybody trying to open the door would feel the push of the legs and simply go away, thinking whoever was using the john could not lock it from the inside.

Margo went upstairs and found Giveadamn talking to Boots again. She took her man's arm and said, 'We better head over to Gracie's.'

'What the hell for?' Boots said. 'This shindig gets better and better, Margo. Wait until Harry picks up the phone and calls a high-priced deli and tells them to send over the works.'

'I just gave him the works and I don't want to be around when he opens the package.'

Giveadamn never learned what the package was. But from that time on, he thought he could discern much more hatred in Harry for Margo, and much, much more respect.

Harry wheeled the Rolls-Royce onto the East Side Highway and gave it lots of gas.

'Now there are four names in and around Harlem I want you to know. I want you to know the names and that's all. Don't touch them even if you happen to have one fall dead on top of you.'

Giveadamn said nothing, but his eyes showed interest.

Harry raised one hand to tick off the names with his thumb. 'First, there's Sonny Roberts. He's good at his profession. And that's a lot more than I can say about the rest. He's the last of the big dealers that was taught by the old numbers bankers.

He's polished and maybe smart. But he's been in damned near every prison the State of New York got to offer, so maybe he's not so smart after all.

'Then there's Doll Baby. He's crazier than J. Edgar Hoover. And he's about the freakiest thing that ever hit a jailhouse. Now the reason they call him Doll Baby is important. What his real name ought to be is Cry Baby. But no one, and I mean nobody, is gonna call him that to his face or even behind his back. So everybody calls him Doll Baby. Doll Baby is a euphemism for crybaby. Get it?'

'Wow.'

'And he's the insanest of the lot. That man will cry when he's glad. He cries when he's mad. He cries when he don't know something. And whenever he cries, he tries his best to kill somebody for making him cry. He's a faggot, but acts more mannish than the craziest bulldike in Harlem. On top of all that, he's coal black and weighs three hundred pounds.'

'A man hasn't got a right to be all those things at one time,' Giveadamn said. Harry glared and went on.

'And the next nigger, Jimmy Adams, lives in a twelve-room apartment with a TV set in each room which is never turned off. If he turned one off, he wouldn't know if it wasn't working. He dresses well, kills well. He's over sixty and carries his age well. He's the only bigtimer I know who ever was a user, but he got cured in Attica, came out and started dealing. He's a big wheel now, although he hasn't been in the real racket for long.

'And the last is a bitch. I mean just that. Studs Thompson is a woman, but she's as bloodthirsty as Dracula's mother. As far as I know, she never had a male friend in her life. She hates men. But she don't argue with any, she kills them the moment they get on her nerves. The first man she killed was when she was thirteen. She and her mother was walking down the street. This drunk makes a sort of compliment to her mother and the kid sticks a knife in the man without even bothering to see if her mother knew him.

'When she came out of prison, she was right into every-thing. I heard she's the one who greased Biggie's fall. He's the first of these men the judge set a five-million-dollar bail on.'

'You would be a doggone sight more convincing if you didn't exaggerate so much, Harry.'

'Exaggerate!' Harry said quietly. 'Boy, Doll Baby has given at least one girl a douche with hot lye. Jimmy Adams, who is the boss of Brooklyn – if the Ankh-Amens aren't – has a deep freeze. He puts people in it and leaves town. While he's out of town, his men take the victim out and let him thaw someplace else. Understand what I'm saying to you?

'And I actually believe Studs Thompson gets an orgasm every time she wastes a man. Boy, the drug racket is operated by wild people today. Not goons. Wildmen! It was because they were stupid and crazy that the cops let them take charge. The cops thought that even the craziest of niggers could be controlled by a white man in a uniform and a gun in his holster. But this is a real case of the animals taking over the zoo.'

'Wow,' was again all Giveadamn could say.

'Doll Baby and Studs are ignorant. I mean, Studs can't even count money and yet she's always killing somebody over money. See what I mean? So only a crazy person would get involved with her. And these are the people who could suddenly decide one day that you have what they want. It don't make no difference if what they want don't exist. You can't tell a crazy man that what he wants don't exist.

'Oh, one more name. Connie Dubois. She ain't a name you're apt to hear much about, but she's brains, the only brains in that bunch, and Studs's got her. It's because Studs's got her, Studs is the one you got to worry about the most. You ask your "ho" about her. She knows her. And Boots knows her. Funny girl, takes her clothes off to think. Will do it right in a roomful of people and not high or nothing. Just don't give a damn. Got a face like a hawk and that's what she's called, the hawk. A beautiful girl and never fucked a man in her life or I'da fucked her myself. Don't know her, but she intrigues hell out of me – only self-made woman on earth. Crawled out of a wine bottle at thirteen and never looked back. Connie Dubois did it all herself.'

'Connie Dubois,' Giveadamn said, like a good student.

'The hawk. If Studs is moving in on Eighth Avenue right now, she's masterminding the move.'

'How come nobody hears about her, or ain't apt to?'

'Because Studs, that stupid bitch, is jealous of her, hates her just because she's smart, won't let her get any credit. One of these days Connie is going to kill that Studs and take over. Then watch out.'

12

Giveadamn's schooling was suddenly interrupted – not unex-pectedly, not completely. But it was a matter of high concern.

'You got it all together?' Harry asked Ossie, who was in the front seat beside the hired-limo driver.

'Everything,' Ossie said.

Giveadamn glanced at Margo, sitting between him and Harry. She was worried about him, too, he could see that. They all were. The wound in his stomach had had plenty of time to heal – but he wasn't feeling well at all.

'Don't worry, Harry,' Ossie said. 'Everything is under con-trol. I filed my flight plans yesterday. And we have hotel reservations ... if you decide to take them. Now that we are on our way, I'm sorry we didn't keep Giveadamn under a heat lamp for a day or two. This trip might not have been necessary.'

'Why don't you stop kidding yourself and go to med school?' Harry snarled.

'I can't stand being away from you that long.'

They swept into Teterboro Airport and parked. Ossie said to Harry, 'You go warm her up while I'm in the office.' He disappeared.

Harry led Margo and Giveadamn to a sleek Skylander that seemed to have been specially parked for his convenience. They got in and Harry began to rev up the engine.

As soon as Ossie came back, they were off. Foxy laughed out loud and then began to talk rapidly, chattering away.

Giveadamn settled back as the plane zoomed higher and higher, aimed for the clouds. He sort of lazed in Margo's chatter. And then the damned thing happened! His breath was gone. He saw stars. He was already dead, but he kept on dying. He reached for Margo's hand. And the black-ness came.

Margo glanced at him and she saw death. She screamed. Harry turned to see. His heart stopped.

Harry struck the panel with his fist, 'Get this goddamn thing down! Down! Down! Down!'

Ossie turned, and he was cursing. He looked back at Giveadamn and Margo. Giveadamn looked dead to him, too. He circled back calling on the radio at the same time for an ambulance.

Ossie looked back and saw that Margo now had Giveadamn stretched across her lap.

'He's not dead, Margo,' Harry said. 'It was only the altitude.' He turned back. They were coming in now. He could see that the ambulance was already on the field.

Ossie said, 'You know where we're going?'

Harry nodded, then looked to him for confirmation. 'Knicker-bocker?'

'Logan now. Used to be Knickerbocker.'

The plane landed and Harry had Giveadamn up in his arms. Much later, Margo realized that Harry had picked up Giveadamn and run to the ambulance in the same way a fullback lugs leather.

Harry placed Giveadamn on the stretcher, and the men in white jackets lifted him into the ambulance. Harry did not get in with Giveadamn. He ran to the front and jerked the driver out of the vehicle. Then he turned to Ossie and snarled, 'I want this boy breathing when we get there!'

As Ossie got behind the wheel, Harry ran and got in the back with Foxy and Giveadamn. Foxy was on her knees with her head on Giveadamn's chest, holding onto what life was left in her man.

Harry began to cry. He did not know who he was crying for. *He should have knelt that time before,* he thought, *and held onto Francis.* There was no room now for him to kneel and hold onto this boy, his real son. He thought maybe he should be crying for himself. Sickle-cell anemia was what was in Francis, and he had not been able to see it. Of course, Francis was no junkie, any more than this boy was a junkie. Sickle cell. That curse of the black race was hiding under that wound that wouldn't heal. The knife had hit his spleen!

He did not feel tired or worn or sixty years of age. He had too much to do. He owed Francis an epitaph. Francis had said he was going to erect a monument. And Francis had. Only Harry Brown had come along and first shit on it, then ordered it destroyed by fire. He thought of Francis all the way to the hospital.

At the hospital, it did not seem long before Dr Wethers came and told them Giveadamn was coming out of the crisis. 'Of course you did not know. So few people do know,' she said softly. 'It is fortunate, in a way, that not many black people have the opportunity to fly in private planes with unpressurized cabins.'

Harry wheeled on Ossie. 'Let's go. We don't have all day.' As an afterthought he turned to Margo. 'What you want to do?'

She smiled grimly. 'I got a choice?'

'People like you always have.'

'I kept one deathwatch over Giveadamn. I kept it by myself. I did not need anyone. You hear me, Mister Bastid? I did not need anyone!'

Ossie took her hand and squeezed it. He looked at Harry. Then he followed Harry, who was bulling out of the place.

Rage saved Harry's mind in the days that followed. His mind was forced through some changes that would have destroyed a lesser man. Giveadamn was only one of his crosses. Francis Williams was now a constant nightmare.

And Francis and the woman had as much as *told* him! He had seen it and had not known. It was like he was too mean to see. Too goddamn dumb to see. Hadn't Francis once said he had a *white* line of defense? Hadn't the woman's sores told him? Hadn't she said that she and Francis were blood kin? Sickle cell blood kin! How could he have been so blind?

Junkies don't have a yen crash down on them suddenly, the way Francis had been stricken. The man had gone into crisis and Harry Brown had stood there and made up lies just like the most ignorant nigger in Harlem.

And everything Francis had said had been so right. If his daring had been known, had been made legend, the police would never again rush in blind, killing first, asking questions later. Harry Brown had destroyed destiny. Harry Brown had torn a page out of the black history book before the page was finished.

And nothing could resurrect Francis, or put his big move back into perspective. Francis was dead, and his big play was dead. There would never be a monument.

He could go to the *Amsterdam News* and tell it like it was. He doubted they would believe him. Well, he had his punishment. The junkies on the street believed Harry Brown had paid the police to murder Francis. And it damned near was the truth.

But Giveadamn was something else again. The boy had to be his son. He had run out on the girl, and his brother had stepped in and done what Harry had not been man enough to do. But she had insisted, at least, that the birth certificate read the way it was supposed to. She wrote and told him that.

And there was this goddamn Foxy Cool Momma. He did not know why he had not killed her personally. The idea of her keeping watch over his boy was unbearable. But he would not be the first saint to be surrounded by whores. The thought cooled him a bit.

And then there was Stella. She came into his thoughts every time his mind grew weary. There had been no forgetting her. The thing had started naturally: he had summoned her. She had come. As natural as turning on a light. Even so!

He picked up a vase and smashed it on the floor.

13

On Giveadamn's tenth day in the hospital, Harry was in his barroom brooding. He picked up the phone and called a bar near Stella's. He gave an order, and in ten minutes he was talking to her. She did not seem surprised to hear his voice. 'I want to see you,' Harry said.

Stella said she'd meet him on the corner of 125th and Eighth Avenue in thirty minutes. His immediate reaction was mixed. Mainly, she had no right to sound so casual about meeting him. He had rubbed her face in horseshit that last time. She could have shown a little more pride. He went down to the garage and started up his MG, a car he hadn't used in six months.

When Stella got in the roadster, he decided he could see nothing in her eyes but honesty and good humor. And her smile was so friendly it tore at him.

They drove along 125th Street, past the wig carts, and the record store with a singer blasting out a recording. Every now and then she would touch his arm and smile.

'I've been getting kicked in the teeth right regularly for the past ten days,' he said gruffly.

'That's why you want me to be with you?'

'That's about the size of it. I can't exactly figure it out myself, but I guess that's about it. I was rough on you the last time. I still feel that way about junkies, but maybe I shouldn't.'

'How old are you, Harry?'

'Sixty.'

Her lips twisted. 'See?'

'See what?'

'I'm twenty-three. I shouldn't come running to a sixty-year-old fart – but here I am.'

The way she said it, there was nothing to get mad about. If anyone had a right to be uptight, it was she. But she wasn't.

'A man I practically never knew existed sits in a room and

looks at me. I go to him like some zombie. Then he calmly tells me that I'm the scum of the earth. After the first shock is over, I still want to see him again.' Her eyes were wide as she looked at him. 'I'm just asking myself what's happened.'

He hunched over the wheel. 'I'm sorry things went the way they did,' he muttered.

The girl grinned. Then she murmured, 'If I screw you, will my sons go to college?'

He was furious, but he believed rage was exactly what she wanted, so he cooled it and said, 'I never bought a woman in my life and I don't intend to start now.' It occurred to him she had not been talking to him anyhow. Not really. 'Why did you say that anyhow?'

She laughed. It was a beautiful sound. 'What you tell me to do, I do. It's a job. You are a job. I had jobs before.' She cut her eyes at him and still grinned. 'I do not mind it. But I still am not your slave. Never.' She leaned back and rested her head on the headrest. She looked as if she had gone to sleep.

When he braked the little speedster to a stop in front of his building, Harry turned to tell her they had arrived, noting again the calm and arrogant beauty of her face. Arrogant, but serene. Her features were totally unmarked by heroin; that was another part of it. He felt he should resent her loveliness, but he couldn't. And he wondered if this girl was making less of a man out of him.

They went up to his apartment. He led the way through the house and down the stairs to the barroom. She gasped when she looked around the lounge, but to his surprise she said, 'Have you read all the books in that room we passed upstairs?'

'A lot.'

'Except for Giveadamn, I never knew a man who read books before.' She glanced at him curiously. 'Why do you do that?'

It made him wonder. He was still wondering when she came to him and kissed him. She stepped back and looked at his face for a long time. Then she laughed, a deep laugh of release.

'We haven't had a drink,' Harry said.

She laughed again. 'Since I quit heroin, I'm a wino.'

'So?'

'It would be against the local law for you to keep the kind of wine I drink in a rich room like this. It's called Wild Irish Rose.'

He had never heard of the stuff, but he went behind the bar and started the ice machine. He made her a green crème de menthe frappe.

She tasted it gingerly. Then she rolled her eyes as she patted her lean belly. 'Good.'

Looking at her then, Harry knew that for one of the few times in his life he was hooked on a woman.

She did not know the changes he was going through. She came around to his side of the bar to kiss him. Then she said, 'I got to be a brand-new thing to you ... or I will not be anything to you. You got to believe that, Harry.' She waited for his answer. Her face and eyes were warm and seductive, yet her tone was businesslike. 'I got to leave in about an hour. The kids, from school.'

'You can go anytime,' he snapped.

Now she was angry, hurt. He had begun to think she was incapable of that reaction.

'What's the matter, Harry?'

He stepped back from her and shouted, 'Why've I got you here?'

'C'mon in the bedroom,' she said.

He did not move.

'I see,' she murmured even more quietly. And Harry wanted to slap all that dignity off her face.

But she said, 'I found out a long time ago that tomorrow is the only day that counts. And yesterday don't have a damned thing to do with the day after tomorrow. When I saw you today, I only thought of what's coming next ... and about how much I was going to enjoy it. But you don't think like me. I don't think you can. But if you ever do start ...' She shrugged as if to emphasize the hopelessness of it all, 'I'll come back.'

She walked from behind the bar. He watched as she went

to the winding staircase. He saw her beautifully muscled legs as she climbed the stairs.

She paused one moment. 'I understand exactly how you feel, Harry,' she said. 'If I was a man I don't think I could ever forgive a woman like me either. But that's the only reason I came. I thought you were a hell of a lot more man than I could ever be even if I had the chance. I loved you for that.'

He did not catch up with her until she reached the front door. She was trying to make the intricate lock work when he grabbed her. Like a wounded man, he shouted, 'If you ever go back on shit, I will kill you!'

'Does that mean you want me?'

But he did not know it as surrender. He thought of it as attack. He thought he was going to invade this one ex-junkie's world and render it asunder. He would not take her out of her world. He would smash her world so that she had no other option but to come into his. He pulled her, but not roughly, toward his bedroom. Once in his bedroom she began to strip with an angry efficiency. As if at last she was back on her own stomping grounds.

She reached up her arms for him as if to break his fall. He lay beside her and began to kiss her. It seemed a long time before he stopped and then got on her.

She began to jabber in Spanish. He did not understand a word of it, but she was swearing . . . and praying. Her legs did not enfold him. They chafed and rubbed his sides, his flanks, in a search for more of him.

And now her head was jerking and she yelled 'Eyyieee!' A benediction. It was like she was praying for him when he came in her.

A little later she seemed contented as she slowly got out of bed and began to put on her clothes. He said nothing and got up and began to dress, too.

He glared at her. 'You're never going to tell a damn soul you love me,' he said coldly. 'You like me all right. But if it wasn't for my money, you tell them you wouldn't be able to find the time.' He didn't want any argument.

'I understand.' She grinned. 'Your friends would all say you are making a fool out of yourself over a little half-white junkie 'ho'. And my friends would all say that a rich nigger can make a 'ho' outa any dumb spic bitch.' She laughed merrily. 'I expect to see you tomorrow.'

He smiled. She had intimated from the first that she possessed him. She had just proved it. Nothing was upside down any more – just a little bit unusual.

So it came to him that Foxy Cool Momma possessed Giveadamn the same way. And it was none of his business.

He put his arm around her and walked her to the front door.

In the car, she said she wanted to go to Central Park West and catch the local train to 135th Street.

As they were going through the park, he said, 'You want to go back to school? I got a friend who has a friend.'

She feigned indignation and struck at him with the side of her fist. 'You screw a dumb "ho." But then it gets good to you and all of a sudden she got to have an educated pussy, eh?' She hit at him again. Then she moved as far from him as the little car allowed.

He was still laughing when he drove out of the park to stop at the Seventy-second Street entrance to the subway. 'I guess a million thoughts struck me the first time I saw you,' he said. 'But I'll be damned if I thought about you being a comedian.'

'I'm too busy telling you like it is to be bothered about how I sound. And anyhow, you don't sound like you got a whole roomful of beautiful books home either.'

'You're going to need a more private telephone from now on, maybe a more private apartment,' he said.

She glanced at him with calm unconcern. 'Okay. It's no big problem.' Then she grinned. 'I'm rich, you know.'

He glanced over at her. She had not said it like a joke.

'I am rich,' she repeated. 'I don't need nothing. Like a phone, I mean.' She saw he did not understand and so she explained. 'I married poor is all. My father is a big man. How you think me and my boys dress so good if my husband is a stupid junkie spic?'

'I never saw the way your boys dress!' Harry said. 'What does your father do anyhow?'

'He owns two bars and three Spanish moviehouses. Plus a lot more. He lives in Great Neck with his woman. My mother is dead a long time. He hates José now because I went on dope. He blames José. But I asked too much of José.' Her smile was pure roughhouse. 'I insisted that my childhood playmate play house for keeps. He did. I ruined him. And all the time I should have been out wrestling gorillas like you.'

He grunted. The kid had diagnosed her situation.

Harry touched the ignition key but did not turn on the motor. 'I still do not see why you have to get out here. You could get on the train at 125th just as easy. Or even take a taxi.'

But she was out of the car and walking rapidly toward the kiosk. He started to get out and go down and talk to her until the train came, but he was too touchy for that.

Harry was still sitting in his car brooding when three youths ran up out on the kiosk and crossed the street. He watched them run into the park. Instinct told him they had just snatched something. That was unimportant, a dull scene. What did interest him was the boys were unprepared for running. Each of them wore sissy high-heeled shoes.

The subway train below began to bleat. It sounded lonelier than a train rushing through the Georgia night.

Two ancient women came up. They were wailing. And he wondered if Stella would come up to tell him what the boys had pulled. Then he jumped.

He got out of the car, ran across the street and rushed up to the ancients. He grabbed the arm of one. 'What happened?'

'She fell . . . in front of the train. They was grabbing her. She's dead.'

'A tall Spanish girl with a real short skirt?'

The woman's eyes focused. 'She was Spanish?'

Shortly he came back to the roadster, got it started and headed into the park. He caught sight of a bushy head moving awkwardly along a path half hidden from the road. He swerved the MG onto the path and gave it gas.

One of the boys looked back and saw him coming. He shouted and the boys split three ways. The tallest lit out for a clearing. Harry chose him. Twenty feet behind the kid, he slowed a little, trying to decide whether to run him down or stop and stomp him to death.

The boy dashed for the stone wall above the crosstown drive. Harry no longer had a choice. The kid was going to get away. He zoomed in on him, hit the brakes and something went wrong with the car. Harry had a bad temper, but he knew better than to do what he did. No matter how mad he was at the kid, he knew better than to hit that stone wall at forty miles an hour. The tiny car and big Harry Brown mashed the kid against the wall, exploded up against him. Harry and his MG came down out of the air, first Harry, then the car, Harry under it.

The first person on the scene of the accident, its sole witness, was Sonny Roberts. Sonny walked up to the car and squatted down for a close look. Then he stood up slowly and straightened the cuffs of his pants around the tops of his high-heeled shoes.

Behind him, on the path, two boys appeared, winded. They stood and watched and waited until Sonny looked over toward them. He nodded. Then they joined him and stood staring at the car and at Harry.

'Now look what you stupid bastards did,' said Sonny.

The three strolled casually away and out of the park like a hip father and two sons taking a Sunday stroll.

14

The phone rang in Giveadamn's old hotel room and Foxy answered it.

She heard Gracie say, 'Stella's dead.'

Margo took a reeling step back. Her eyes blurred. 'No!'

Gracie was relentless. 'She got shoved off the subway platform. I think I'm going crazy.'

'Harry Brown?'

'How could you say that, Maggie? How *could* you?'

'I know Harry's reputation. You don't. You only know he approves of you and your damned babies.'

'Don't be like that, Maggie. We are all gonna hurt the same. I was standing at the window looking at nothing at all when all of a sudden the police drove up and went in Stella's house. Then they came out with José. He was crying. I could tell from the way he was kind of sagging that Stella was dead . . .'

'What else?'

'So I went out and asked José. But, Maggie, those police treated José like a dog. I think they had him under arrest. They know if he's an addict he's got to be guilty of something and they might as well find out. You know what I mean?'

'Well, who did kill her?'

'The radio says some teen-agers. There was lots of witnesses. They was trying to grab her, force her to leave with them.'

'Why Stella? What she do to them, Gracie?'

'Maybe they just went to snatch her purse and she jumped back, not realizing she was so near the edge. That makes a lot of sense in New York City, Maggie. And then there's her father, Maggie.'

'There you go again!' Foxy stormed. 'All that poor man ever did was hustle his butt off like an ignorant spic is supposed to do. And now you're gonna come rushing up with your goddamn prayerbook and start blaming him.'

'Well, that kind of man has enemies.'

'Harry Brown has one million enemies. Every mother, father, uncle, aunt, brother, and sister of an addict would like to see that man dead. So maybe somebody saw Harry with Stella and how his big lips were drooling over her. What better way to even things up? Huh?'

'Yeah.' Gracie sounded doubtful. 'How's Giveadamn?'

'He's okay. I'm taking him back to Harry's next week. But the way I feel right now, I got a great mind to bundle him up and bring him back here tonight. This is not one of those nights I want to be alone. Dig it?'

When Foxy reached Giveadamn's bedside in the hospital, she saw that he was asleep. She was tempted to wake him, but just then Ossie walked into the room.

'That little Spanish stallion Harry had eyes for is dead,' she said right to the point. 'Mugged in the subway, I think. Fell and got run over by the train.'

'Oh shit,' Ossie said softly.

The phone rang. Foxy picked it up. Then she said to Ossie, 'It's for you.'

Ossie took the phone and said, 'Yeah?' After that he was silent for a long time as he listened intently. Then he asked a few sharp questions and hung up. He thought for about a minute, then said to Foxy, 'Harry is dying in St Luke's Hospital. He jacked up his car in Central Park, or maybe it blew up, nobody's sure. I'll be in touch.' And he hurried out.

Foxy wheeled to stare at Giveadamn. 'How long you been awake?'

The urgency that the Logan Hospital staff put behind Margo's and Ossie's request to have Giveadamn transferred to St Luke's so he could be with his uncle carried a lot of weight.

A little after six that evening Giveadamn, in a wheelchair, was rolled into a two-bed room in St Luke's. He stood up and walked for the first time since he'd got on the airplane, went to Harry's bedside and took Harry's hand. For a moment he doubted the wisdom of his insistence on coming to Harry's side, because one look confirmed the hospital report: there was nothing he could ever do for Harry.

Harry's arms and legs were in casts, one leg was mangled. His spine was broken. His face was bandaged, his eyes swollen shut. There was a tube up his nose and another in his side. He could not live much longer.

But Giveadamn held Harry's hand for a long time – until Foxy came with Ossie and led Giveadamn to his bed. In a little while he was asleep. Foxy and Ossie looked at each other and shrugged.

'Let's take a walk over to Vincent's Place,' Foxy said. 'Seems like we ought to drink to three different people tonight.' Her voice was oddly crisp and take-charge.

'You said the right word when you said walk,' Ossie replied. 'I want to walk more than I want to drink.'

On their way Foxy mused: 'They said the man is going to be dead as a vegetable from now on.' She then said to Ossie, 'You don't feel nothing, do you?'

At Vincent's Place they sat down in a booth in the bar. Ossie sighed, and only then answered, 'What's to feel? I never met Stella. I can understand why I should feel for her. But Harry is something else again. He did this by himself. I mean, you can't honestly even judge this thing. I only know Giveadamn is going to need the hell out of me from now on in.'

'Harry told us to run like hell the day of his ... Harry's ... funeral,' Margo said. 'Think we better?'

'We got some time. That's why there are no cops at Harry's door. I managed to talk a friend of mine by the name of Morris out of it.'

'Why?'

'I don't want anybody to know where Harry is. Not even the hospital knows who he is. That's been arranged, too. And I don't want anybody to know his condition. I mean: we *can't* let anybody know Harry's true condition.'

'But police report all accidents,' Margo said doubtfully, a little later.

'I'll see there's no report. We'll make a few calls, spread

the word,' Ossie said. 'The police aren't always stupid; they don't want a dope war. We say Harry ain't hurt at all. He's just clearing the decks for his getaway from a homicide rap. Shee-it! And why not call the newspapers and tell them the same thing? I mean, if the bad boys hear that Harry ain't hurting at all, they might not make any waves right now.'

'Somebody's going to recognize him sooner or later. There's a lot of black staff at St Luke's.'

Ossie shook his head. 'Not in all them bandages. And we'll shift him and Giveadamn to a private hospital I know as soon as we can. Giveadamn's our problem. Somebody's going to recognize him a lot quicker, from his first stay, you know.'

'Okay, let's get going. Did you ask for dimes?' Foxy asked.

'I got, babee. I got,' Ossie said with a grim smile.

They had four drinks apiece, and after each drink either Foxy or Ossie made three phone calls.

The only thing was – Sonny Roberts had witnessed the action in Central Park. But the man was dazzled by his golden chance, and he did not care to share his knowledge.

Almost as soon as Foxy and Ossie left, Giveadamn woke with a start. He had been mulling things over, even in his sleep. Giveadamn looked over at Harry. His head in bandages, he was breathing heavily. His upper lip was flecked with blood. He was in a deep coma. Giveadamn tried to remember the last time he had been near a mortally wounded person.

He decided it was right for him to have come here. Even if Harry could not see him, hear him or smell him, it was his duty to be with Harry ... but at the same time, it was his duty to get up on his feet again and start taking care of Harry's affairs. The sooner the better.

He pushed the buzzer for a nurse. In time, she came.

'I want to ask some questions about my condition, ma'am,' he said slowly.

'You'll have to ask your doctor.'

'I don't have one.'

'Everyone has a doctor.'

He sighed. He would never get anywhere with her. He lay

back. He would see a doctor in the morning and, with or without his permission, get out of here.

Although Giveadamn and Foxy had lived briefly with Harry and Ossie, neither had really felt free to inspect all the rooms and cupboards and chests and closets in the apartment. Now they did. Giveadamn was on his feet again – but weak. He sat down a lot, but the first chance they had, with Ossie gone somewhere, they took a tour.

Harry's apartment contained sixteen rooms, nine up and seven down. There were seven bedrooms. Giveadamn was feeling a little too weak even for sex – and wondering if he'd ever enjoy it again. And so all those bedrooms amused him. Giveadamn and Foxy stopped in each one to laugh, and Foxy vowed it would not be long before they made love in all seven of the beds. Giveadamn really hoped so.

And there were lots of other adequate rooms for loving. There was the lounge with its two bars. There were several long couches. In the library, one of the smallest rooms, there were two BarcaLoungers Foxy insisted would get a good workout. There was also a book that lay open on a small table in the library, but because it was open Giveadamn ignored it. He thought he wouldn't be too interested in books Harry read.

On their first inspection, each chose a favorite room. They decided to sleep in Harry's bed, although Foxy took the pink room as her own: Harry would never leave the hospital.

Giveadamn more or less took the library for his private retreat. He decided he would go there to read or when his pain got so bad he didn't want the others to know.

Since childhood Giveadamn had been amused when he heard someone say he ached all over. It was, he'd thought, an overstatement, because if anyone could take the time out to say he ached so, then surely he didn't. But now Giveadamn understood.

Right after lunch that first day back at Harry's, the phone rang. It was a crisp voice that said, 'To whom might I be speaking? This is Sonny Roberts.'

'Harry's not home right now,' Giveadamn said and hung up fast.

'Who was it?' Ossie said.

'Sonny Roberts.'

'Maybe somebody ought to talk to that guy.'

Giveadamn and Foxy looked askance.

'Well,' Ossie said, 'I know the man is acting crazy, but the fact is we don't know for sure he's crazy.'

'Yeah,' Foxy said doubtfully, 'but if Harry shot out his tires, I don't think I'd want to talk to him. Or Giveadamn shouldn't either.'

Ossie looked directly at Giveadamn. 'Is it okay if I talk to him?'

It was then that Giveadamn realized he was now Harry Brown's surrogate.

Like fear, the potential of real pain is unknown to most people. It is at times a dynamite narcotic. Pain will destroy all fear of death and even make one long for it.

Some days Giveadamn's limbs burst with agony. He could see his legs and feet swell with it. Not soreness, not infection or inflammation – his limbs swelled with misery. Even so, once Giveadamn was out of bed and dressed, he never lost his cheerfulness.

The first thing every morning he called the hospital to see how Harry was, and at least once a day he went to see Harry.

Sometimes when they were alone, Giveadamn talked to Harry, told him what was happening. Harry never moved so much as a finger or quivered a lip, but Giveadamn thought he could hear, though the doctors said not. It was a sad daily visit for Giveadamn, but he had to make it. It was decided not to shift Harry to a private hospital, since the dying man seemed well concealed. It began to look, however, as if Harry had refused to die, that Death stood by him waiting, but that he was so ornery he denied even Death.

Or perhaps, Giveadamn thought, Harry's pain was so intense not even Death could overcome it.

15

The day that Giveadamn, Foxy and Ossie returned to the apartment after talking to Harry's main lawyer, they were met in the lobby by Freddy Morris. Giveadamn didn't know Freddy; Ossie made the introductions. They did not speak again until all four were seated downstairs in the lounge.

'I came to ask around,' Freddy said. 'Everybody is waiting for this man to tip his hat.' He nodded to Giveadamn.

'I haven't got a hat to tip,' Giveadamn said to Freddy. 'Harry Brown left the narco rackets a long time ago, Lieutenant Morris. I think you know that. And you must also know I know exactly nothing about the heroin trade. So I know you are going to believe me when I say that I am not only not a fair-haired boy, but a bareheaded one.'

Margo and Ossie showed different kinds of disapproval.

'Harry was clean,' Giveadamn went on. 'But I got a hunch a lot of people are going to get hurt before I can convince them of that.'

Freddy nodded. 'The heroin business is run by megalomaniacs, Mr Brown. If they ever came to believe you were clean, they would kill you out of contempt. I mean that.'

Giveadamn grinned softly. 'I'm even beginning to believe that God wants me to come home ahead of time.' He stared at Freddy. 'I got me as good a case of sickle-cell anemia as you'll ever want to see. I got a hole in my belly that is never going to heal. And out of it leaks pus and water twenty-four hours a day. There's a joke folks like to tell back home in Wiggins. It's about this poor colored guy who is sitting on the train with his pretty daughter, a teen-age son, and twins, a boy and girl of two. The conductor comes up and asks for tickets. The man says he ain't got any more.'

Giveadamn took a deep breath and went on, 'Well, the old cracker of a conductor is used to these kind of jive plays and he is bored. He says that he is going ahead and collect tickets from the rest of the people, and when he gets back this man better have himself some tickets or he is going to be in trouble.

'Well, the little dried-up nigger looks him in the eye then and says: "That's my fifteen-year-old girl there and she's pregnant and ain't got the slightest idea of which of her boy friends did it. That other boy there got the clap. These two twins of mine ate up the tickets and I ain't got no more money. My wife is in a coffin in the baggage car. And I just got a telegram before I left home saying that my wife's family home got burned up where we is headed." The guy stood up then. "Now, Mr Conductor, what makes you think you can give *me* trouble?"' Giveadamn stopped. Margo giggled softly.

Freddy nodded again. 'I just got my orders to look around and listen around and report back. That's all. Report back. And that's what I'm going to do. I'm going to make a full report and tell it like it is.'

Ossie laughed. 'Huh!'

Freddy ignored him. 'I'm going to say what I know – that Harry paid off to keep everybody off his back. I'm going to say there is no golden empire.' He paused. 'But that won't help you with the dealers.'

After Freddy had gone, Ossie said, 'He's right.'

'The thing to do is give the dealers what they want,' Giveadamn said.

'You don't have a narco operation to give them,' Ossie pointed out. 'And when they find out you haven't, they'll kill you – like he said – out of contempt.'

'I don't have one yet, but damned if I'm not going to find one and give it to them. It's the only way out of this,' Giveadamn said.

The three of them sat and thought for a long time.

'What you want we should do, Giveadamn?' Foxy asked.

'Depends on what's happening,' Giveadamn said.

And so they sat back to wait and see what it was that was happening.

*   *   *

Things began to happen, and very shortly – but not what any-one expected or where they thought trouble might appear.

The next morning Giveadamn had gone alone to the hospital to tell Harry what he'd decided, figuring if Harry didn't approve he'd be so mad he'd sit straight up and cuss him out. So when he told Harry he'd try to find a narco racket to give the dealers if they insisted on one and Harry didn't move, Giveadamn had a feeling he was on the right track. No trouble so far.

Trouble, when it did come, was sudden and violent. It was waiting for him at Gracie's. And it was more trouble than Giveadamn, a fledgling prince of Harlem, knew how to handle.

That evening he got up and went over to shake Margo gently. She'd been depressed and gloomy lately.

'How about a little bit of Gracie this evening?' It was about seven o'clock.

She gave him a sidelong glance. 'You really for it?'

He grinned, 'Would I be asking if I wasn't?'

She gave him another glance and this time seemed reassured that he really felt okay. She went upstairs to dress. Ten minutes later they were in a cab headed for 137th Street.

Gracie came to the door with one of her infants in her arms. 'I got me a little tummyache here,' she moved her head toward the infant. 'I'm going across the street to Dr Jenkins. I'll be right back.' She came out of the house and ran down the steps before Foxy and Giveadamn entered.

They went into the parlor. They put ice in the ice bucket and mixed a couple of drinks, and had sat down to relax when Toni let herself in the front door.

The almost imperceptible stiffness of the child's gait hit Foxy in the gut. She came out of her chair to brace Toni. 'Who turned you on?'

Giveadamn had seen only a cute kid walk into the room, munching a candy bar. Almost idly he wondered what Margo had seen.

Toni laughed. 'You mean I look that fly?'

Margo slapped her across the face. Giveadamn thought he heard the child's nose crack.

Foxy's next blow was a fist from the floor. The Hershey bar sailed out of Toni's hand and landed in a corner, then Toni seemed to go up on her toes and her body took off after it. Foxy followed like Toni's shadow. She landed astride Toni and began to choke the child, at the same time banging her head on the floor.

'You only gonna live if you give me my answer,' Foxy said, banging Toni's head at almost every word.

Giveadamn did not begrudge Margo her wrath. Turning a beautiful child of fifteen onto drugs was a terrible thing, especially if the child meant more than life to you. He looked at the two women struggling on the floor. It hit him that Toni was in danger of being choked to death. He got up and pulled Foxy off Toni.

Foxy took a deep breath and heaved her whole body at Giveadamn, and Giveadamn landed on the floor beside Toni.

'Take a walk,' was all Foxy said.

Sitting on the front steps, he realized he, too, might have died if he had disobeyed Foxy. He began to tremble as the truth eeled up into his brain. Foxy was out to kill. She was either going to kill Toni or she was going to kill somebody else.

The moment Giveadamn walked out of the parlor, Toni, still conscious, cried out for the first time.

Foxy clawed beneath Toni's flimsy shirt to grab a breast. She squeezed and twisted. Toni screamed, but Foxy's grip was forever. The pain shot to Toni's bowels. Her head waved from side to side with nausea, but she would not let her lips form a name. She fainted.

Foxy stomped on her. 'Wake up, bitch!'

Toni could not hear her.

Foxy grabbed the ice bucket. She pulled down Toni's pants and panties in one savage jerk. Then she knelt and went to work on Toni with ice cubes. The child gasped, moaned and began to blubber. She tried to get to her feet.

Foxy's knife was at Toni's throat. 'You are going to die, but not until you tell me,' she said.

'Ranger,' Toni lisped. Her lips were swollen, but it was the dryness in her mouth that choked her.

'C'mon,' Foxy said.

They left the house together. Giveadamn was sitting on the steps. 'Stay here,' she said to him quietly.

Giveadamn's eyes were empty. There was nothing to say. Nothing to do in this terrible game but sit and wait.

He saw Foxy step quickly down the steps, then go next door, Toni right with her. Foxy rang the bell, then stepped aside. Ranger came to the door, saw only Toni, and immediately opened it. At the same moment, Foxy stepped forward and whipped at the side of his neck with her blade. It was not a slash or a stab. She hit Ranger on his neck with so stern a vengeance the knife seemed to rebound. Foxy had not butchered the boy Harlem style. Foxy had flayed Ranger with the blade of her knife.

She flayed him again. Then she bent low, she lunged, and five inches of steel split Ranger's heart. She straightened then and she and Toni came quickly down the steps.

'Let's go,' she said to Giveadamn.

The three went over to Seventh Avenue and hailed a cab. All during the trip to Harry's, Giveadamn marveled how a woman could preach a jeremiad with not a word spoken. Only heaves, grunts came out of Foxy, and some sounds like hisses. And her eyes burned with fervor as her head bobbed around.

Just as wordlessly Toni took in that sermon. At times she even raised her hand from her lap as if she would push back some of the gut truths, but each time Foxy would make a louder grunt and Toni would drop her hand in surrender.

When Giveadamn opened the apartment door, Foxy pushed past him and yelled, 'Ossie!'

She paced through the foyer and on to the back living room, pulling Toni behind her. She flopped in a chair and motioned for Toni to sit opposite her, but Toni remained standing.

Foxy again shrieked Ossie's name. In a moment or two he came up the spiral staircase from below. He walked over. What he read on Foxy's face changed him. He turned on Giveadamn with a look of sorrow and resignation that Giveadamn would never forget.

'Not him,' Foxy said.

So Ossie turned to Toni. She stood there in her beauty, whole, yet sundered. 'My sister,' Ossie said. He did not know why he said those words.

There were more than five minutes of silence before Foxy said, 'Let's cut the shit. There ain't nothing but us and love in this house.'

Her knife came out and she went to Toni, moved around her with quick savage slashes and pared the clothes from Toni's body. When Foxy put her blade beneath the strap of Toni's bra and sliced it, the girl stood perfectly nude.

Giveadamn and Ossie dutifully watched. It was an impersonal thing Foxy had done. It was like a call to worship, only different. It was just as if Foxy said aloud, 'Here, my brothers, is a work of God which we now destroy to save.'

And Toni was a wonderful work of God. Her little shoulders were square and straight, her jet breasts no bigger than porcelain teacups. Her skin was not coal black. It was black-red. But it was the utter simplicity in the beauty of her face that made the three believe she could be saved.

Foxy heaved a sigh. 'Where?'

The two men considered her question. Giveadamn was about to suggest they use the barroom lounge when Ossie said, 'Mine is best.'

He was right. His room led off the barroom and it held not only a king-sized bed, but also a leather couch. For three days one or all of them could stay with Toni. And that's what it was all about.

Giveadamn did not know, but Ossie and Foxy knew they had seventy-two grueling hours ahead of them. Seventy-two hours to keep the child imprisoned while she went through hell. Ossie had seen it. Foxy had experienced it. Giveadamn had not even read about it.

The four went down the winding staircase. In Ossie's room Foxy went to the big bed and stretched out. Giveadamn and

Ossie each chose a rocker. Only Toni remained standing. And no one told her to sit down.

Giveadamn's mind began to review what had happened since Toni, Foxy and he had come home. Over half an hour had passed, yet not one of them had spoken more than a few words. But they were now four minds completely attuned. Even Toni knew exactly what was happening now.

Suddenly, into the silence, Foxy laughed. It was a very gentle laugh, sweet and bitter too. Her voice sounded faraway, like a weary blues singer moaning low. She began to tell about her first fix. The beauty of it. The vile arrogance. And then the scrounging, the death in life. She spoke gently of Harlem, the only streets she knew.

Her thoughts were a moth; they flitted here and there through her past. The picture grew. It was she, Maggie, Margo, Foxy Cool Momma. She was all three and now they knew why. She grew silent, but all in the room knew her.

Then Ossie began to talk. He was ten. His mother took on more work so they could move into a flat with one more room. He must sleep alone from now on. He was man. In the quietness of his room, he came to accept his maleness. He had decided he liked it.

He had gone to Nam. He came back to resume a career in basketball. College. And he was one long tall nigger who would have gone to college anyway, even if he couldn't toss a ball in a bushel basket three feet away.

He filled in a portrait of his sister. Giveadamn could see her plainly. She smiled out from the past at him. The girl he saw looked exactly like Jean Terrel of the Supremes. Only Ossie's sister Joan was taller and darker – a female Ossie.

Toni was now on the bed beside Margo. She seemed to be asleep. From time to time, Foxy would caress the child's face. The hours passed. Then it was six.

Toni began to writhe. Foxy held her tightly. The sobs began, increased. Foxy lay crosswise atop Toni. The girl's body glistened eerily. And then she began to retch. The muscles of her flat belly contracted and convulsed. Her lips held foam in the corners. She began to vomit snow-white meringue.

Toni gave a sudden shriek, then her body convulsed into a black stone arrow. Foxy's mouth flew open. She thought the girl had died. In terror she pounded on Toni's chest, willing it to heave.

Toni rolled over. She sprang. One arm caught Foxy beneath the chin. Toni was making her way to an exit with the flailing strokes of a drowning swimmer.

Ossie caught her around the waist and flung her back on the bed. Foxy grabbed Toni's Afro bush and pulled, and Toni was pinned to the bed.

Foxy raised her eyes to Ossie, 'Got tape?'

Ossie went out of the room and returned with rolls of two-inch tape. He held Toni's ankles and Giveadamn taped them together. After that they bound the girl's hands in front of her. Then Foxy rolled Toni over and sat down on the small of her back. The only thing Giveadamn would recall was how Foxy's feet dangled eight inches above the floor. Toni was apparently asleep.

Suddenly she shrieked again. Her eyes swiveled. She stared down at the mattress as if helpless to ward off a mouth nipping at her from the bed.

Foxy sobbed and lay beside the girl. She put her arms about the slim body as if she were Toni's lover. While she held Toni, her eyes looked into those of Giveadamn as if she did not like what she saw there.

'We been here a long time without eating, Giveadamn. You want to go make coffee and eggs?'

'You go.' Ossie said it, not snappishly, but just as if it would be best for Margo to fix the food.

She sighed. 'Yeah.'

When Foxy went out, Ossie said, 'Margo thinks you're going to break. But I'm not going to let you. Toni is still living. Joan's been dead so long that I'm just about used to it. I mean Toni got to mean more to me than my sister now. Understand?'

Giveadamn looked incredulous. 'You mean you think I'm going to do something dumb?'

Ossie shrugged. 'My mother tried this very same thing with Joan. But she broke. She let Joan get up for one more fix. A little one, Joan said. My mother even walked with Joan to get it. They came back home. Joan overdosed right there on the bed, my mother looking at her.'

'Ossie, Toni could never bullshit me into getting her anything. And you and Foxy are here.'

'You've not been thinking like that. For the last couple of hours, I haven't had to look at Toni to know what's going on. I can look at you and tell exactly what she's doing. The only thing you have not done with her is puke. And maybe you'll do that after we eat.'

Instead of denying anything, Giveadamn said, 'You think we should eat in front of Toni?'

Ossie's laugh was bitter. The muscles in his jaw hardened. 'From now on this kid don't belong to us, Giveadamn. The devil in hell's got her. I mean it exactly like I say it. That girl is gone, and the devil in hell's got her. He's going to turn her brains into puke and let it drip out her nose. She's going to shit all over herself and stink worse than if she'd been dead a week. But you got to understand that one tiny little fix is not going to help. It just means we got to start the job all over again later.

'Now Toni don't even know we are here. So she can't hold anything against us after it's all over. Lots of people can't remember that. They get guilty and think they have no right to deprive anyone of something, if depriving them causes what Toni got to go through. So what this all means is Foxy don't have time to watch and to nurse you, too. Understand?'

'I'm staying. And I'm not pleading for anything for Toni. Like what you and Foxy forget is I'm a country boy who was born despising dope fiends. If I had so much as suspected Margo used drugs, I wouldn't have spoken to her in that bar the night we met. And I'm glad as hell I didn't know . . . now.'

Toni's teeth were chattering. When Foxy returned with the food, she got out a blanket and covered the sweating body of the child. After that she and Ossie talked while Giveadamn tried to read, then fell asleep over his book. When he woke, Ossie drifted off. And when Ossie woke, Foxy took her turn.

She did not stretch out beside Toni. Instead, she reclined on a bolster in a sitting position with Toni's head in her lap.

As Foxy slept, Giveadamn, racked again with pain, saw for the first time that his woman was really thirty-eight years old. He wondered if this ordeal had aged her or if he had been blindly in love, or blind with the need of love, all the time. She was still cute, but her neck seemed scrawny. And there were lines in her forehead.

The ordeal had affected all of them. Ossie Winbush was no longer a vague figure to Giveadamn. He now knew Ossie's money did not come from crime or from Harry. Ossie was a cool cat who moved in circles with people of mystery, but his money came from several business investments — the largest of which was, of all things, coin-operated laundry machines.

The Ossie Winbushes, and Giveadamn had now come to know one, give the impression they're big in whatever it is they're in, but few know for sure what that is. They'll drop into a bar like Vincent's Place at any hour, always short visits, and never buy a drink. They're conservative dressers in tailored suits. You see them at good downtown restaurants no other blacks frequent and they'll be with someone, a girl, a woman, any age, a different companion every time.

Ossie Winbush was born rich. He did not have a father. And that was important. As he had observed as a boy, only children in Harlem who had fathers, a man about the house, suffered. It was the children from homes where a father reigned who were half-fed, half-clothed and half-witted. Hard and cold facts for a child to absorb, but from the first grade on, Ossie was unable to deal with the nonfactual. He could not countenance make-believe. Ossie was a born realist.

From the cradle on, Ossie was the end product of what the black mothers of the ghetto can produce. The neighborhood and the school taught Ossie that the home without a father is the best. Later on, he learned that the family that prays together eventually comes to despise each other. Like the holier the family, the meaner their hearts. It was some time before young Winbush was able to distinguish one kind of holiness from another.

And because he loved, feared and obeyed the long black arrow that was his mother, Ossie eventually formulated the opinion that the state of matrimony is the most unnatural state humans can enmesh themselves in.

The Italian Mafia has never been able to understand or respect black men. The Mafia holds that black men do not respect their women, but black men hold that all Italians are stupid because no man in his right mind is going to enter a life of crime without the consent and advice of his woman.

The cool black cat knows women of all colors are natural-born criminals. The only way women know how to fight is dirty.

So Ossie grew up a cool cat. When the gamblers approached Ossie after he became a college superstar, Ossie looked upon the gamblers as angels of mercy. Ossie resented the public's betting on his prowess. Racehorses got fed and lodged and cared for like jewels, so what was he? Less than a god-damn racehorse? Ossie took the gamblers' money without the slightest qualm. Harlem taught Ossie many things, but it had not taught him puny white armchair athletes had morals — the kind of morals that made them wish to send others to prison for not trying their best to win by the highest score.

And so it was that the basketball scandals were the last fiery crucible to anneal Ossie Winbush. Afterwards, he was no longer just a cool cat. He was an ice-cold dude.

Harry had appeared unbidden. And Harry had worked so coolly behind the scenes of that scandal that he saved Ossie from much unnecessary hassling, probably from prison. But if Ossie felt he owed Harry anything, he soon considered Harry repaid simply because he endured Harry's company.

As soon as Harry held the first open house in the new apartment, Ossie was fair game to the women who flocked around, but every one of them was anathema to Ossie. They were young, less than thirty, skilled in some way. And they were nice to look at, proficient and very much self-made ... women who had pulled themselves to the top by their garter belts. Once in exasperation Ossie labeled all these sexy young dolls 'heroin widows.' In a very real sense they were. The men of their age, all the promising men who should have been their husbands and lovers, were either dead or among the living dead of heroin addiction in New York City.

Ossie had to contend with a dead ideal. He had loved his sister Joan. Joan Winbush was a great kid. In every stage of his growing up, Ossie had never been ashamed of his kid sister or unhappy to take her to the movies, Sunday school, things like that. And when he was told Joan had died from an overdose, a lot of love inside the cool-cat Ossie died, bitterly. If a beautiful and brilliant kid like Joan could not keep away from heroin, then nobody in Harlem could. Ossie had to live with what was real.

This was the Ossie Winbush who slowly revealed himself to Giveadamn and Foxy in the room with the bed where Toni lay in agony. All of them had sat there for two days in that room, slowly revealing themselves. When Foxy signified the passage of forty-eight hours by cutting the tapes that bound Toni, they stood unveiled, stood known to one another.

The child on the bed was still tossing and muttering in delirium. Though Ossie and Foxy thought nothing of this, Giveadamn looked askance.

Foxy saw his look. 'If this room was right in the middle of a blazing building, she ain't got the strength to walk out of it. She's not going nowhere. It's practically over.'

'Over?' He couldn't believe it. If it was this simple, why was there a junkie left in Harlem?

'Yeah,' Ossie said. 'She's exhausted. She wants a fix still all right. But if you handed her a needleful of the finest dynamite in town, she would not have the strength to pick it up, much less push it into her arm. She's coming back now.' He slumped deeper in his chair. 'It's like coming home, keed. Toni's on her way back.'

And so far the dealers, not sure what Harry was up to or where he was, were holding off. It couldn't go on forever. It wouldn't either. Giveadamn, almost as exhausted as Toni, was sure of that.

More trouble was coming – or maybe it was help – from another unexpected quarter. Did Lawrence Brown give a damn? He was beginning to.

16

The ferry was nearing the dock on the Staten Island side and Connie, leaning against her car, waiting, looked at the car ahead of her and grinned. The grin was unnatural-looking. Her thin lips drew down at the corners, her lower teeth showing. She had interesting features, but they came from a white mother and a black father. She was black but did not look black. She looked like an ancient Egyptian queen. With her beaked nose and reflective eyes, she looked also like a hawk, and killer. She happened to be both.

She was grinning because the left rear tire on the Jag in front of her was rapidly going flat. Connie had studied the head of the hinkty-seeming black bitch at the wheel of the Jag and hadn't liked what she read. Connie disliked rich black bitches. They were all dead-end women. They had a wonderful present, but no future. Not only that; they did not want a future. When you give a black bitch a fine pad and a fine hog, she immediately sets about stopping the clock. She wants time to stand still. She begins to shove the world away from her, can't stand seeing her friends age. She even gets to robbing the cradle, a little boy or a little girl. More than half the time a little girl.

Connie got in her car and politely honked the horn on her Stutz Bearcat. The fine black bitch turned her head to see what was happening. She had a coal-black face with keen features. She looked oddly familiar.

The fine black chick in turn saw the crooked grin and recognized Connie's hooked nose and classic looks. She got out of her car to go back. The last time she had seen Connie, the broad had been leaning against the front fence of a house on 132nd Street, puking her guts out. Drunk as Cooter Brown. Shee-it! It was not just that Connie was driving this fine car, but that she was sober enough to drive it, that made Boots go back to renew an old friendship. Her smile was sincere. 'Hi, Connie. Who the hell ever thought we'd be meeting up again like this?'

Connie said, 'You got a flat.'

But Boots was not going to play it dumb and look at her tire. She said, 'You look like a million, Connie.'

'Way back when,' Connie said, kind of carelessly, 'everybody wore long gray cloth coats over their clothes. Called them dusters. They came in right handy keeping grease spots off your duds. You know.' And she looked pointedly at Boots's magnificent pink gabardine pants suit.

'I don't get flats!' Boots hollered, and she still refused to look at the wheels of her car.

The ferry bumped into the pier. Motorists began to start their motors. Connie started hers. 'One thing I always liked about you, Boots,' she said, 'you don't play. And I don't blame you. If I was you, I wouldn't take no crap from that tire either.'

Boots finally let herself look at her rear tires, then she began to swear. She went on in a steady monotone of cursing that made Connie feel nostalgic. You got to be born on 132nd Street in Harlem, U.S.A., to know how to cuss for real.

Boots was working herself up into the finest of rages, and when she ran out of invective she jumped into Connie's car and sat there like an ebony fixture.

'Goddammit, bitch, get the hell outa here and go move that car,' Connie said.

Boots stared straight ahead. 'No,' was all she said.

She had paid the last note on that fine hog with blowout-proof tires, and now she was sitting on the Staten Island Ferry with a flat and not the first idea of how to change it. They do not teach tire-changing in Harlem or the women's pen.

'No,' she said again.

'Don't sit there and keep saying no when you damned well have to get that car off this boat,' Connie said. She once more liked Boots. She divined all that Boots had put into the purchase of that car. She imagined all the manless nights Boots had to sleep to pay for the car. If the night hadn't been without a man to touch you in bed, there would be a man at the wheel of the damned thing now. It is expensive as hell to sleep with a man every night. Any black woman can tell you that. Especially a black woman like Boots Haley.

Sure. And Connie could imagine how Boots would get her kicks out of driving on this ferry every evening after work and just sitting cool, calm and collected while all the whiteys stared at her and wondered if maybe she was Diana Ross or somebody. And now that she was driving on a flat, Connie figured Boots felt like a black Cinderella sitting in a simple-assed pumpkin instead of a big sports hog.

'I'll get out and drive it.' Connie had to. Boots had made her stand. Boots had as much as said the car was unworthy to be driven off the boat. In a way, that was true. It was all a matter of somebody saving face, so Connie scrambled out of the car and got in behind the wheel of Boots's car. She drove it, hobbling on one rear tire, off the pier and parked.

Boots drove up behind her. Then, after Connie got back in the driver's seat, the two girls rode through the town.

'Where to?' Connie asked.

'Drive me to a taxi stand,' Boots said.

'How about driving you to a Jag dealer or to a gas station?'

Boots peered morosely through the windshield. 'If the damned thing wasn't paid for, I'd call 'em and tell 'em to guess where it was.'

Connie allowed a sidelong glance at her buddy, half admiration and half awe. 'I'm gonna drive you by my place,' she was reflecting aloud. 'I'll call our garage man. Have him go fix the flat and then bring the car to you while you sit and visit awhile. Okay?'

'Okay,' Boots muttered. After that, Boots relaxed and grinned. 'I never had to fix a flat. Hell! Even when we stole a car, we checked out the tires first off. You know.'

Connie smiled too. 'Yeah. I know all about it. There's no forgetting. It wasn't such a bad life, was it?'

Then Boots had to ask, 'What you putting down these days, Connie?'

Connie shrugged. 'Nothing. Just loafing and trying to stay sober. It's a full-time job.' Then, 'What the hell you doing yourself? You pull one of these bigtime dope dealers or something?'

'Naw.' She looked at Connie. 'You know I did a stretch up the joint?'

Connie said nothing.

'I come out and got me some computer training. I got in on the ground floor like. You know. I got me a real job making some real bread. Not like dope, but there's no fuzz to keep up with. You know.'

'How's your maw?'

'Dead. Long time. I never think about it exactly. She died before I could get out of the joint.'

To Boots, Connie looked real good. Tanned and healthy. And even if she was sitting behind the wheel, it was still very plain that Connie had a boss figure. 'You should have made it to the top toot sweet, Connie.'

'I am the heart and brains of the world's super-ambitionist,' Connie said as if to the windshield.

Boots gave her a quizzical smile. 'What the hell is an ambitionist?'

Connie shrugged. 'It's something like the dude that is born with a limber dick. You know. So he's gotta keep on kicking everybody in the asshole so he will finally be able to get it up. You know.' She had whipped the car into a long driveway and in a moment slammed on the brakes and skidded to a stop in front of a huge colonial mansion.

Boots expelled her breath. There was a touch of envy in her smile of appraisal and congratulations. But she said wistfully, 'One more fine dommie that narco built.'

Connie did not even bother to shrug. She led the way to the front door, unlocked it and then pushed Boots toward what had to be the big room of the house. 'Go on in,' she said. 'In this house you walk in and introduce yourself. I'm going to go get outa these damned rags.'

Nothing Connie had said suggested to Boots that she was walking into the front room of the world's foremost dope queen, Studs Thompson.

*　　*　　*

Studs Thompson stood amid five glorious girls in that huge living room of her seventeen-room Staten Island mansion. The girls were all reclining on massive pillows somewhat like an E. Simms Campbell harem scene. But the five were clad in far less clothes than E. Simms would have provided. These girls wore bikini briefs and a few wore bras. Studs was dressed in a severe, yet feminine red-and-black-threaded Harris tweed skirt and jacket.

Studs was a big girl, but her shape was good. Her wig was costly and shoulder-length. She was about five feet ten and a rock-hard one hundred and seventy-five pounds.

Boots came into the room, smiling brightly, but still with a bit of reserve.

Studs showed genuine surprise and pleasure. 'What the hell you doing here, Boots, and who you come with?'

'The goddamn tire on my car went flat right there on the ferry. Connie was parked behind me. She drove the car with the flat off the boat and parked it. Connie said she'd take me here and call a mechanic.'

Studs came closer to touch Boots's breast.

Boots stepped away and at the same time brushed Studs's hand off. 'Jailhouse love is for the birds, Studs.'

'How the hell you making it now?' Studs's curiosity was real.

'I give the orders to a roomful of bitches on computers.'

'Good goddamn. I always thought some man would come along and fuck you up for sure. What the hell you know about computers? Where the hell they teach you?'

'Harry Brown sent me to school after I got out of the joint.'

Studs's eyes coolly measured the girl. 'You screwed him?'

'Who hasn't?'

'Where's he now?'

'I don't know.'

Studs stepped forward once more. She grabbed and squeezed Boots's left breast. She twisted it with a jerk, but Boots didn't scream. She grabbed Studs's wrist and twisted back in reverse. It eased the pain a little but not much.

Studs let go and smiled. 'Why the hell should two tough-assed bitches like you and me come to blows? Sit down and relax. I got to talk to you. All I want to know is what Harry Brown's up to. Is he retiring like the wire says?'

'I don't know, Studs. I honestly don't know. And not a goddamn soul in Harlem except maybe Ossie Winbush or that son of his ever knows what Harry Brown is up to.'

'Son? He got a son? You seen him?'

Boots nodded. 'They call him Giveadamn. Damned if I know why. He looks kind of scarecrow-y.'

'So that's what all this weird shit is about,' Studs said softly. 'Giveadamn,' she spat the name. 'That whitey name is a giveaway. He's a faggot that wants whiteys to punk his rear so bad he'd be willing to give every damn cent of Harry's bread to help the downtrodden. Get it?' Studs's eyes narrowed and deepened with anger. 'You lie!'

Boots was looking down and trying to massage the pain from her breast. 'Everybody thinks it's a lie, but the kid's got to be Harry's son or he wouldn't be in Harry's house. I know the setup in and around that apartment as good as anybody.'

'Harry Brown would never stick his dick in a junkie, Boots.'

Boots gave her a level look. 'Did I look like a junkie when I got to the joint?'

Studs chose to say nothing.

'I was sent up for dealing, not using. I was guilty as hell of dealing, but the law didn't prove it. They had to frame me. Harry didn't like it, and so when I made parole he fixed it so I went to business school instead of working is all. And that's why I am willing to do anything that man wants me to – anything. Dig?'

Studs changed her ground. 'Harry Brown is retiring because all of a sudden he found himself a faggot who is so in with them Rockefeller whiteys they call him Giveadamn. Well, all of a sudden I'm gonna give a damn too. Now Harry and his son can't suddenly be good-dealing politicians and sell dope, too, dig? So I'm stepping in and for once in my life I'm going to make a man a offer. I'm simply gonna go to Harry – or this simple-assed son – and tell 'em I want the names and addresses of every single connection they got. Dig it?' Studs grinned.

'No,' was all Boots said.

'Goddammit! Even if this son is so respectable he gives all these damns about the ghetto, he can't whitewash Harry Brown. And a man as rich as Rockefeller is too damned square to believe that a holy bastid like Giveadamn Brown could have a father who is the biggest dope dealer in the world. So I blackmail 'em is all. Goddamn! No wonder I got millions and you work your ass off in a office from nine to five.'

'Studs,' Boots said slowly, 'when you got to the joint, I was just about ready to leave. I wanted to like you. All the girls did. You weren't even menstruating, but the whiteys laughed in your mother's face and put you in the joint with grown-up hard-assed women and studs. And when a fourteen-year-old kid can walk in a prison like you did and damn near take over a wing of it in less than a month, she is hell. And I mean pure hell. But, Studs, please believe me, for your sake and for mine. Harry Brown is pure hell, too.'

Boots stopped to organize her thoughts and feelings, then went on. 'You got to sit around Harry's apartment for a while to dig him. Like there's a nationally syndicated columnist, a whitey, who is likely to be up at Harry's anytime. And the two of them fight like cats and dogs. Talk, I mean. And you wouldn't think there was a damned bit of love lost between those two. But that's not the way it is at all. You got to be there and see it and hear it to know. And there was a Mafia boss got wasted a while ago. I swear Harry Brown did it. I swear it, Studs. And it's not from one single word I heard passed between them. Only it was like things Harry said and did not say when he and I were alone that makes me know. Studs, I honest to God believe you're going to get hurt if you fuck over Harry or his son. You got it good; why take risks now?'

Studs laughed carelessly. 'Harry Brown is retired. His son is taking over or Harry Brown would not risk having his son kidnapped by suddenly announcing out of the blue he has found himself a son. Only the thing you don't see is Harry don't know this mother-fucking son of his is a punk, and I do. All I did was hear his name and I read the action loud and clear.'

'Harry Brown is the establishment, Studs,' Boots said simply.

'Harry Brown is no big thing. Never was!'

The five girls around Studs gravely nodded agreement. Studs had told it like it was.

Boots noted those grave nods and did not laugh. She only said, 'I like Harry. He's a man. And Harlem is a damned sight shorter on men than it is on money. You know that. Shee-it! I wouldn't ever tell this to a whitey, but sometimes I think Harlem got a hell of a lot more bread than it got wise men to know what to do with it. Hell. There's so many niggers walking on 125th Street most afternoons you got to walk like a snail. And you think a single one of those women out there shopping for wigs and shit is broke? You think any of those kids out there is broke?'

Studs nodded. 'Yeah. I know. And that's the main reason I'm going over on Eighth Avenue. It just don't seem right to sit back and let the stupid-assed men rake in that long bread. They don't got enough sense to know what to do with it after they get it. You know.'

'You can say that again,' one of the girls on the floor said. She was a baby-faced Oriental with the body of a thirteen-year-old boy. 'Move everything to Manhattan, Studs. Keep this pad and the one in Manhattan too. Connie and I can run things here on the island until you get your New York operation running like grease.'

'Smart thinking,' Studs murmured. But her mind was still on Harry Brown. She had never liked to hear a woman insist that a man could be decent and brave. Women who did were usually freaky as hell. 'What's Harry Brown's pad like and where's it at?'

Boots told her. Harry's address had never been a secret; no one ever went there cold turkey. Either Harry or Ossie took you the first time, or somebody Harry and Ossie liked took you and introduced you. It was kind of the same deal as the White House, or maybe even the Pentagon or State Department. You either belong inside or you don't. Secrecy's got nothing to do with it.

'He's not in town,' Boots added.

'He's not?' Studs said eagerly. 'Just that simple-assed son and Ossie Winbush? I don't like that Ossie bastid no way. Thinks he got class. I killed a bitch for fucking with him one time.'

Boots did not know why she added: 'The son seems to have a thing going with a broad named Margo Hilliard. You should know her. She was that little knife freak up there the same time as us. I don't remember how long. She was one of those old bad broads ... until you got there ...'

'She still using?' Studs's voice was eager.

'I don't know. She's one of those bitches who never nod. And naturally everything she wears got long sleeves. But that's not the point. The point is if she *ever* used, she would not have her ass sitting around Harry's joint.'

'What you think all this means, Boots?'

'I don't know. I just don't know. I mean if Harry was dead, all hell would be busting loose. You think Jimmy Adams, Sonny Roberts and Doll Baby would be living in peace? I mean those vultures would be tearing up Harry's empire like mad, mad. And so would all the white boys be playing position. No, Harry's not dead. Nothing says he's dead; it's something else. Maybe Margo got something they want, but I sure in hell can't figure what it is.'

'Pussy!' Studs snarled. 'Pussy, what else?'

'Margo is no teen-age bitch, Studs. She's cute and tiny, but she could be fifty. I mean, she's been here ever since I can remember and been grown.'

'I never leave this place,' Studs said bitterly. No one seemed to know why she suddenly said it.

Boots had always had a foreboding sense of sorrow for Studs, and Studs's sudden remark magnified that feeling. 'Can't blame you much,' she said. 'This is a fabulous place to never leave. Wish I could do this well.'

'You can live here if you want.'

'Thanks. But I got my own. I bought further out in the woods.'

'A eighty-thousand-dollar home for termites,' Studs sneered. 'You know what this pile of rocks cost me?'

'Plenty, I know. But for the first time in my life I am somebody. I mean, I meet a few people as equals and we share. You know what I mean.'

'Hinkty kind of bitch when you want to be, ain't you? Well, me and you are the same age about ...'

Boots could not help it; she had always been short-tempered. 'How stupid can you get, Studs? The law called your mother a liar and said you had to be at least twenty. But you were only fourteen. Damned near every woman in the joint was more than seven years older than you. Hell, I'm thirty-one.'

Studs grinned broadly. 'I deserve that one. I can be stupid as shit sometimes. But you look so goddamn young I nearly forgot. Hell, I'm twenty-four ...'

'Twenty-six,' the little Oriental said.

'Okay, okay. So I'm not so good at numbers. But that ain't what it's all about. What I mean is this girl looks like twenty-four.'

'I only hope I can keep my looks like goddamn Hilliard.'

'You bring that little stud to me.'

Boots did not look happy. 'Studs, forget it. I got me a diploma from NYU that says I am a systems analyst. I grow corn in my backyard. I don't eat it. I raise it so my mother will know I'm free. She died in an all-night prayer meeting her church had just for me. They were praying the parole board would not shit on me one more time. I don't bring nothing to nobody.'

'The 'ho' is cold,' the Oriental girl said and jumped to her feet.

Boots looked at her levelly as the two stood facing each other, each on guard.

'You're a real cold bitch.' A stiletto was suddenly in the Asian's hand. 'Your blood cold, too?'

'Knock it off. Both of you,' Studs said.

But Boots had already started her swing, and as the one-and-a-half-pound glass ashtray landed on the girl's head, the crunch of bone was heard.

Studs cursed and stepped in to land a karate chop on Boots's neck. Boots dropped, as good as dead.

Connie Dubois stepped into the room, her only garb a pair of see-through bikini panties. She went straight to Studs. 'Hold it. Lots of people saw her ass get in my car.'

Studs wasn't listening. 'You brought the "ho" here so you take her out of here, and you take yourself out too – for good, bitch. You're through.' She turned and walked out of the room.

Connie shrugged. She stood up straight, then clad as she was, bent down and grabbed Boots under the arms and dragged her out of the house and down the driveway to where a car was parked.

Keys were in the car. She managed to hoist Boots into the rear seat of the Mercedes sedan. Then she got in and drove away. She was crying and grim. She was confused.

She drove the back roads that would take her eventually into New Jersey. After about five minutes of fast driving in the whisper-smooth car, she said softly, 'You dead, Boots?' There was no answer. 'I don't want you to be dead, Boots. You know that. You and I licked on the same ice cream cone on 132nd Street, Boots.'

She heard Boots move. And then: 'You're deader than I am, Connie.'

'I know.'

'I'm going to tell you how to get to Harry Brown's,' Boots said. 'It's the only place in the world that butch can't get her hands on us . . . if Harry really is still alive. There's lots of shit in the air, Connie.'

'Yeah, I know.' She took a quick glance back. 'Your neck broke?'

'I wish the hell it was. I wouldn't be hurting all this much if it was. Goddamn, that Studs can hit.'

'Well, cool it until you get me to Harry's. He'll get you a doctor and all, won't he?'

'Yeah. Only . . .'

'Only what?'

'I would never lie to Harry. So when he asks me how I got chopped in the neck, all hell is gonna break loose in Harlem, Queens and Staten Island. I know it is.'

'This thing with me,' Connie said, 'it was coming anyway.'

17

When a man sits in a poker game, he's not going to win unless he makes the other guys call his bets,' Giveadamn said petulantly. 'You aren't supposed to be the one who calls the bets, see? You make them.' He'd been feeling much better lately.

'I know, daddee, but it's not for real you're sitting in at the table,' Foxy said. 'I know how you feel.'

Giveadamn looked at her sternly and said, 'There's nothing wrong with far-out ideas. Like inventing the telephone was a far-out idea.'

Foxy sighed with resignation. It was a fact her man was a hard-luck guy. 'You been going downtown with Ossie to the pistol range. I suppose I'm supposed to back that idea somehow?'

He nodded.

She frowned. 'S'help me, daddee, if I knew any way to attack ... with some sense ... I would be the first to say so. But I know how you feel, just sitting still and waiting for them to prove how bad they are.'

Giveadamn frowned. 'Who is the baddest?' he asked Ossie.

Ossie thought a moment. 'The cards are getting shuffled so fast you've got to sit and analyze it. That bunch from Staten Island is fierce and rich. And nobody is crazier than Doll Baby. You can't tell, Giveadamn. I don't guess nobody knows, and that's why everybody is willing to believe Harry was the tops.'

'Well, that makes me the devil's own son. And I am going to make all these chumps who would gladly kill their baby sisters for a piece of pie-in-the-sky know who I am, Ossie. Let them all know I am dealing.'

'It's not going to be that easy, Giveadamn ...' Ossie began.

All three were silent for a while. Then Ossie went on: 'And

it's not like we was alone. We got Toni to think of. I think we ought to keep her out of this.'

'No!' It was Foxy. 'Toni is in this as much as I am. Her life is not a damned bit safer if she is out of it.'

Ossie turned to Giveadamn, 'What you think?'

Giveadamn said, 'We got to do something, and we do it all by the book. The Good Book. Those who live by the sword are going to die by the sword. Now, if we maybe let it be known there is a big delivery being made, we would have everybody's nose open, wouldn't we?'

'There haven't been any big deliveries made before,' Foxy said.

'Huh?' Giveadamn was startled.

She gave him a bitterly quizzical look. 'I think it's time for you to learn what I discovered: Harry Brown has been out of dope for years. And that's where the danger lies, Giveadamn. Once you stop dealing your life's not worth two cents. Harry continued to pay off the fuzz so he could keep on living.' She shrugged. 'Only it's not going to be that easy for you ... and me.' She added, ''cause I'm in this 'cause the street says I'm in.'

'She's right,' Ossie said.

Giveadamn sat on the floor at her feet. 'Foxy, no one knows what Harry's been doing for his daily bread for the last three years. Right? So we tell them. We tell them Harry really had that formula. We tell them Harry could add one ingredient to some raw heroin, or whatever you call it, and produce the finest synthetic dynamite in the world. And this one mysterious ingredient costs less than thirty-five cents a pound.' He cocked his head to one side and smiled gently. 'I like that price. Thirty-five cents.'

'But you don't know any one mysterious ingredient.'

'Harry ain't got no dope empire.'

Foxy sighed.

'Now, the first thing I want you to do, Foxy, is spread the word. Put it in the ear of some bigmouth. Then we'll see what happens.'

*　　*　　*

Margo pranced into the bar. She looked to Deep Freeze as if she was back on the stuff. He watched her closely. He knew he had been right the first time. He also noted she was not hurting. But there was no reason why she should. The rumors had it Harry Brown was dead and this old-time junkie had got Harry Brown's nephew and heir's nose open.

Deep Freeze sat and pondered fate. Margo was not a bad chick. She was a smart little operator, but with these cute kids of fourteen and fifteen hitting the street every day, a chick who had been around as long as Margo had a lot of extra hustling to do for her daily bread.

'How you making out, Deep Freeze?'

Here she was speaking to him. There had to be a reason. He looked at her as she stood by his booth. 'What's happening?'

She shivered her shoulders. The broad had a real classy kind of sex about her. 'A stupid mother-fucker got me uptight.' Her eyes sought understanding. 'We, out here on the hustle, got only one responsibility. Right?'

He nodded. 'When I eat, my whole damned family eats. And it's always gonna be like that. Nobody gets a free ticket to ride my train. Never. So what's really happening? You hearing about Harry Brown?'

'There's been talk.'

He spread his arms in a gesture of anger. 'Talk! Hell. Nobody knows anything but talk on this street.'

Foxy nodded sympathetically. 'There's talk because nobody knows for real who the hell Harry Brown is.'

'Was.'

'Is! You been to his funeral?'

His eyes widened. 'It's like that, eh?'

'Could be.'

'What you know?'

'I know how Harry made it.'

'Who don't?'

'Who does?'

'What the hell are you trying to say, Margo?'

'Everybody says Harry was a dealer. Well, who did he deal to?'

'To who?' Deep Freeze yelled. 'Everybody! That's who. Everybody!'

'You know the name of *anybody?*'

He thought about that. He shook his head. 'You mean, Have I ever heard anybody say they were going to meet him or something like that?'

She nodded but said nothing; he could make up his own fairy tale. He would believe it more better anyhow.

'You figure he only sold to whiteys?'

'You're telling me now.'

Deep Freeze accepted the invitation. 'Man!' he exclaimed softly. 'Imagine that? A nigger selling to the whole damned Mafia, and then the Mafia selling it back to us. Damn! That man had to be worth one hundred million dollars if a cent!'

Foxy nodded. 'Wrong. Two hundred million. And he didn't sell to the Mafia. The Mafia brought it to him.'

'Huh?'

Foxy looked at him indignantly. 'What's the matter, can't you understand English?'

He wanted to yell at the dizzy bitch to cool it, but he had to keep it cool himself. He smiled. 'I understand. I understand completely what you said. You know me, Margo. There's nothing goes down I don't understand. Me and you are with it.'

She remained unruffled. 'Harry took their stuff and boosted it a couple hundred per cent. Maybe even more. After Harry got through with their stuff, it could be cut a thousand ways and still be dynamite. Nobody knows Harry was a professional chemist.'

Deep Freeze grinned broadly, though he tried to show indignation. 'Margo,' he said reprovingly, 'I know that better than most. I told lots of people Harry Brown started out with a drugstore on 125th Street. But nobody wants to believe me. See? The fact is junkies die so quick there's nobody around to check these kind of facts out with but me and you. Now, I bet you didn't know he owned a drugstore once, did you?' His smile was proud and arrogant.

Margo looked at him almost wistfully. You don't even have

to ask a Harlem dude to spread a lie. Sprinkle one drop of water on his head and he'll make a river all by himself.

'With Harry gone, there is only one man who knows how to boost heroin. He's my man, but he got this bug up his ass.'

Deep Freeze saw millions floating in the air. He leaned forward, not daring to speak.

'He's one of these black is beautiful chumps. He thinks he owes something to *the* nigger. Imagine!' She was apparently too angry to go further.

'Margo,' Deep Freeze said sincerely, 'I want to help. I know now why you sat down here at my table. I know and you know. How about going up to my place and talking some real heavy shit?'

She looked thoughtful. 'Maybe not yet. What I want you to do is think, Deep Freeze. I want you to think out all the angles and details for me. I know I can trust you. I been watching you since both of us hit the streets way back when. And you know I'm a woman.' She stared him in the eye. 'And you know I only go for one man at a time. I took my time and thought as much of it out as I could. And I chose you. Dig it?'

The doorbell rang. Giveadamn and Ossie were in the library. Both rose, then looked at each other in an after-you way.

The doorman had just called to say a couple of practically naked girls were on their way up to see them, one of them Boots Haley, a friend of Harry's.

'I'll get it,' Giveadamn said.

Ossie stepped out into the hall from the library and watched Giveadamn as he went to the door and peered through the mirrored peephole into the vestibule and open elevator doors.

'Well, I'll be a little more than just purely damned,' Giveadamn said in a loud but reverential whisper.

The elevator man, as always, was waiting to be sure the visitors were welcome.

'What the hell you looking at?' Ossie said impatiently.

'Sex on fire.' Giveadamn turned to grin at Ossie. Then he went back to the peephole with all the attention an uptight dude would give to a downtown peepshow. 'Wow! And it's really on fire,' he marveled.

Ossie came up to shove him aside and take a look for himself. And he did not believe what he saw, because he knew damned well Boots Haley would not come knocking at anybody's door in a torn blouse. Neither was Ossie prepared for the odd-looking beauty beside her in the briefest of panties and no blouse at all. He knew her at once.

Boots ducked in past him and the fine hawk of a girl followed along behind her, under Ossie's outstretched arm.

He whirled to glare, but Boots was not looking at his face. She wasn't looking at anybody. He shut the door.

'I'll be damned if I thought we would make it,' she breathed. 'Where's Harry?'

Ossie returned her stare, then looked away. It was a confession of something, but Boots did not know what. She decided to treat Giveadamn as the master of the house. 'We've had it,' she said to Giveadamn. 'I think I killed Studs Thompson's favorite concubine. I caved in her skull, I guess.'

Giveadamn looked at the long naked limbs of the girl with Boots. She was skinny, maybe, but there was just enough flesh and muscle to give her symmetry if not real curves. He noted the briefness of her panties – more like a G-string. He then allowed his eyes to wander over her upper parts. But when he looked into her eyes, he was warmed by a feeling of kinship, of brotherhood for the girl.

'What the hell is this shit?' It was Margo speaking. She had come quietly up the stairs from the lounge. And she did not bother to hide her stiletto. 'What the hell is this?' She turned on Boots. 'When the hell did she get sober enough to find her way to the East Side outa Harlem?'

'Shee-it!' Boots muttered between her teeth.

Margo turned to Ossie. She pointed at Connie. 'This bitch was the pride and joy of my whole goddamn block. I used to change her diapers. I watched her up until maybe she was something like twelve or thirteen when she took and crawled into a cheap-ass wine bottle and never came out again. Shee-it!'

She stood with arms akimbo now and directed her anger at Connie. 'What the hell you come here now for? Why? What for? I said.'

The girl did not quail. She did not even act as if she was being hassled. She smiled in a slow, lazy way.

Then Margo smiled at her. 'You dizzy bitch, you really are sober, aren't you?'

Connie nodded. 'I stopped working at being drunk about four years ago.'

Surprisingly, Margo was less dubious than Ossie or Giveadamn. In fact, Margo, in a Mother Hilliard role, herded the two girls down the stairs to the lounge. It was Margo who went behind the bar and poured five stiff brandies over the rocks. When she passed them out, talking all the time, no one but Giveadamn noticed that Connie accepted her drink quickly, but did not touch it to her lips.

As they drank, Foxy said casually, 'Why the hell you two stupid bitches come here with your simple-assed lies?'

Boots told their story.

'That's the way it was, Margo,' Connie said. 'That's the way it was.'

'How come you came along?'

'Studs loved that Ming Toy, that Mai-Tai bitch, Margo. I should be dead. I'm as good as dead. Oh hell, Margo . . . Studs has been looking for a good chance to kick my ass out of there for about a year now.'

Margo put her knife on the bar and said, 'If you two came here on a wolf ticket, it's time for you to leave. You know? This goddamn apartment is a fucking fortress. Dig it? Especially you, Boots. You know damned well your lives ain't shit if I even get the idea you are full of shit. So if you is: Walk! Walk on out now. Or you are going to die right here.'

'Margo,' Boots said coldly, 'I came here because the owner of this apartment is Harry Brown. Where is he?'

Foxy picked up the knife. Boots stared at her.

Ossie stepped forward. 'Margo,' he said quietly. 'Raise up, Margo.'

Boots marched out of the room. The rest exchanged glances,

then followed her. Boots walked down the hall to the last room on the floor, took out a key and unlocked the door.

'Shee-it!' Ossie said in a whisper, behind her. He gazed at two huge safes that faced each other.

Boots went to the one on the right and worked the dial. In no time she had it open. She reached in and took out an envelope with her name on it. Inside was a bundle of hundred-dollar bills an inch thick. 'This is mine,' Boots said. 'If we have to leave here, I'm going to need it.'

Foxy went to the safe and slammed it shut. Then she said, 'Let's go.' They all filed back to the lounge.

When they were seated in a group around one of the divans, Foxy said to Giveadamn, 'It's time you told everybody like it is.'

The room was silent. Connie was peeling off her bikini. She was now completely stripped.

Boots said to Giveadamn, with a slight shrug, 'From a kid Connie was always like this.'

'There's one thing I think you don't know, Boots,' Giveadamn said. 'How long you think Harry's been out of the racket?'

Boots let her disgust show. 'Don't come on like that, man. Give me a break. I know Harry Brown.'

'Margo?' Connie said lazily from where she was reclining. 'What the hell you doing here?'

Margo tried to look ferocious. She also tried not to grin. She partly failed in both. 'Me and Harry had it out.'

'That's as reasonable as *my* story,' Connie said. Then she asked, 'Who's the other person in this house?'

Margo gasped.

Connie said, 'It's a chick and she has crept to the doorway over there,' she nodded with her head, '. . . and listened and then ducked back. So whoever she is, she's in. So why don't I have a right to ask?'

Toni's face appeared in the doorway, ravaged, dazed, puffed up.

'It's not seventy-two hours yet,' Foxy hollered.

Connie got up from her place on the couch and went to the

child. She took Toni's hand and led her back to what had once been Ossie's bedroom.

'Connie will save us or sink us,' Ossie said. 'I say we go with her.'

Foxy nodded.

The men who collared Deep Freeze had not been too rough, so during the ride uptown to the Riverdale section of the Bronx, Deep Freeze made a change in plans.

The thing to remember and stay cool with was he did have the info. And that info was not like something could get a man time. His life was not in danger, just because a loose-lipped bitch had given it to him. What he had was valuable. All he had to do was stay cool, go into his deep freeze and wait to hear from the highest bidder, the highest bidder being the dude these goons were taking him to. He sat back and enjoyed the rest of the trip.

They stopped in front of a big Tudor-style house. Deep Freeze thought it was an extra-fancy brownstone. There were more trees around it than in all of Morningside Park.

The three of them got out. So far the men had not said a single word, and Deep Freeze admired that. It wasn't they considered Deep Freeze wasn't there, it was as if these two young cats weren't even there themselves. Outasight! Outathis world. Young and cute. They had on handmade basketball shoes that even Walt Frazier didn't wear.

So there was nothing to do but stay in his deep freeze. The kids unlocked the door of the big house and entered, shoving Deep Freeze into the darkness ahead. One of them flicked on the lights. And damned if they weren't in a real lobby. Just like an apartment house. The three of them waited for an elevator at the foot of a grand staircase.

They went to the second floor and emerged into a freakish bedroom. It was the kind of room a smart black boy would fix up after having Hugh Hefner's pad described to him.

Deep Freeze let out a sigh of awe and appreciation. This pad was the living end. The main issue. The kind of thing that would keep a guy's rod hard even if a chick never walked into the room.

His glance traveled to the bed and then his eyes bulged. There were three hundred pounds of solid black fat on that bed. It wore pink pajamas and a yellow wig. Deep Freeze shivered, then began to tremble. He was living a crazy nightmare. He had to be making it up in his own head: he was looking at the bloated black corpse of Jean Harlow.

And then the corpse rose up and smiled. Deep Freeze's guts quivered. But he couldn't take his eyes off that smile. The corpse was not smiling at him, but with charming falsity at the two boys. It was a beautiful smile even if it was false. It told the boys not to worry about disturbing this fine lady's beauty nap. She was going to forgive them if they went right away and let her finish her little nap.

Then the corpse looked at Deep Freeze for the first time. Not exactly *at* Deep Freeze, but at his fly. Just as if it could see what was behind the fly. The corpse sent up a big bass man's voice that said, 'Who's this?'

And then Deep Freeze cooled it. This big black ugly queen suddenly made things right and safe. This had to be Doll Baby.

'Hello, Doll Baby,' he said. He summoned the correct amount of awe and servility without even thinking about it.

Doll Baby's smile drooled upon him. 'You never saw me before.'

'Everybody's heard of Doll Baby. My name's Deep Freeze. I been around Eighth Avenue for years. Lotsa years. I'm the last of the old-timers.'

Instead of looking at Deep Freeze, Doll Baby beamed his thanks at the two boys. He was so graciously appreciative that Deep Freeze began to ponder the true reason this faggot had sent for him. But he stayed cool all the way.

'Doll Baby, we was in the bar and this girl named Margo comes up to Deep Freeze in a booth and says something. Then she sits down . . .'

'I'm not interested in any "ho",' Doll Baby exclaimed petulantly. He rose to sit on the side of the magnificent bed.

Without looking, he moved his feet around until they found some pink fur mules. Then he sat primly and waited, hoping no one was going to get him upset.

'Margo is the old bitch who got that young boy's nose open. The boy everybody is talking about now that Harry Brown isn't on the scene.

'We couldn't get what she said, this chick, but we were watching. And what she said suddenly made him start to cream in his pants right there in the bar. Then she split. And Deep Freeze right after her, like he don't catch. But we catch him,' the second youth said.

Doll Baby smiled at Deep Freeze. Deep Freeze returned his smile. Doll Baby's face screwed up in a thousand little black puckers. He began to cry. And then he was beating the living hell out of Deep Freeze.

Way back in a fading reality, Deep Freeze heard the hysterical voice screaming, 'You know I don't like to ask nobody no questions!' And then there were more thumps upside his head. But the voice was louder even than the thumps Doll Baby was laying on him. Deep Freeze was very ready to tell it all, only he went unconscious before Doll Baby gave him a chance.

Doll Baby wiped the tears running down his cheeks and glared spitefully at the boys. 'Now look. He can't even talk no more. Why didn't you tell him that it makes me mad when I have to ask questions?' He began to sob piteously. He blubbered, 'A queen don't never ask no questions. She's s'pose to be tol'. You men should be happy to tell me every little thing like that.'

One of the boys went to him, put his arm around him and said softly, 'We got the answers, Doll Baby. We heard it all. We just wanted you to see how hard we try to make you the biggest. The biggest, Doll Baby. You are gonna be the biggest from now on in. Me and Tommy here is gonna see that nothing stops you from being the biggest and the most fabulous. There is a heroin machine for real, and the Browns got it.'

Doll Baby's tears stopped. He smiled his benedictions upon both his lovers. 'You boys are good to me,' he said simply, sincerely.

* * *

The little bitch had to be old, but she had an old-fashioned funky something that made you feel like freaking off. Sonny sat alone in the booth and pondered Margo. It had been a long time since he had seen such a high-stepping walk on a chick. She stepped out like an Arabian stallion. Fine. And her skin was like rare sherry. And she was aged, too. Nothing to sneer at. She was just aged enough not to be a pain in the ass.

Then it hit him. This bitch was smart. The 'ho' associated with Harry Brown's son or nephew or whatever he was. And she did it with Harry's permission. Nobody did anything around Harry unless Harry approved. And that meant she and Ossie were running a game.

Sonny grinned appreciatively. The answer could be simple as hell. Like Harry never did the usual. Harry was an original all the way. Harry Brown's ass had visited a few prisons, but Harry had never done time for narco. Harry *operated*.

There had been the time Harry left Atlanta and the grapevine had it Harry had bought out that stupid Jew's drugstore just to make it right with the parole board. Harry was always in and out of that drugstore; Sonny had seen him coming and going when Sonny was just a kid playing around, hoping to glimpse a big star going to the Harlem Opera House. Stuff like that. But nobody could prove Harry owned the joint. Nobody could prove Harry knew a damned thing about a pharmacy or even chemistry; but old-time Harlem had always figured he did. Looking back on it all now, maybe he actually had a heroin-enriching process of some kind. Harry couldn't have just been supplying that druggist with all that illegal booze he sold over the counter on Sundays. Sonny had been to Harry's pad. Nobody lives in a building like that without both bread *and* prestige. Joe Namath would not be too welcome a tenant in that building. So Harry had money. And Harry had respect. So maybe Harry was in on big narco. Only it had to be something like a Meyer Lansky thing, like maybe Harry was bankrolling every other man in narco except Sonny Roberts. If that was true, then Sonny Roberts was sitting on a time bomb. But if it was a heroin machine, then Sonny could move freely again.

Meanwhile, he believed he was the only one outside the people in Harry's apartment who knew for sure Harry was dead and buried. Question was, How long should he stand pat, waiting? He could make his move now while everyone was sitting around wondering. But where?

He rapped with his knuckles on the paneling behind him. The boys in the next booth got up and came to sit.

Studs Thompson stood in the middle of the floor and gazed angrily at nothing. Three glorious girls sat on pillows on the floor and silently waited to see and hear just what was bugging Studs. And whatever Studs wanted to be done about what was bugging her would be done.

Life around Studs was simple that way. In fact, life without men is simple, good, and a hell of a lot of fun too. No hassles. When you live in a seventeen-room house with six embossed snuff jars always full of fine cocaine, it is impossible to be hassled. No man on earth is worth giving up a life like that.

Once Studs brought in some way-out whitey bitch. Not that whitey bitches were anything unusual around Studs. One of the three awaiting Studs's orders was white. But this one dug the scene and announced this was a commune. The girls damned near killed her. Hell, this was no crazy bunch of kids starving on a ranch. This wasn't even a sex thing that way. There was sex enough for everybody, but that was just a part of living, no big thing. The thing Studs offered was peace. And there could be no peace ever if there was a man in the house.

Studs was a good girl. Studs was no bulldiker. Studs liked to play around sometimes – who doesn't? – but she was not one of those butches who would kill a girl for not wanting to.

'I've heard enough about Harry Brown and this young kid he's been schooling. Everybody is talking about Harry Brown, and nobody is saying a goddamn thing about the man that can be proved or that even makes sense.'

She glared around at the girls.

'Now, I see what men don't see. What nobody realizes is for the first time people have been *thinking* about what things would be like if Harry ain't around. Dig it? Dig it?' Her voice rose shrilly. 'That's all there is to it: *Harry is nobody if Harry ain't around!* Everybody else gotta put an *if* in it, but why should we? There's nothing in the book says any man *has* to be around.'

'That old mother-fucker's at least seventy right now!' one of the girls said.

'If he ain't dead, I say kill him, but we don't do any killing until we get facts. All the facts,' Studs said. 'Whether there is or ain't this machine ... and where Harry gets his stuff and who he deals it to. So that means we got to put the snatch on the bitch.'

The pretty white girl jumped to her feet. 'We mail in her left nipple and then ...'

'Then they would think she was dead.' That was the darkest one.

The one who looked like Nona Hendricks of LaBelle said nothing. She never did. But she reached up and stroked the back of Studs's powerful legs.

Studs sat down on the padded floor and the girls then proceeded to touch and caress all of Studs's body. Studs relaxed even more. Finally, she stretched out on the floor and gazed at the ceiling. Her eyes and her voice got dreamy. 'I want to do this man-to-man. Man-to-man.'

'I know where he lives,' the Nona-type said.

The other women stared at her.

'I didn't know you knew that,' Studs said. Her words chilled the group.

'It's no big thing, Studs,' the girl said quickly, breathlessly. 'He has party time up at his house anytime. Ask around. I've been took up there lots. Lots, Studs. Every pretty girl in Harlem been to his house sometime or other.'

'Let's just the four of us go up and talk to Harry, then,' Studs said conversationally. 'We go up there and ask questions. That's all. We only ask questions. If I don't like the answers, we are not going to leave anybody up there still breathing. Now, is that clear enough for all of you?'

'How?' It was Doris.

Studs got off the floor and went to a sideboard and took out a huge Mauser automatic pistol. 'When you get hit with this, you don't do nothing heroic. Like, say, there is no machine – I am going to start shooting, and when I stop it's all going to be over. No police are going to ask too tough who did it. We just leave and come back here, and then we go on doing our thing like before. Only there will be no more Harry Brown. We don't have to go out and ask who he did business with. When his people hear Harry is dead, they going to go out and look for a new connection. See what I mean? We don't need any info from Harry or Ossie or that little bitch Margo. All we do is sit tight and the people come to us.' She paused to glare. 'Now all these sonsofbitches who claim I don't know how to read and write don't seem to realize that the only problem is to kill Harry Brown and his nephew and Ossie. I don't need no goddamn Connie Dubois to tell me that.' She grinned. 'Maybe if I knew how to write I would be dumb enough to want to negotiate. But I ain't that smart, so all I got to do is do it the easiest way. Now, ain't that thinking?'

The ringing of the phone woke Ossie at seven in the morning.

'Ossie? Ossie, is that you?' It was a woman's voice and vaguely familiar.

'Yeah.'

'Deep Freeze and Big Frank are dead.'

'Huh?'

'They got them, Ossie. They beat Deep Freeze black and blue. I saw his body in the morgue already. They shot Big Frank through the head.'

'Is this Mona? And Mona, who is "they"?'

'You know. You know better than I do, Ossie. Everybody knows Harry Brown is not out in the street. Everybody knows. People who never spoke to him in their lives miss seeing him wheeling by in one of his cars. You know that. And they figure if there was nothing serious, you and the rest of Harry's friends would be telling the world he had a stiff neck or something. You should have announced, Ossie.'

Ossie sighed. It was no time to quibble. 'So what happened for real, you think?'

'They picked them up yesterday.'

'Goddammit! Who is "they"?'

'Doll Baby's bunch. They got Deep Freeze. Jimmy Adams' bunch shot Frank. I know them all. They all come in the bar and drink a lot.'

'Don't too many people know Frank was ever in any deals with Harry Brown. You know that as well as I do. There's got to be more. Nobody knows Frank and Harry were real gone buddies from way back.'

'Yes they do, Ossie. Yes they do. I mean like when you're behind the bar, you get into conversations. You know. Like somebody makes a false statement about Harry Brown, like, say, he don't fool with women. Well, naturally, Frank would pick that up. You know. And if the thing gets heated, Frank would say he knows more about Harry Brown than any man alive. After all, nobody ever said it was a secret that Harry was a friend of Frank's in Florida, then sent for Big Frank to come up and help him out in his business. You know, Ossie. And why don't you give it up anyhow?'

'What?'

'Give up that process Harry's got? And don't tell me he ain't. I heard it too many times. I heard it years ago. And where there's smoke there's fire. Like Harry Brown gets richer every year. You ever hear of a black gangster getting rich in the stock market? Huh? Did you? And that's what that crazy Frank told everybody who would listen.' She suddenly choked up and then the sobs began.

'I know how it is,' Ossie said quietly. 'You forgot he was dead. That's the way it is though, Mona.'

'That man had dignity, Ossie. Deep Freeze was nothing. You saw Big Frank and you knew he was somebody. In a way, Big Frank could attract more attention than Harry. He sure in hell attracted more women than Harry. And I'm here to testify.'

'I'm going to hang up now, Mona. I'll be by your house before eleven this morning for sure.'

Mona said goodbye. Ossie sat on the side of the bed and brooded. Word was out. Margo had done a good job.

If Jimmy Adams knew that Big Frank used to be Harry's right-hand man, he also knew that killing Big Frank meant war. Jimmy Adams was demanding that Harry Brown's secret formula and all narco lying around Harry's premises be turned over to him.

This first murder was a concrete declaration in that Jimmy Adams knew Ossie must avenge Big Frank's death. If Ossie did not fight, if he turned over all Harry's narco assets and secrets, then Ossie was a pussy. Ossie would get killed as soon as the secret formula was in Adams' hands. And if he did not give up this nonexistent formula, he and Giveadamn were still dead.

There was also the very tricky kind of bind he was in with Studs Thompson. Connie Dubois was not Studs's brain trust any more. And it was pretty clear from what Connie said last night that she alone was responsible for keeping Studs from declaring war on Harry Brown and/or Harry's heirs and associates.

So Connie was no longer able to keep Studs this side of sanity. What was worse, Connie was a fugitive from Studs's kind of justice and currently hiding out in the fortress of Studs's sworn enemies. It would seem only death would settle that issue.

What the hell was wrong with Sonny Roberts was anybody's guess. The man was actually crazy, the way he had been dogging Harry's footsteps.

A sudden thought hit Ossie. Was Sonny tailing Harry when Harry jacked up the car? That was the million-dollar question. The only consolation was that Sonny was one of the originals, the last of the numbers men to move into heroin. Sonny was not a killer; he was a give-and-take man. He took a hell of a lot more than he gave, but he gave in . . . when necessary.

Ossie decided to get in touch with Doll Baby. It was time to negotiate.

18

That morning Boots went to the hairdresser's and had her hair cut and slicked down in a permanent. Her once great Afro plumage was a shiny black nightcap on her head now. And it made a difference. It hardened Boots's appearance. Boots worried about herself more than people knew. She worried she wasn't smart enough or hard enough or black enough or sexy enough. She was never comfortable with herself.

When she came back to the house, Giveadamn saw her first. 'That's a boss hairdo you got there, Boots.'

'Shiny black all the way. Why don't you get one? It's unisex time now.'

He smiled but said soberly, 'If Harry wasn't laid up in the hospital, I would. I got a kick out of not agreeing with him. I know he doesn't like slick-headed niggers, but it wouldn't seem like fighting fair now.'

'Do you like to make people mad for real, Giveadamn?'

'No. I just refuse to get serious over the trifling things in life. I think the only real difference between blacks and whites is that blacks are not as able to get het up over nothing as whiteys. You know. Like Watergate.'

'Well, what did you and Ossie do to Doll Baby?'

'Doll Baby? Heck, I've never seen the man . . . or should I say "young lady"?'

'The Baby is a lady,' Boots said grimly. 'But a lady with sledgehammers instead of claws. Why did you fuck over Doll?'

'I don't know this Doll Baby. I have never met him. I never saw him. I do not know who his associates or intimates are. And from what I hear about him, he and I live in two different and separate worlds.'

'Didn't he call you up?' she said.

'No. And I doubt he would be able to get hold of this

number anywhere. I mean, the people who know Harry Brown's phone number are not people who would hand it over to Doll Baby.'

'He called you after he talked to Deep Freeze. I'm sure of it. I got it through the grapevine, but it was pretty dependable people who told me.'

Giveadamn sat down. He looked bemused. 'I'm beginning to get the picture of just how far out Harlem can get . . .'

'Like?'

'Supposing Doll wants my phone number and offers big bread for it. Well, why shouldn't a real gone dude give him a number for that kind of bread? Any number, anybody's number? Doll calls the number and issues an ultimatum without even bothering to make sure who he's talking to.'

Giveadamn leaned forward insistently. 'Figure it, Boots. The wise guy at the other end of the wire could have called Doll a million different kinds of mother-fucker. But Doll will never be convinced that it was not me who answered the phone and who subsequently cussed him out. Wow!' Giveadamn slapped his forehead.

Boots was just as insistent. 'You got to turn it all over to Connie, Giveadamn. This ain't your kind of game – or Ossie's either. It's Connie's. She was Studs Thompson's mastermind, she might be the only person in the world who can make sense out of what is happening to you . . . gonna happen to you and Margo. Please, Giveadamn.'

'I already made up my mind about Connie, Boots. She's my kind of people.'

'I'm beginning to dig you all the way,' Boots murmured.

The day after Ossie reported that the dynamite and more hand grenades were at Giveadamn's fix-it shop, Connie came into the lounge. It was 11 A.M. but she still looked sleepy. She sighed contentedly though and said to Boots, 'How 'bout some coffee?'

Boots shook her head at Connie's innate laziness. 'You and strong black coffee deserve each other,' she said and went into the kitchen.

Connie said to Ossie, 'I been doing some rethinking. We don't exactly need no dynamite.' She suddenly feigned self-righteousness. 'Law and order is the name of our game, so why not build us a heroin-processing laboratory?'

'How?' Giveadamn exclaimed.

'We got to have ourselves a machine because seeing is believing. Then we invite Doll Baby and all the others to inspect our laboratory for refining crude heroin into the finest grade obtainable in the world.'

'It won't work,' Ossie said. 'It can't work. It's too easy.'

'Easy does it all the time,' Connie told him.

Giveadamn had already decided things were getting like Margo always said they were: he always got the best kind of bad luck. But Giveadamn wanted to try. To Ossie he said, 'You know how to get in touch with Doll Baby? Before we go building a machine, let's sound him out.'

'I know a gay bar where I heard he drinks,' Ossie said dubiously. 'I heard he tore it up a while ago, but there ought to be somebody in there who can contact him and have him meet us somewhere.'

In the Mercedes driving toward Harlem, Giveadamn said, 'Connie's right. I see the play already. We make the exchange in a bank. Doll Baby can't make a muscle move in a bank.'

Ossie glanced at him quizzically. 'What makes you think he can't? In fact, what makes you think Doll Baby has good sense?'

'Yeah,' Giveadamn murmured thoughtfully. 'Yeah. According to the way I heard it, Doll Baby just might go berserk.' He smiled. 'But Jimmy Adams is not crazy. I mean, he wouldn't go berserk, would he?'

'Not as likely as Doll Baby.'

They had barely ordered drinks at the gay bar when a regular customer sidled up to them and asked if he could spring for a drink. Ossie and Giveadamn accepted his offer. But when the bartender brought the three drinks, Ossie put a fifty-dollar bill on the bar and said, 'This gentleman's money is no good while my buddy and I are in this place. Okay?'

The little nance of a bartender smiled roguishly and said words to the effect that such gentlemen as Ossie and Giveadamn were always welcome at the Gay Blade.

When the bartender had swished away, Ossie said to the faggot who had joined them, 'We're here on business. We want to get a message to Doll Baby.'

'You picked the right place. He just bought out this bar yesterday.'

Ossie grunted. 'With his prison record?'

'You think the Italians who owned it don't have records?' The little guy's name was Alice – at least that's what he called himself. 'And anyhow, I said the Doll Baby bought this place out. I didn't say there was going to be any changing of names on the liquor license. You look like you been around. You ought to know what's happening at all times.'

'I do, but Doll doesn't trust anybody enough to let the name on the license stay the same,' Ossie said.

Alice leaned closer. 'Doll killed the bartender and shook up half a dozen other girls in here. He bought the place to buy silence. See how it goes, love?'

'So you figure he'll be in sometime soon to inspect his new investment?'

'Well, the rumor is the Doll will be here any minute.'

'So let's drink to that,' Ossie said.

Giveadamn, Ossie and Alice were on their fifth drinks when two handsome youths came in the bar and planted themselves on each side of the entrance door. Both boys had their hands on guns stuck in their waistbands. If they gave any signal, it was not apparent to Giveadamn, but a few moments later Doll Baby entered, swathed in mink, although it was more than a little warm for September. The sheer bulk of the man made Giveadamn think of a hog in human form.

It was one of those masculine days for the Doll. He neither swished nor spoke in high mincing tones. He came to the bar and in a deep voice ordered the bartender to set up the bar.

Alice sidled over to Doll Baby and whispered something in his ear.

The Doll roared an oath and slapped Alice halfway across the floor. 'I hate faggots!' the Doll hollered.

Two of the pretty boys in Doll Baby's entourage picked Alice up and ushered him to the door.

The Doll turned to Ossie and Giveadamn, 'Don't mind me. It just so happens I hate men who try to be girls all the time. Shee-it!'

Ossie went headlong into his approach. 'We want a man-to-man talk with you, Doll Baby,' he said. And then: 'This is Harry Brown's son. I want you to meet him.'

All of a sudden the Doll was a simpering woman. 'Pleased to meet you, love. It's wonderful.'

Giveadamn followed Ossie's lead. 'We have some merchandise to sell to the highest bidder.' He took out a card and scribbled a number on it. 'Call us when you want to make a bid.' He turned as if to leave the bar. Ossie did the same.

'Wait, dears. Let's go in the back and take a booth.'

Giveadamn looked at Ossie, who shrugged noncommittally.

In the booth facing the Doll, Giveadamn said, 'We decided not to quibble. We're going to let everyone who's interested know we're open to offers and we're going to take the highest bid. It's as simple as that.'

'No it's not, love. My bid is one million dollars more than anybody else bids.'

'You realize what you're getting?' Ossie asked.

'It's all over town, love. Harry had a secret for making "H" four or five times stronger than when he put it in his thingy. I want that thingy, dears. And nobody but me is gonna have it. Now that's fair and clear, ain't it?'

Giveadamn did not look at Ossie as he said, 'As soon as I get the highest bid, I'll call you and let you up it. We'll set up the heroin still and show one of your men how to work it. It's a tricky kind of thing to run, you know. Explodes to hell and gone if you fuck up.'

'Jimmy Adams will bid,' Doll said. 'And Studs will bid.' Doll Baby grinned hugely. And then just as suddenly, he began to weep. Through his tears he moaned.

Ossie had often heard that when Doll Baby weeps, it is time to get away from him, so Ossie rose from the booth.

'Don't go, babee,' Doll Baby blubbered. He whipped out his

forty-five and as the tears came even harder than before, said, 'I want you all to give me that thingy. It's mine.'

Doll Baby's entourage was now making a half circle behind him.

'You done made me cry,' the Doll slobbered. 'Don't nobody do that to the Doll.'

'Let's talk it over,' Giveadamn suggested. 'I'm not a hard man to deal with. You can look at me and see that, can't you?'

Like a dutiful little girl, the Doll said, 'Yes.' Then he put the gun in his waistband.

Now that the maniac was quiet, Giveadamn could not think of a thing to say to him.

But Ossie said, 'How do you want us to make delivery?'

Tears jumped out of the Doll's eyes once more. 'Even if you give it to me, you wouldn't show me how to work it right.'

'Don't cry, Doll,' Giveadamn said gently. 'We are on your side. We don't like anybody else in the racket to have what's rightfully yours. We're going to give you that machine and show you how to run it and then maybe if you appreciate what we've done for you, you'll give us a nice little taste. How's that?'

But the Doll's tears flowed more copiously. 'You want to cheat me outen what's rightfully mines,' he blubbered. And then the tears suddenly stopped. 'Git up!' he commanded in a deep masculine tone. 'You's gonna go and gimme what's mines right this minute!'

Giveadamn and Ossie exchanged glances. And both men were meekly led out of the bar and into the street at gunpoint, each believing that the other would come up with a move that would get them out of this fix.

Giveadamn finally got tired of waiting for Ossie to act. When he saw three Muslim sisters, in flowing robes, he fell to his knees in front of Doll Baby and began to scream, 'Mercy! Allah be saved and have mercy on me!'

He did not know if the Harlem Muslims cried 'Allah be saved,' but that was the only thing he could think of.

Three or four neat young black men with the sisters were

silently staring at Ossie, Giveadamn and the Doll. The young warriors in conservative suits, close-cropped hair and black ties, said not a word.

But one of the little sisters came to Giveadamn and extended her hand. He took it and she walked beside him down the street. Ossie followed. They walked silently to the corner of 135th and Seventh Avenue. When they reached the corner, the Muslim girl smiled and turned back to rejoin her sisters whom she had left staring the Doll down.

As soon as the girl was out of earshot, Giveadamn yelled, 'Why the hell didn't you do something?'

'What?' Ossie looked both stubborn and mad.

'Anything!'

'If I'd got down on my knees like you did, everybody would have thought that goddamn Doll had a perfect right to kill me. You can do crazy things and nobody gets excited about it.'

'You've had more experience with egomaniacs than I have. You were Harry Brown's closest friend.'

'Harrh!' It was the only sound Ossie was capable of at the moment.

Giveadamn stared at him. 'You sorry I went down on my knees? 'Cause if you is I can gladly walk back and introduce you to Doll Baby again.'

'Bullshit!' And then it was Ossie's turn to frown. 'So what the devil are we going to do now?'

'You are going home and get that dynamite. I am going to the shop and start setting up the thingy, as the dear Doll calls it.'

Ossie was truly amazed. 'You intend to deal with him again, don't you?'

'What have I to lose?'

'Everything!'

'A victim of sickle cell don't never have nothing to lose.'

'And what makes you think the Doll is going to pay us?'

'He won't.'

'So?'

'Somebody will.'

*   *   *

The hawk slowly pulled off the bikini while gazing at the ceiling. 'We are going to need big bread, Ossie. I got over three hundred thousand salted away. Boots has fifty thousand. What can you raise in hard cash?'

'Maybe a million. There's safety deposit boxes in my and Harry's name all over town. I checked out those safes Boots showed us, but there's nothing negotiable in the one Boots can open. I think the two million in cash that Sonny Roberts had to come up with is in this house somewhere, but don't ask me where. Probably in that other safe.'

Two questions at once were deviling Ossie, and he did not know which one to ask first. Finally he said, 'You skimmed three hundred thousand off the top of Studs's bread?' And then: 'What the hell we need big bread for?'

The hawk said, 'We got to have a genuine-looking contraption if we're going to sell one. A real good fake. You and Giveadamn or someone you can trust must go to Chicago and buy three stills. I mean something shiny and brand-new and complicated-looking in stainless steel. If we are going to put down murphy for millions, we got to look like millions.'

Ossie saw the play forming in Connie's mind. 'I take it you want some shiny laboratory equipment,' he said slowly. 'I can get that here. I can get anything money can buy right here in New York City.'

'I beg to differ with you, my confrere, but the Windy City hawks everything in the world that can be got hold of. In New York you have to dig out the sellers of the truly exotic.'

Ossie turned to go. 'Have it your way, but if we don't have everything you want parked in Giveadamn's shop by eight o'clock tonight, I'm going to make you wear clothes for a week.'

The hawk suddenly laughed. 'It's funny how ignorance is based on truth. I mean, Did you know that the chemical molecular weight of heroin, diacetylmorphine, is 369? But the morphine that heroin is distilled from only weighs in at 303. Anybody who distills heroin out of a kilo of morphine is going to have more molecular weight in heroin than the amount of morphine they started with. Crazy, huh?'

'How the hell you know all this crap?' Ossie said.

19

Ossie and Giveadamn found all the equipment they needed in New York for Giveadamn to concoct a dazzling, compact, six-by-seven-foot computerized heroin-refining machine. The contraption would have impressed a board room of IBM directors, let alone five stupid narco dealers. Since it only had to look good and act impressive, Giveadamn had it almost finished within a week. During that week all was quiet with the dealers. Too quiet, thought Ossie and Margo. Connie guessed so too.

The hawk, fully clothed, sat in Giveadamn's shop and watched him at work.

'It surprises me,' Giveadamn said seriously, 'that a kid as mental as you should brush off sex the way you do. I tell you, Connie, sex is a mental game.'

'Might be,' she said agreeably. 'Just might be. And it just might be I got a blind spot or I'm a coward. You know.'

Giveadamn nodded. It was clear. Connie could not stand to be hurt like that. Maybe she could not stand the idea of his trying it once and then politely refusing to try it again. Something like that.

He shook his head. 'Even if you got on your knees and cried, I would never touch that glorious frame of yours, Connie. May your mind rest in peace.'

'Giveadamn, let me explain something. I love the hell out of you. I mean that exactly like I'm saying it. But don't ever touch me and I promise I won't ever touch you.'

Giveadamn sighed.

'All us geniuses have really stupid kinds of blocks,' she said. 'I bet Einstein was as scared of black cats as you are.'

'I'm not afraid of black cats,' Giveadamn said, looking up from his work. 'Heck. I'm not too scared of two-legged black cats either . . . although some of the tales I've heard about this crazy Doll Baby are scary as hell.'

'I'm glad you brought that up, Giveadamn. I don't think we ought to let Doll Baby or Studs bid on that machine. They're both too unstable to deal with. We got to wipe them out, real soon. Understand? Think you can help?'

'The key to my entire being is self-preservation. I'll do what I have to.'

'I'll remember that,' the hawk said.

'Well, it's getting there.' Giveadamn stepped back from his work. The apparatus rose higher than his head and rested on a slab of concrete. He'd made it big so nobody looking at it would get the idea they might pick it up or wheel it away.

It looked something like a still and something like a bank of glass tubing filled with lavender liquid, the liquid a concoction of Kool-Aid and wine Boots had brewed in the kitchen. There was a control panel and it had two meters, along with a half-dozen knobs of various kinds and sizes.

Giveadamn flicked three toggle switches. Lights glowed. The machine began to hum; bubbles started to circulate through the tubing. At that moment, a throb of pain went through Giveadamn's body. He knelt on one knee and held his breath.

Connie hadn't seen the pain hit him. She was watching the bubbles with the wonder of a child. 'It's real beautiful,' she said. 'I buy it. Where you put the skag in?'

'That opening up front there.'

'And where's it come out?'

'Around back.'

'Five times as good, huh?'

'You gotta believe it.'

'Not me,' she said. '*They* got to.'

Ossie gave a quick discreet rap on the door, then pushed it ajar. She looked at him with displeasure. He had been a fool; there was absolutely no reason why he had even considered this kid to be alive, much less a weight on his back and his mind. He stepped back and closed the door. But her voice caught him.

'Ossie!'

He opened the door again and looked at her.

'I don't want you to go.' Her eyes still seemed unhappy.

'Yeah?'

With her hand she smoothed a place beside her. He came and sat gingerly on the bed. She placed one hand on his thigh. Then she nodded her head.

From way back, from long ago when Harry was into one of his historic diatribes against all junkies, Harry had said drug addiction was a sexual problem. And Harry had said more; he had spoken of the awful yen for sex that the nerves create in the aftermath of withdrawal.

The pressure of Toni's hand on his thigh was heavier and so was her voice. 'Ossie?'

'Yeah? I'm here. I can hear you.'

'I was diddling myself.'

He jerked his head around and started to ask her what she expected him to do about it. But instead he raged at himself. Up until now he had got himself enmeshed . . . fucked up! . . . with tough-assed broads, but today, like a dirty old man, he was a candidate for a child molester.

But now her hand was stroking his crotch.

And then his hands were on her.

He pulled back the covers. Her dark body still gleamed with a light sweat. He lay beside her and the tiny body rived. Her breath, her eyes, every thing about her was violent now. And he began to think she was a whirlpool of deadly black waters.

But he could not stop. She would not let him.

She reached orgasm first and cried out, 'That's it! That's it, Ossie!'

They both lay on their backs and stared at the ceiling, afraid to look at the other.

'Am I a 'ho', Ossie?' She moved a little, but still gazed up at nothing.

'I don't know,' he said heavily. 'I don't know.'

'Why?'

'I mean I don't know if you are a whore.' And then he was angry. 'What difference does it make?'

She turned on her side so she could put her arms around

him and put her head on his chest. Her tears dropped on his skin and ran in a tickling little pattern over his ribs. He moved his hand toward his chest, then rested it on the back of her head. Her once beautiful Afro was a matted horror, but it still felt soft, clean . . . and like his. It really did. It was like the kid belonged to him. So he knew he was fucked up for real.

'If I got to be a 'ho', I'm going to be your 'ho'.'

Again he wanted to put her down, but he couldn't. He still was not able to take her in his arms and comfort her. Not yet, but he knew he would. He had to. Just like he'd had to be born black. When you got born black, you got born with shit in your face. And the only real thing wrong about Toni was she had been born black.

Margo did not seem to be standing so much as frozen there. Her dark eyes drove hatred into his.

It was not exactly fear but a kind of anxiety that choked up Ossie's words. 'Hi, Margo.'

And then she shed her hatred like a dirty pair of drawers, and her smile was tough, rugged. 'First come, first served. It's my fault. I forgot.'

He really did not know what she was talking about, yet it seemed he should. 'What's it all about, Margo?'

'Ossie, you got there first. That's all. And maybe she could have done a whole lot worse.'

'If you're looking for promises, Margo, I'm not promising a goddamn thing.'

'She's not a "ho"!' She spat the words as if the venom burned her own lips. 'I swore to God no man would ever make her a "ho".'

'If you use that word one more time, I'll kick your simple ass.'

She remembered one of those crazy songs the church niggers used to sing in the storefronts down the street where she had once lived. The niggers were crazy. Punched out by all the jive that went down around them. And so they gathered together in their little punchy church and sang and shouted and beat their goddamn drums as if the noise itself would scare away sin and hard times. But the punch drunks in that church had this song that was crazier than all the rest: 'The Blood Done Sing My Name!'

She turned and walked away from Ossie. He went to watch as she marched through the lounge to the stairway, and he continued to watch her legs as they went up the stairs.

Connie had taken the bedroom that led off Toni's room. As usual, she was all but nude when Margo opened the door and slowly walked in. Margo's face was cold enamel.

'Hi, Margo,' she said.

'You got this thing for Giveadamn, Connie. But it's not gonna be like that ever. Like you think you're smart. I think you're not.' And now Margo's knife was in her hand. 'I'm gonna put a stop to it, Connie.'

The hawk looked away. 'If your mind's made up, there's no use telling you like it is, is there?' Then she laughed, a lighthearted sound that both surprised Margo and angered her.

'What's so funny, bitch?'

Connie would not look at her. 'Giveadamn would never forgive you, Margo. Never. From now on out, you and Giveadamn are going to have a dead chick sitting right between you. Dig it? I'm nothing to Giveadamn now, but the moment you stick that blade of yours in me, I'm gonna be somebody. Somebody you can't kill again. Dig it? Giveadamn's got imagination, Margo. You don't. But you better hurry up and get some.'

The sound from Margo was rage. She threw the knife to the floor and leaped to grab Connie by the throat.

Connie was ready for her. She leaped and jabbed both of her feet into Margo's lunging body. Margo hit the floor, but was up in an instant. This time she came more carefully.

They clinched and then struggled over the bed. Then Margo was on top of the hawk, pounding her fists into the girl's face.

But Connie wasn't helpless, and with a heave and a twist she was on her stomach, Margo still astride her. Connie got hold of Margo's hair and yanked, and Margo came off her back. Then they were both on their bellies, banging at each other.

They grappled. This time Connie broke away and got Margo in a mugger's necklock. She brought her forearm up hard against Margo's windpipe and kept it there. She felt Margo begin to collapse. She opened her grip and shoved hard. Margo's forehead banged against the wall. She fell dazed at Connie's feet. Connie got out of the room.

She went to the library, hoping to find Giveadamn there. He wasn't. Everybody in the house seemed gone. She dropped herself into the recliner chair and tried to get her breath. Melancholy hit her, and for the first time in years she wanted a drink. A lot of drinks.

She was about to leave the library to go get a drink in the lounge when she heard footsteps – too light and too firm to be Margo's, she thought. Margo would have walked slower and heavier after that banging her head got.

But it was Margo. She paused at the library door to stare at Connie. She opened her mouth, but no words came. Then she shrugged and passed on toward the front door.

Connie heard her open the door, then heard it slam shut. She closed her eyes and tried to forget that vacant, yet all-too-disturbing look on Margo's face. Connie had seen that look at least a dozen times as she grew up in Harlem. Connie always knew, even as a child, that the look was the face of a murder going someplace to happen.

Foxy glanced at the windows of the house next door. She did not see the front door open or see Lupo step out on the stoop. But she heard the sound of the closing door. She was halfway up Gracie's steps now.

Lupo gazed at her.

She was smiling. 'How's Ranger?'

Was the bitch crazy? All bitches got crazy after a big sting. Didn't she know he had a contract out on her? He invited her to have a drink. There might be a few crumbs in it for him, whatever it was she had ripped off. Then he'd kill her.

She came back down the steps, then came up his.

'Yeah, Lupo, a drink is just what I might need.'

She passed him and entered the house. He was right behind

her, a puzzled look on his mangled face. He could almost smell some kind of success. This kid had been into something. She smelled like it. Walked like it.

He turned a moment to secure the latch. When he turned back, she had her knife in her hand.

'One for you and one for Ranger,' she said.

The knife flashed high and then she was driving it in low. He grabbed her neck with both hands, banging her head against the wall even harder than he squeezed her throat.

And Margo's knife was cutting a V across his stomach. Then she pressed real hard.

They fell into each other as they both went down to the floor. She died first.

20

When the burial was over and the muted talk had ended, fear came like a dark night. Still and stolid black fear. The world outside the apartment began to push at his door. It was panic time, but Giveadamn was too depressed even to panic.

When he sat in the hospital room beside the bed where Harry lay, he no longer had the feeling everything was going to turn out all right. Harry no longer had to have tubes in his nose; that was hopeful, but Giveadamn felt no hope. And talking to Harry no longer helped.

At first, going to see and sit beside Harry, talking to him, had given him a kind of energy, as if Harry could hear him and send that energy back to him. He'd had the feeling that as long as Harry lived, nothing could really go wrong.

But something had. Margo was dead. If Margo could die, they could all die. And they were all going to. No use pretending.

He stared at the side of Harry's bandaged face, black and ferocious-looking even with his eyes closed. There were deep frown lines between his eyebrows, set there over his lifetime. His jaw was short and wide, like the end of a brick. His nose was kind of flattened now, and it had already been broken a couple of times.

'Harry,' Giveadamn said, 'just move a finger or something.'

But Harry never moved. Only his chest rose and fell, ever so slightly, rose and fell.

Giveadamn sat on, missing Margo.

In death Margo had not been a Foxy Cool Momma. She was a far cry from the perfectly proportioned nymphet beauty who liked to putter around the hotel room clad in nothing but panties and one of his old shirts. In that crazy coffin she was a gnarled and gnomelike dummy. And the hideously purple-tinted thing in the coffin was all that Giveadamn's memory would give him. His memory cheated him even of a decent image of his Foxy and Cool Momma.

He never went out now except to sit beside Harry. There was no need to. When he wasn't at the hospital he would go into the library and pick up a book. He did not read much of it. He tried to, but melancholy thoughts took over his mind.

He tried to spend time in the lounge too, but it was as if, at night in bed, he could only recall the hours he spent alone in the library. And all the crazy brooding he had to go through by himself. It hurt especially when he tried to make plans and came to a gut sort of problem with no Margo around to interpret for him. He did not even care what Doll Baby or any of the others might be up to.

For a few days, the girls had consoled him and he was grateful. But they had changed. Each in her own way seemed to think it was his duty to give meaning to Margo's death. It was as if each girl now lived with a fear of death just as he did. They did not know he used to dread death and dying more than they did.

He knew that they were not ready to have him tell them that Margo's death had been a common Harlem demise. Margo's death was a 'nigger's death.' An exquisite form of self-lynching. But no one in this household of his wanted so simple an answer.

Truths like that were especially hard when they were all living in this apartment as if it were a besieged fort. They were at war with the entire black underworld. It wasn't just their old enemies now. Lupo had friends. An open contract was out on all their heads. Everybody wanted to be in on the toppling of the tyro king, the heir of Harry Brown. Everyone in Harlem wanted a piece of the action. Threats were coming at him in the meanest ways.

Crippled old women came to the downstairs with packages of shit. Joe the doorman received vicious letters, to be given to him. Ossie had changed the phone number twice, yet the phone still rang with unwanted and obscene callers. It was as if the C.C. Riders and all their lesser kin had an open line to the inner workings of the phone company.

In the crisis of Margo's murder, Boots had retired into the kitchen. She came out only to watch the afternoon serials on TV and then again at night to watch at prime time. Bright and brassy no more, Boots was now a drone. She scrubbed floors. She did the windows. She boasted no more of being in charge of a roomful of stupid whitey girls manning computers in a brokerage firm on Wall Street.

It had been insidious, barely perceptible, the way Ossie began to defer to Giveadamn. For some kinky reason, Ossie needed Giveadamn Brown, aged twenty-six, to be the natural father of Toni, aged sixteen, and the father-in-law of big bad black and damned near middle-aged Ossie Winbush!

Ossie, he knew, was ashamed of his courtship of Toni. Maybe he saw her too much as his little sister. There was no other explanation for his shame at being in the sack night after night with a teen-age ex-addict, an angel with a dirty past.

Little Toni's moods were just as disquieting as Ossie's. Sometimes Giveadamn would catch her eying him sullenly, reflectively, searching for something inside him that would explain why her mother died for nothing.

Connie was the only salvation. The tall and willowy beauty demanded nothing.

'You're not even making a bluff of talking to the old man,' Connie said as she opened the door to Harry's room and sauntered in. When she took off her coat, he saw she wore only a thong of a brief and no bra. His grin widened. Didn't she care if a nurse came in? But he was glad she had come to interrupt his thoughts.

'You come here looking for the answer. But the answer is none of your business, Giveadamn.'

He knew exactly what she was talking about. 'I do not sit and brood over the circumstances of her death. I know what killed Margo: she lost her cool. Two violent people met and disagreed.' He opened his hands wide. 'Nobody can make a conspiracy out of that.'

'But it's possible,' she said, 'that the big dope boys set the whole thing up from the git go. From getting little Toni hooked all the way to the funeral parlor. You understand me? The period of mourning is over.'

He said nothing.

'But first we have to deal with attitudes. The sum total of attitudes.' She stopped, then went on: 'We're going to go get the three hundred thousand I got stashed away at Studs's. You come with me.'

'What about Studs?'

'I'll take care of her.'

21

The hawk anxiously glanced at Giveadamn. 'You sure you've told me exactly how to do this?'

It was the first time she had ever shown doubt. Either in him or herself. It gave him a queasy feeling and made him want to pray. He nodded his head toward the back seat of the rented Ford sedan. 'Those things are the latest model. Darn near foolproof.'

He had never thrown a hand grenade. He had never even seen one until Ossie gave him these six and told him how to use them. He tried to grin. 'If anyone's got a right to be scared, it's me.'

Good sense told him that he and Connie were wrong to try to take on Studs. 'Connie, we got all the bread we need. More than the whole gang of us will ever be able to spend in our lifetime. So what right we got to go about bombing a house for your measly little three hundred thousand dollars? It's really nothing but peanuts.'

Connie hunched her shoulders doggedly. 'I stole that bread in good faith. Good faith to myself. I promised myself I would show myself a good time with that money. You can dig that, can't you? But try to understand this, Giveadamn. It's more than money. You got to put fear in people. You got to make a show of strength just to stay alive.'

He nodded.

'Furthermore,' Connie added, 'I'm after something else. We need thirty keys of heroin for bait. Thirty keys is bait for real, Giveadamn. Any man on earth holding thirty keys of dynamite shit is rich as Rockefeller. Dig it now?'

He sighed as she turned a corner. 'Okay. I'm letting you have your way. But there's going to be one little change in plans. I'm going in with you.' He reached inside his jacket and pulled out the huge pistol Ossie had given him.

It was Connie's turn to sigh with regret. 'Giveadamn, you'd only be in the way. I know that terrain with my eyes closed. I don't want to be tied down with having to lead you around. On top of that, the dogs would tear you to pieces before I could calm them. On top of which, they are not going to be eating you up in silence . . . you realize what that means, don't you?'

Connie turned off the main highway and took a dirt road. She drove about half a mile, then braked to a stop beside a wild hedge. All Giveadamn could see were thick berry bushes, but he knew without being told that in the midst of these thickets ran a barbed-wire fence.

Connie cut off the motor. There were dogs snarling and growling on the other side of the thicket. The hawk now looked like a little girl in the coveralls she was wearing. But she also looked efficient as she took a pair of wirecutters from the glove compartment and left the car.

Giveadamn watched. She picked a thin space in the bushes, got down on her belly and wiggled forward. She paused and Giveadamn assumed she was cutting a space in the fence. Then she was out of sight.

The dogs got quiet. It simply was too quiet, too deathly still. And there was nothing to do but wait.

In about five minutes he heard the first grenade go off. His fears grew. He listened in vain for the roar of another grenade.

Time to move now himself. He got stiffly out of the car and made for the space Connie had wriggled through. He came out on the other side. The dogs were still silent. It wasn't too painful to move. The excitement must be good for him, he thought. There was nothing to see but a vast expanse of not very well-kept lawn. Beyond the lawn were trees, and he supposed Studs's house was just beyond them. Bending, he ran forward. It was hard for him to keep from shouting Connie's name.

When he got past the trees, he saw her. He could see only the back of her figure. She lay crouched with one arm upraised to throw again. The grenade arced up, and over to the house.

It landed on the old-fashioned slanted cellar doors. It blew. Then Connie was up and running. She reached the blasted cellar doors and disappeared from sight.

Giveadamn thought of Margo, of how death had overtaken her. Connie had four more hand grenades, but if she had to grapple with someone she would not be able to use them.

Then Connie reappeared, lugging a large suitcase and what looked like an old army duffle bag. She was not running fast because of the weight she carried. She came on toward Giveadamn.

Then from around the corner of the house strode a Juno. Even in this moment of stress, Giveadamn knew that the giantess had to be Studs, and that she was more than ordinarily handsome.

Connie ran toward, and past, him. He was not sure she had seen him. Studs was running toward them both, a look of rage on her face.

Giveadamn jerked out the pistol and fired carefully in the direction of Studs's feet. The first shot didn't faze her, but she felt the earth spit beneath her as the second bullet struck the turf. She stopped. She was no more than fifteen feet from Giveadamn. He raised the pistol with both hands and aimed directly for Studs's eyes. He did not know if he could pull the trigger. But he aimed and waited for her to come on.

But she turned and hurried back around the house. Giveadamn ran to catch up with Connie, who was scrambling through the hole she had made in the fence.

Connie already had the motor started when Giveadamn reached the car; and then she was speeding away up the country road before he had the door closed on his side.

'Where does this road lead?' he asked.

'Don't ask me,' the hawk said. Then, 'This Ford is no match for her Jaguar.'

He looked back and saw a foreign-make car coming closer. 'And you can't drive any faster?' he asked.

'Not on this road. We don't got a chance.'

Out of the corner of her eye she saw him pull out the pistol and refill the magazine. She also saw up ahead a sort of deadman's curve. She slammed on the brakes and headed in a straight line into a tree-dotted meadow. She got out, saying, 'Okay, Giveadamn. She'll be here in a second. Better shoot good.'

He nodded, tight-lipped, then fell on his belly just around the corner of the rear end of the Ford. Resting on his elbows, with both hands he raised the big gun and began to fire at the windshield of the Jaguar coming straight at them. He fired four shots.

The Jag swerved but quickly straightened and came on. When the car was a dozen feet from him, Giveadamn took careful aim again and got off the last two slugs. He rolled and kept his eyes shut until he heard a loud thump and a crunching of fenders. He opened his eyes and saw the Jag totaled up against a tree.

He looked around for Connie. She was coming toward him from the other end of the Ford.

'I saw Studs's face as she went past to greet that tree,' she said in a tight little voice. 'That Studs was driving with three eyes – the middle one all red.'

He felt sad. His only glimpse of Studs had been as she rounded the corner of her house. Studs had been a beautiful girl. He wished he had not killed her.

'Well, let's get it on,' Connie said crisply. 'Let's get it on.' And then she added, 'Just as if you did not have to kill her.'

He looked at his hands. They were shaking. He looked at Connie. She was coolly composed as she once more got behind the wheel of the Ford. She drove back down the dirt road the way they had come.

'You going back to her house?' He tried to sound incredulous, but he knew she was.

'We got things to do. Lots of things to get.'

'Don't you think somebody heard those explosions? Don't you think a single person at least heard me shooting?'

'And what's that got to do with us?'

This time she took a road that led to the front of the house. She got out and Giveadamn followed her to the front door of the mansion. Connie said, 'You better go unlock the trunk,

Giveadamn. There's nothing inside you can do until I bring things out ... Everybody in there is dead.'

Connie was upstairs about ten minutes. It seemed like an hour to Giveadamn. When she came back, by the look on her face, it would seem she had picked the house clean. Clean of whatever it was that she wanted.

They drove back to the apartment. Once she had all the stuff from Studs's house stowed in the library, Connie seemed to put all the blood behind her. Down in the lounge she said to Ossie, 'We got thirty keys of pure dynamite.'

Ossie said slowly, 'While you were out with Giveadamn trying to get yourselves killed, I got a call from the police.'

'What? The fuzz? You mean they want in?'

'They want it all,' Ossie said quietly. 'They do not want us in New York City as either objects or victims of a heroin war.'

'Well, thirty keys should get them off our backs,' Connie said. She grinned, her lips dropping at the corners. 'Sure, thirty keys will do it. The only thing is, we don't have them.'

'Huh?' That came from Giveadamn. 'What you mean now, Connie?'

'We will report our stuff stolen. I've always said the police in this town are good for something. Why not send the damn fools on a chase?'

'And why not just give it to them?' Giveadamn asked. 'At least we would have them on our side.'

'Shit,' the hawk said. She pulled off her blouse, then her slacks. 'They would immediately accuse us of holding out. All thieves are thieves because they believe all other people are bigger thieves. You can't hand a cop thirty keys and tell him that's all you got. They would say you gave up too easy; you got to have twice as much stashed away.'

'You're right,' Ossie said. 'But what are we going to do, Connie?'

'Okay, Connie,' Boots said. 'I got a feeling maybe no one of us is gonna come out of this alive. Or maybe I should say: *none of you*. You realize I'm home free? Studs is dead. I can go home and go back to work too.'

'But,' Connie said, 'even though I saw blood gushing out of

a hole in the middle of Studs's head, you got no proof Studs is dead. In fact, Boots, you got no proof any of the girls in that house is dead. Just like nobody got any proof Harry Brown is dead.' And then: 'Get me Jimmy Adams on the phone,' Connie said to Toni.

Toni gasped. 'I don't know Jimmy Adams. I don't even know where he lives. Gee, Connie, why you ask me to do it?'

'If you're going to hang around, you got to learn to think. This is a thinking folks' party we got here.'

Toni stiffened, then said quietly to Ossie, 'Come to the phone with me, Ossie.'

Boots left with them. Connie turned to Giveadamn and said, 'Next move is to get Jimmy Adams softened up. We gotta move fast now. Giveadamn, tell me something, why'd you kill Studs?'

'I guess because I was scared.'

She nodded slowly. 'From you I've got to have something more . . . a whole lot more.'

'Why?'

'Because I don't want to take up with somebody who likes to pull north when I'm pulling south.'

All he said was, 'I see.'

'Do-gooders are natural-born fuck-ups. I want to know if you are ready to admit you killed Studs because you maybe wanted to. Not for the good of the community. And not to save our youth and way-out shit like that.' She took a deep breath and went on. 'You didn't kill for revenge or even in self-defense. The real reason you kill someone is because they are creating a disturbance.'

He eyed her. He knew where Connie was coming from now. The girl was honing rough edges Margo had left. Giveadamn took a deep breath.

'Murder has nothing to do with the ghetto,' Connie said coldly. 'It's got no more to do with the ghetto than sunshine has to do with the rain. Murder belongs to everybody, Giveadamn. Since the beginning.'

After Connie left, Giveadamn doubled over with the pain he had felt coming when she asked him why he'd killed Studs. A damn-fool question – although he knew what she was getting at. He made his way to the library, shut the door and sat down to wait for the pain to stop.

In about ten minutes he got up and went down to the lounge. Connie got up and shed the thong of a brief, the only garment she was wearing. When she was completely nude, she lay down on the divan and stretched luxuriously.

'I have spoken to Jimmy Adams on the phone. I am expecting him shortly,' she said absent-mindedly. 'Giveadamn, from now on . . . since Studs has said her fond goodbyes, all of the hoods who want you dead are men. The female is the deadliest of our species. Jimmy Adams is deadly, but I am deadlier. If I can't flim and flam and slam that man, then my name never was Constance Dubois.'

22

Jimmy Adams was said to command as much firepower as the Cuban Army. Whether he did or not, he carried himself as if he had that much authority or more. Tall, straight and thin, Jimmy inspired thoughts of well-honed razors rather than firearms. Jimmy disturbed the people who saw him. Sometimes those who saw him were scared as hell.

But Mr Adams was not a mean man. He did not hate people. Like Ossie, he was a realist. He believed, furthermore, that the good life is achieved through a continuous culling of your personal world. Graveyards are inhabited by noxious people. And noxious people and graveyards deserve each other. That's the way he thought of Big Frank and a dozen or so other men. But Jimmy never thought of himself as an anointed hangman. In his own mind he was simply a born survivor, strong on charity. He liked to give a pretty girl the shirt off his back. Girls knew that. Lots of pretty girls said that's why Jimmy wore such pretty shirts. He also liked to send pretty girls to expensive colleges, especially if they called him Uncle Jimmy and thereby became related to him.

All the girls were in the lounge – little Toni, Boots and Connie. They looked at each other expectantly when the doorbell sounded.

Boots stood up nervously. 'I'll get it.'

'Okay,' Connie said, 'but be sure he's by himself. I don't want him to have any army at his side. Dig that real cool, keed.'

'Don't worry,' Boots said as she went up the staircase.

'I still think Ossie and Giveadamn should be here,' Toni said to Connie.

'Jimmy is a ladies' man. You got to remember that and you got to treat him like that. Now before we get through with this murphy, he is going to be asking all of us to come in with him. Maybe not as partners, but damned near it.'

The two sat in silence until Boots descended the winding staircase with Jimmy Adams in tow.

For the first time since she had been around Connie, Toni was embarrassed by Connie's nudity. She made a furtive gesture for Connie to get something on. But Connie wasn't thinking of anything so trifling. She smiled coolly at Jimmy and lay stretched out on the divan.

Jimmy took a chair and sat gingerly on the edge of it. He had a close haircut, not much longer than clipper length, the kind required of all black waiters before neo-Africanism and equal opportunity. His eyeballs were naturally red and not from all-night poker sessions. His teeth were good.

He smiled at Connie. Jimmy smiled most of the time. Fools mistook his smile as a sign of truce and were comforted, but Jimmy smiled best when he had a gun in your back.

'I know who you are,' he said to Connie. 'And I've seen Boots here around for years. How you all doing?'

'Fine.' Connie looked at Boots. 'Did you show him the layout?'

'I didn't think it was necessary.'

Connie said to Jimmy, 'What you think of this sixteen-room duplex? What you think of never having to worry about some rookie cop banging at your door any night at any hour and asking for a handout? This is serenity, Jimmy.'

He nodded. 'Yeah. I heard a lot about this place, but Harry ... God rest his soul ... never invited me.'

'Harry's not dead!'

Jimmy did not dare to look surprised.

'Harry Brown is alive,' Connie repeated. 'But the thing is, Who grabs his territory? You? Me? Or Doll Baby?'

'Yeah,' was all Jimmy said. She'd said 'me' not 'us.' He looked at Boots and Toni, but they said nothing – so she was running things.

'Harry and his son Lawrence want out. The price is six million. For that you get all his connections. This apartment. All his processes for refining heroin to up its street value five hundred percent. And the real kicker is that thirty keys of dynamite "H" go with the deal.'

'Thirty keys?'

Connie nodded. 'Thirty keys today will give us our money back. We will then own this town.'

Jimmy began to understand. 'You and me? You can get your hands on six million cash?'

Connie stared at him as if he were simple. 'What you think I sent for you for?'

'That's what I'm talking about,' Jimmy said. 'Studs is dead. You got something out of her, maybe the whole six million. I don't know. So what you send for me for?'

'I need an outside man, but I take him only as a full partner. You only got to raise four of those six million in the next three days.'

'Where's Harry?'

'Harry is not going to deal with you. You know that. I shouldn't even have to tell you that. Now if you don't trust me, say so.'

'Four million is a lot of bread to hand a woman you never saw before in your life for a machine nobody's ever seen and a process no chemist I've talked to says can exist.'

Connie turned to Boots. 'Go get that briefcase Giveadamn and I brought in the other day.'

Boots left the room and returned with the huge old-fashioned briefcase, the one Ossie had called a schoolbag. She put it on the floor near Connie's feet.

Connie raised up from the divan and with one foot shoved it toward Jimmy. 'Take that,' she said.

Jimmy opened the suitcase and saw what had to be at least a kilo of heroin neatly packed in the bag. He raised his eyes to Connie. 'Take it? Where?'

'Test it. Deal it. You don't trust me, but I trust you because I know Jimmy Adams. Your credit's good.'

He wondered if she really was on the level. And he wondered if it would pay to find out. On the other hand, if she had six million in cash, she had exactly two million more than he did. And with things as tight as they were now with the CIA under suspicion, there was no telling what thirty keys of uncut horse would be worth tomorrow morning.

But it was too damned easy. Something was wrong. She was giving him over one hundred thousand dollars' worth of merchandise to deal. And she only wanted him to put up four million in cash for a deal eventually worth a hundred million. Crazy!

Then the answer came. Every whore needs a pimp. It was a tale told a thousand times a night. Well, he had started out as a pimp, and now maybe he had a whore here who possessed a four-million-dollar money-maker.

He stood up. 'I can get four million. Some of it will be in paper.'

'Any paper has to be signed over to Lawrence Brown,' Connie said. Her tone was so cool and businesslike it reassured Jimmy that here was a woman of the world with a keen mind who was on the up and up.

'All right, say we're partners; then what?' he said skeptically.

'Then next we auction off Harry's process to the highest bidder. That's if Sonny Roberts and Doll Baby want to bid.'

'What's the point of that?'

'We make like dealer rings do in Parke-Bernet and other auction houses. You and I buy from Giveadamn and Harry, then hold a knock-down auction among us dealers for three or four times what each paid to buy the right to bid. Losers get their two million back minus the auctioneer's house cut. We say Giveadamn wants eight million; we got to get it up. Hell, that operation of Harry's is worth two hundred million easy and we all know it. But the auction gives the proper perspective, Jimmy. It makes it plain that everyone else had a chance but couldn't come up with the bigtime bread. After that we have no trouble with them. You know what I mean.'

He said nothing, only gave her a hard quizzical smile.

She looked at him levelly. 'We run the show and that gives us the right to take an auctioneer's cut. Or more rightly, I run the auction. I just want you nearby with lots of guns to be sure it's all run proper. You know?'

'What's the dealer's cut?'

'Anything we want to make it.'

Jimmy was thoughtful again. 'You got your two million yet from the others?'

'No. But I don't think I'll have any trouble. Do you?'

'Where's this machine that refines the heroin?'

'It'll be at the auction.'

He scratched his chin. 'It would be easy,' he said, 'for you and me to walk off with the whole bag, wouldn't it?'

'Anything's possible, Jimmy, when we put our heads together.'

When Boots led Jimmy up the stairs to the front door, Connie got up and stretched. She looked at Toni and grinned, her nipples standing out like turret guns. 'Gawd! That bigtime city slicker is so het up he forgot this sack of goodies. Run up and take it to him, Toni.'

But before Toni reached the stairs, Jimmy had come back down.

'I got to thinking on the way out,' he said to Connie, 'I don't know what kind of condition Harry's in, but the very fact he wants to sell out is proof to me he don't believe in himself no more. Understand? Harry wants to get paid for something a child could take from him.'

Connie's nod of agreement was most amiable. 'You got something there, so why don't you just pull out all your muscle and snatch it? You don't even need me in the act.'

Jimmy studied Connie. The woman was so damned slick it was scary.

'Like first of all, where the hell are you going to hit Harry and his son? You got his processes? You know his connections? You know how he keeps every single law-enforcement agency off his back. Like, suppose you did take all you saw, what then? I mean, you take it over and all the big gravy Harry is paying out suddenly stops; what you think the big brass is going to do to you when they have to put their yachts in drydock country?'

'If they came to me, I'd pay,' Jimmy said, like a blustering child.

'They like dealing with Harry better. Harry is a known

quantity. You pay, I know, but do you know who you really pay? You pay a bagman, don't you?'

Jimmy nodded.

'The machine is real. I've seen it work and you will too when I see some of your money. So, Jimmy, you get up four million in cash or bearer bonds now and come see me like a good dude should.'

'Or else . . .?'

'I'll find me another partner and that partner just might get the idea that once he owns Harry's muscle and savvy he can lean on you till you're flattened. They have milk wars, gasoline wars, any kind of price wars. You think maybe Harlem and its environs needs a heroin war?'

The king is dead; long live the king. It ran like a counterpoint in his mind. But what he said was, 'I heard you killed Studs on that back road. Did you?'

'What kind of question is that? And what kind of answer you expect?'

'Just want to keep the record straight.'

'I don't have a record. And that's something you ought to keep in mind before you throw your millions on the table.'

His answer was a shrug. He picked up the bag and started for the stairs. Boots followed him to the front door.

As she unlatched and opened it, he said, 'I know you pretty well, Boots, from the old days. What's happening for real?'

She did not smile. 'It's the end of things as they have been, Jimmy. It takes a special man to put up four million dollars on what just might be a murphy. But if a new combo does take over the entire racket, what good would that four million do you? They wouldn't trust you; they would have to kill you.'

She gently closed the door in his face.

In the elevator going down, Jimmy had a moment of trepidation. He could get knocked off toting a bag of pure heroin. But then it came to him that he was already under the protective umbrella of Harry Brown.

His euphoria was so great that when he got to his car, he simply opened the trunk and tossed the bag in. He would not even have to scurry home. He had faith in that brainy

Giveadamn Brown | 181

little half-white-looking girl, Connie. She would see that he got home safely.

And if she had invisible bodyguards following him, it was up to him to act smart, un-uptight. He knew that whoever the girl put on his tail would report back to her.

He decided to drive to Wall Street and get all the negotiable paper in his account put in the name of this Lawrence Brown. As he drove down the East Side Highway, his thoughts turned to love. Like, what other reason could this Connie have for picking him for a partner? And he was such a logical choice.

Doll Baby was a faggot from way back, and she needed firepower to hold the Doll off. Studs just might have made it, but she was dead. And Sonny Roberts was a little too cute for his own good. On top of that, Sonny was damned near as white-looking as Connie. So where Sonny would be like a god to the average dark-complexioned woman, he was just so much half-white trash to Connie. For the rest of the drive, Jimmy dwelt on this new-found love that had dropped out of the blue and into his pocket.

Yeah, this kid Connie was bringing with her a dowry worth more millions than maybe Harlem itself was worth. He decided on his way back uptown he would stop off in the fifties and order Connie a Rolls-Royce as a show of his appreciation for her generosity to him.

He was so engrossed in his loving reverie he did not see the car that pulled up beside him. The two plainclothesmen in the car were about to pull him over for a quick search and shakedown. But because Jimmy's countenance was so serene, the cop next to the driver said, 'We're wasting time. He's not carrying anything at the moment. That black bastid looks too cool. Go ahead and pass him up.'

Down on Wall Street, Jimmy was still so full of self-confidence he parked by a fireplug on Pine Street, went into a sporting-goods store and bought two knapsacks.

From there he went to his broker's, and once in the inner office, he said abruptly: 'I want two million squeezed into these rucksacks.'

The broker stared aghast. 'You can't pull that in broad

daylight.' Then it came to him that Jimmy had more than two million in negotiable paper in the company's vaults. 'You mean . . . ?'

Jimmy's cold black eyes fixed on the young broker. He nodded his head. 'I don't want no crap. There's been a snatch and I want that money clean as a newborn baby's soul. You get me? I mean I want that paper now!'

The young broker acted. It had never occurred to him black people would ever get so far up in the world that one of their worries would be kidnaping. But neither had he dreamed that young blacks who couldn't even write their names would every day come into this brokerage house and buy hundreds of thousands worth of negotiable bonds and bearer notes. Right now the company had thousands of dollars' worth of securities held for young black punks, some of whom had disappeared without a trace, leaving the company holding securities of men who were probably dead. It occurred to the broker that a man with eyes like this Jimmy Adams could help him peddle these unclaimed stocks.

In less than half an hour Jimmy left the office with one of his rucksacks filled with negotiable paper made out to the bearer for three hundred and fifty thousand dollars; the rest was in cash.

Connie picked up the phone near her bed and dialed. As soon as she got her number, she said, 'A Rolls is a little too much, Jimmy. I don't like it. I don't like it at all. You disappointed me.'

'How?'

'I picked you because I thought you were like me . . . without sentiment. We are partners in business, partners in crime, if you want to put it that way. I don't want presents. Any chump can give presents. I want smart action and nothing else.'

He decided to come on strong. 'I figure to give a smart girl her due. And from now on, I'll call some of the shots. That's the way I am, Connie. If you don't like it, say so.'

'I got a plan for you to make back most of your bread in one deal,' she said offhandedly. 'I got a buyer for you. He's going to lay three million on you for the thirty keys. What do you think of that?'

'Give me time. Just a little bit of time and I can deal that stuff out in the street for four or five times that kind of bread, babee. What's the sudden rush?' He got worried. 'You ain't trying to renege on our deal, are you? What kind of business is this anyhow?'

'The name of any business is a quick cash flow. I can get more and better keys anytime I want. Don't forget I'm the person who is next to the guy who inherited all Harry Brown's know-how and the machinery to turn the saddest narco into pure dynamite.'

'Yeah, babee. I guess I forgot. So what gives?'

'I'm going to set up a date for the auction. So you give me two million now and bring the rest to the auction. I'll be there to see you get your thirty keys as well as Harry's business. How's that?'

'Anything you say goes, Connie. I'm sorry I sort of went off there.'

'Think nothing of it, Jimmy.' And she hung up and contemplated the ceiling.

Little Toni came into the room. 'Hi, Connie. What's up?'

Connie jumped off the bed and smiled fondly as she impulsively put out a hand to touch the girl's tall Afro. 'You look pretty as a brand-new penny this morning, keed,' she said. 'Fact is, I think you are going to be my little lucky penny today. You don't have to go to school if you don't want to.'

Toni smiled slowly, 'Something big for real?'

'Kinda,' Connie admitted. 'Just kinda. But any day you play with fire like we got at our door is likely to be a big day. I think I kinda owe Margo one. I think she would want you to be right on top of this weird shit. Like she would want you to see first-hand how greed can kill a man . . . or woman . . . or child. Did you ever meet up with anybody at all in the narco trade?'

Toni shook her head. 'I let Ranger make all the connections.'

'Well, today you look like you never touched a drop of

heroin in your life. You look like a little angel. So I think I will send you to church.'

'Church? This is Monday.'

'The Doll goes to church every morning to pray. I have that on the best authority. I can't reach Doll by phone and he knows I want to talk to him but won't call me. So – I want you to go stand in front of his church. And when he drives up with his entourage of pretty-faced boys, I want you to step up to him and whisper that Jimmy Adams is buying Harry Brown's business. Lock, stock and barrel. But that the Doll can get it from under his nose if he calls this number and gets in on the auction. And then vanish – fast. I can tell by those pretty legs that you can run, Toni.'

'Sure. I can do that, but why just me? I mean, I might get it twisted or something. I won't, but I didn't think anybody thought I had that much sense.'

'Don't talk foolishness, Toni. Nobody around here has ever called you stupid. But Doll knows the rest of us on sight. He don't know you. Anyway, I want the most innocent-looking person we got to deliver that message. I mean, if some hard-nose delivers it, Doll Baby just might take a dislike to them or something. I'm betting that he will just thank you and let you go. Like he will think you're one of the nice little girls who attend his church on Sunday mornings so they can meet up with one of his pretty-faced little boys. You understand, don't you?'

'Why don't you write a note? I'll hand it to him and then split the scene.'

'Good thinking,' Connie said. She sat down and dashed off the message. She folded it and handed it to Toni. 'I hear he makes it about ten every morning. You'll just about have time to get there on the subway. I don't want you riding in a car, especially an expensive car. I want Doll to get the impression this is an innocent little schoolgirl bringing him a solicitous thank you because of his massive kindness to the Christian downtrodden. By the time he finishes reading it, you be gone. Now git.'

*   *   *

Because she had to walk from the subway station at 125th and Lexington, Toni did not arrive at Doll Baby's church until ten-fifteen. She had only to see the stragglers admiring the huge, shiny limousine to know Doll was inside and at worship with his Gawd. She waited patiently for him to emerge.

It was almost eleven when Doll Baby bustled out of the church. With snarls he brushed aside the neighborhood supplicants. He was about to shove little Toni aside, but she adroitly pushed the note into his hand and turned to run. Neither she nor Connie had figured the illiterate Doll would go into a rage when confronted with handwriting.

His hand shot out to strike Toni. She was too fast for that, but not too fast to elude a grab. He held Toni and shook her.

'What dis?' he bellowed.

She did not know whether he meant what was in the note or what the note was.

'What dis?' the Doll roared.

'A message.'

'I don't take no messages!' He glared accusation at his retinue for allowing this scrawny little bitch to interrupt his heavenly thoughts. He mumbled, 'I jes come from prayin' to de Lawd.'

'A friend thought you would be interested,' Toni said in desperation. 'Just a friend, Mr Doll Baby. They got your best interests at heart.'

'Git goin'!' And he shoved her toward the car. He had no intention of asking to have the message read to him in public. And he was not going to let his little no-butt kid go until he was sure she was stupid.

In the car he handed the note to the youth sitting on the other side of Toni.

'It's jive, Doll,' the boy said as he scanned the message. 'It's pure dee jive. Like it says Jimmy Adams has paid out already to get control of Harry Brown's territory and all. They're going ahead without you. It's the balls, boss. Like nobody's gonna deal off what Harry Brown had without consulting you first. Everybody knows that.'

The Doll grunted and then was silent. 'What else it say?'

'It's got a telephone number here for you to call if you want to buy out Harry Brown's interests at that fucking auction.'

'Who you?' Doll yelled at Toni.

'I was on my way to school when this man paid me five dollars to bring this note to you, Mr Doll Baby. That's all I am.'

'You more.' Whatever that meant, it sounded ominous.

And then the Doll had one of her arms in his hand and was twisting. The pain was so great she choked when she tried to scream. The pain paralyzed her throat, yet if she could not scream, she knew she'd die of the pain.

'Now I guess you tell me who you is,' the Doll said in a placidly bovine tone. 'I guess you is right glad to now, ain't you, little "ho"? Now who the hell sent you?'

'Harry Brown . . .'

She had meant to add 'nephew,' but her breath was still too short. The Doll seemed satisfied. He leaned back in the seat and tucked his mink coat up around his neck.

'So old Harry's seen the light, eh? That old fart shoulda known a long time ago he was too old to mess with this new day.' He shot his glance at Toni. 'Dis de new day!' he howled.

She nodded. And then began to cry, and to shiver.

'Where to now?' the boy at the wheel asked Doll Baby.

'Le's go back to the church,' Doll said. He looked at Toni. 'You came to meet me at my church, so now I'm gonna let you come inside an' pray. You gonna like praying.'

The other youth in the front seat laughed. 'Damned if she don't look like a little Sunday-school pupil. Damned if she don't.'

'And don't you go getting no fresh ideas,' the Doll said severely. 'Don't you dare, because this here little bitch is going back to Harry Brown in one piece . . . if he comes to take her back.'

'What?' The word came from all three youths in the car.

'Harry Brown's gonna come git his property personally! And he gonna deal with me hisself. And then I'm gonna let him take this little bitch by the arm and walk on outa my church.'

'This ain't right, Doll,' one of the youths said. He was smaller than the others and even more baby-faced. 'Harry Brown is dead. I heard it too many times lately, boss.'

'Thass exactly what I mean,' Doll said complacently. 'If he's alive and sending messages, then we is gonna find out. Now this here little thing ain't exactly what you would call a tramp. Looks to me like she might even be really going to school. See? Now if Harry's so much man, he ain't gonna let nothin' happen to this little girl. So you call that there number on that there piece of paper and let's get things hanging out in front.'

'I'll call it for you.' In desperation Toni had found her voice. 'He won't believe you are holding me unless I talk. You know. He'll figure you're too smart to get involved in kidnaping.'

'This ain't kidnapin'!' the Doll hollered. 'This ain't no kidnapin' a-tall!'

'The police will say so, Mr Doll Baby,' she said. It was funny how the ability to now speak fluently gave her a kind of edge of things. 'And you know that Mr Harry Brown don't 'low no dealings with the fuzz,' she added.

'He better not call no p'lice!'

'Maybe it's better she calls. We go home and we let her talk on one phone and we listen in on the other,' the smallest youth said. It was evident he was the only one who had any sense at all.

'Humph!' Doll Baby said. The boy at the wheel translated the grunt into an order, and in another moment the car was speeding toward the West Side Highway and upper Bronx.

It seemed no time at all before they were in Riverdale, a section of New York totally unfamiliar to Toni. Everyone got out. No one took Toni's arm. She thought of flight, but did not know in which direction. As soon as they led her to a telephone, she dialed the apartment and prayed Connie would answer. But it was Boots.

'This is Toni. Let me speak to Harry, please,' she said.

Boots was on the uptake. 'Harry's not here. You want to talk to Connie?'

'Yes.'

When Connie came on, she said, 'Toni, what's happening and don't leave out anything.'

'Mr Doll Baby says he is going to hold me until Mr Brown comes and gets me and makes a deal.'

'That's reasonable,' Connie said. 'Where are you? Never mind where you are. Where does Doll Baby want us to pick you up?'

'I don't know. He's on another phone listening.'

'Tell me the number on that phone you're using, Toni,' she said. Her voice was calm, almost bored.

Toni gave Connie the number.

'Now hang up and I'll call back,' Connie said.

Toni did as she was told. Then she went to a chair and sat down. Already, Connie had the Doll on the defense. A moment later the Doll rushed into the room and yelled, 'What you mean, giving my unlisted number to somebody?'

'She has to call you back as soon as she makes arrangements,' Toni said meekly. 'That's what you wanted, isn't it, Mr Doll Baby?'

He said no more but began to pace about the room.

Boots told Ossie of Toni's call. Ossie rushed downstairs, lunged at and slapped Connie. Connie reeled back. She had not played it perfectly, but she was ready to defend her actions.

'Maybe we are dealing with killers, Ossie,' she said, crouching by the bar, 'but even the craziest killers do not kill messengers.'

'How the hell could I let myself think a silly bitch who likes to loaf around naked all the time got any brains?' Ossie groaned.

'Margo wanted Toni in. You know it. Besides, Toni needs what I sent her into,' Connie said evenly. 'She just kicked and is still full of remorse, Ossie, even if she don't show it. So save the rest of your licks until I fuck up proper.'

It did not make sense. She did not make sense. He and Giveadamn could get on the next train out of town. A train to anywhere, and they would be out of this camp, out of all this crap! Neither owed crazy Harry Brown one iota of loyalty. So why had they hung around this long?

'Giveadamn and I do not need you. Neither does Toni. She's clean as a newborn babe, and you know it. Now that Studs is dead or fucked up like Harry, you are free to go. So why don't you?'

'The same damned reason as before, Ossie. I'm here because I don't want out. And neither do you. And neither does Toni . . . and she don't even really know what this is all about.' And then Connie added wearily, almost disgustedly, 'Give me some cash and the key to a car.'

'You got a bagful of cash.'

'It's all in old one-thousand-dollar bills. I want hundreds at least. Maybe even some fives and tens. And if you want to know what's happening, I'm going out to Doll Baby's house and get his two million personally. I'll find his place if I have to bribe the president of the phone company.'

'You ain't got a chance alone.'

Connie decided to make no retort. Instead she said, 'We're getting what we been hoping for all the time. Let the snakes kill each other off. I already got Jimmy Adams on our side. That's why Doll's pissed off. With Sonny Roberts in, the auction is set.'

Ossie was finally able to put it into words. 'Those young punks Doll Baby keeps hanging around are freaks. Neither you or Toni are going to be able to get out of that house with your insides intact. And you know that too!'

Connie marched off to her bedroom. When she came out, she was dressed in slacks for the street. She thought of asking Ossie for his pistol, but decided against it. If she was searched and a pistol found, she'd no longer be taken at face value by the Doll.

She had another thought and went to the phone and dialed Jimmy Adams. When he came on, she said, 'If you want your bread protected, you've got to get me into the Doll Baby's house. The one somewhere up in the Bronx.'

Jimmy knew the address and gave it to Connie. Then she went up to Ossie's room. He had stuffed both his coat pockets with grenades and was checking his pistol. 'Well, I can use you to cover me,' she said, 'but I want you to stay outside and out of sight. I'm going in alone.'

'Then, how do I know what's going on?'

'We take a couple of Giveadamn's tiny walkie-talkies. But don't ask him for them. He's in the library stretched out sweating cold sweat. Just go to his room and get them, or I will. You know how they work?'

'You get them,' Ossie said. 'I'm going down for the car.'

Connie was driving. As they sped toward Riverdale, Connie said, 'I'll fasten the microphone on me so you'll be able to hear, and naturally I don't want to hear anything you got to say. If I need you, you'll hear me calling you. I'll make sure neither Toni or I are near any window. In fact, if Doll Baby has a cellar or a dungeon or anything like that, I'm going to try my best to get Toni and me put in it. I hear tell you played a little centerfield and got a great arm.' She took a good long look at Ossie. 'Damn,' she muttered, 'you need a drink, don't you?'

Ossie said nothing.

Connie pulled up in front of a phone booth at the curb. The hawk moved quickly now. When she came out, she started the car and for a while seemed to be driving aimlessly. But she was looking for a taxi and when she found one, blew the horn. The taxi slowed. She motioned that she would take it. They stopped, and she slid from behind the wheel. 'Okay, Ossie,' she said, 'follow the taxi, but carefully. I don't have to tell you how, do I?'

Ossie frowned. 'I know already a million trees are going to hide that house from the street and therefore hide me from anyone in it. Anything else?'

'No, just play it by ear.'

Connie got into the taxi and Ossie followed the taxi to a tree-lined street just as he had expected. The taxi slowed, then stopped. Ossie picked a place diagonally across from Doll Baby's house to park.

He took out Giveadamn's walkie-talkie. Connie went inside the house. They were at the door expecting her. The gizmo was working pretty well because he heard Connie speak to whoever answered her ring at the door.

'I came to get my friend, Toni,' he heard Connie say.

Her coolness must have worked because the boy's voice said, 'Yessum.' A little later the boy's voice: 'I'll go get her.' After that, silence. Connie had put her hand over the mike. Either that or she had been silently searched and the mike cut. He doubted that. There would have been talk, a cry of discovery.

No. Connie had created the silence for one reason: she didn't want him to know what was going on. He moved to leave the car.

Connie had covered the tiny mike with her hand. She did not trust her voice. Did not trust what Ossie would hear next as she stared at Toni.

The cleverest-looking and smallest of Doll Baby's young men had led the teen-age girl down the stairs. One look told Connie all. It was not that Toni was broken or tearful. She was very quiet and contained. Relaxed.

Connie did not go to the child. She would wait. As for Ossie, he could sit outside and wait. There was nothing inside this house he could do.

'This is a lovely house,' Connie heard herself saying. 'You have a nice view.'

The remark unsettled the youth beside Toni. He had never seen a cool woman inside this house before. If anything, this broad was more than just cool and collected; she was deadly cold. And like the young minions of all bigtime dope dealers, he knew little or nothing about heroin addiction or the true effects of heroin on addicts. He wondered if she was high on narco. It was surprising as hell that this cool chick facing him now could ever get dumb enough to send a teen-age addict to do a man's job, but she had.

All they had had to do with this stupid Toni was roll up her sleeve and look for the marks. The marks were there, so they took a syringe and hit the kid a good pop. After that, the kid wised up like she had been born knowing where it was at.

But Connie was only thinking of Ossie and whether his walkie-talkie was working. It would be a hell of a note if it wasn't. No matter where you stood in this room, you were in front of or near a window. Ossie was now her one hope. Toni was a walking basket case. The kid was higher than a mountain in Switzerland.

Connie made herself stay cool. 'For someone who is about to make your boss the richest black dude in this life, we are being treated a little shabbily, wouldn't you say?'

This time the young man found the words unsettling, because the strange woman had not addressed them to him. She had not exactly said them to the little junkie either. It was like when his mother used to talk to God.

'Sit down,' he said.

She did not obey. She walked to the window and then quickly turned her back to it. It was the best she could do. Like what the hell else was there to do with that bird-brained Ossie striding masterfully up the walk to the house in full view of any and all sharp-shooters the Doll might have on duty?

The doorbell rang.

'Don't answer it!' Connie yelled. There was real worry in her voice.

The youth turned to seek a clue in her face.

'We ain't shit,' Connie said rapidly. 'We ain't nothing to that crazy freak. He's going to kill us.'

The boy hesitated. He stared at Connie and then turned to stare in the direction of the front door. He was about to call out for someone to come from upstairs, but he had not quite turned when Toni glided up to lock one arm around his neck like the most proficient mugger in town. The boy was strangling. He kicked back viciously at her legs. Toni winced and pulled the armlock tighter.

Connie picked up an ashtray like the one Boots had used to kill Ming Toy. And with the same swing she smashed it right between the kid's eyes. Then both girls rushed to the door.

There were heavy thudding sounds behind them as they struggled with the lock. Two of the Doll's pretty boys were coming down the stairs. When they got to Connie and Toni, they grabbed the girls in the same mugger's hold Toni had used – but before her wind was cut off, Connie screamed.

Ossie heard her and ran back down the walk until he could take a good aim at an upstairs window, then let a grenade fly. It smashed through the upstairs front window and exploded. He threw another. And then the front door came open and two scared young men burst out of the house, followed by Toni and Connie.

'Shee-it!' Connie yelled when they were in the car and headed for Manhattan. 'We just blew up two million dollars.'

23

No sooner had Connie, Ossie and Toni entered the apartment than Connie began to shed her clothes. Giveadamn came out of the library and followed them to the lounge, where Ossie sat down facing Boots. Neither spoke when Toni, Giveadamn and Connie sat down. Ossie was in a rage.

'She put me in a clutch, Ossie,' Toni said anxiously, 'but she came and got me out all in one piece. Maybe a little shitty, but out.'

'Yeah,' the hawk said, 'I sent you in. And you are still in one piece. Now go to your room and get in bed.' That was all Connie said, but it told Giveadamn all he needed to know.

Ossie sat slumped, his head bowed as if he were crying.

Boots got up. She paced about the room. When Toni had left, she said, 'Let's send the kid to Washington. I mean, take her to Freedmen's Hospital and let that Dr Williams take her in charge.'

'Can't now,' Connie said. 'First comes the auction. We got too much going on.'

'Hold off the auction,' Giveadamn said. 'Toni's more important.'

'We need her for the auction,' Connie said.

'What auction?' Ossie said. 'Doll's dead. Sonny Roberts still hasn't put up his two million. Studs is dead. That leaves Jimmy Adams, who is your partner.' He stood up and crossed the room to the telephone on the bar. They sat quietly as he called the airport. They listened without a word as he ordered the plane readied and a flight plan filed for Washington. After that he called Freedmen's Hospital in Washington and made all the necessary arrangements to have Toni admitted immediately.

An hour later, when Ossie, Connie and Toni were aloft, Giveadamn said to Boots, 'Who's this Dr Williams?'

'A black neurologist, one of the greatest.'

Giveadamn shook his head. 'I hope he can work fast, whatever they think he's going to do, because it's just you and me holding down this fort, Boots.'

'Shit, Ossie's right,' Boots said. 'Giveadamn, there's nothing much to hold down any more.'

Giveadamn shook his head. Lately, facing down the Harlem heroin overlords was becoming more important to him than attending his near-lifeless father.

'Giveadamn, let that goddamn Connie have it all. This is more her style. Let her handle Sonny Roberts and Jimmy.'

'She can't do it alone. We got to be here to back her up.'

'Why?'

'Me, for that machine I made. And you and Ossie to back us up. And we can't hold off the auction. Be like telling a couple of wild lions they can't have the beefsteak you just hung over their noses.'

'Give 'em the machine.'

'Boots, the machine's a fake. Which one you going to give it to?'

'For that matter – which of those two killers you going to let win it?'

Giveadamn sat and thought. He shook his head. 'I'll have to ask Connie. She must have a winner up her sleeve.'

'Giveadamn, you just want to hope so. I know Connie. I been watching her. For the last week or so she's been flying around here by the seat of her bare ass. I'm worried.'

Giveadamn was unwrapping the sandwich the delicatessen had sent up when the phone in the library rang. It was Ossie calling from Washington. They were all coming back.

'Toni too? This soon?' That must be some neurologist, he thought.

'We can't leave Toni here,' Ossie said. 'Connie's convinced me we need her more than ever now.'

'What convinced you?'

'We think the Doll's alive. That's a rumor we picked up.

I'm just calling to tell you he may turn up in force. Let me talk to Boots.'

'She's gone out.'

'For what?'

'She said to get her hair done up.'

'When she gets back, tell her to find out what's with Doll Baby. Meanwhile, we got to get little Toni a fix.'

'Where are you now?'

'At the airport.'

'Don't the CIA got a booth there for that?'

'Don't be funny at a time like this, Giveadamn. How you think I feel finding that little girl a fix?'

Ossie snapped on the light in Giveadamn's room. Giveadamn opened his eyes and raised one arm to look at his watch. It was after two in the morning. Giveadamn sat up.

'Boots ain't in her room,' Ossie said. 'Where is she?'

Connie and Toni appeared at the door behind Ossie.

'Staten Island,' Giveadamn said.

'What do you mean?' Connie said.

'She called, asked for Connie. Right after I talked to Ossie. She's cut out on us.'

Connie came into the room and began to pace. Ossie sat down on the side of Giveadamn's bed. Toni, Giveadamn saw, was nice and high. She was riding. She leaned in the doorway, a smile on her pretty face. 'You're all going to need me,' she said dreamily.

'Cut out?' The hawk paced. 'That don't sound like Boots. I know she was scared and feeling low. But still . . .' She stopped and kicked off her shoes. 'Giveadamn, let me tell you what we learned. The Doll's alive all right and he wants in. Him and Sonny Roberts are going to meet you in a bank, as planned, and each hand over two million dollars. As soon as we get their four million, the auction is on. They're going to have it for us no later than the end of the week. Jimmy will then see that everything goes smooth . . .'

'And I will too,' Toni said. 'Smooth is my middle name.'

*   *   *

They were all waiting, and the waiting wasn't easy. Nobody left the apartment unless absolutely necessary. Giveadamn went every day to the hospital to see Harry. He made the trip early and was back before breakfast. Tension built. Obscenely threatening phone calls were still coming in from anonymous men and women who had got hold of each new private number – and more packages of excrement arrived. None of this made Giveadamn feel very hopeful that Connie would get them out of this alive.

'Not just alive, Giveadamn. We'll come out of this the richest niggers on earth.' Then the call they'd been waiting for came. It was from the Doll's right-hand man.

'No, you ain't going, Giveadamn,' Connie said. 'I changed my mind. They'd just love to get their hands on you. And, I ain't going because I'm the mastermind. Joe Glass is going, Harry's moneyman.'

'Don't you know Doll Baby yet?' Ossie yelled. 'He'll grab Joe and the money on sight.'

'No, he won't. He won't because Sonny Roberts will be there, too, with his own two million.'

'Well, I'm going along.'

'Fine,' Connie said. 'I'd been about to ask you to.'

The exchange of money in the bank was made without a hitch; the only puzzling thing was the Doll hadn't been there to see his money change hands. And though rumor had it the Doll was still alive, nobody could be found who could swear he'd seen him.

'He's dead,' Ossie insisted when he and Toni came back to the apartment.

But Giveadamn said, 'My hunch is he's had his head cut up from the grenade and he don't want anybody to see him.'

'What's the difference?' Connie said. 'We got his two million.' She was putting her clothes on, slowly. She would look at each article – each stocking, her panties, her brassiere – and smile. She'd been thinking for several days. Now she was through thinking.

'All right,' she said at last. 'Friday it is. Friday night. We hold the auction on 112th Street. Now at the height of that auction, there's going to be a lot of excitement.'

'How do you know?' Ossie, the constant doubter, said. Worry about Toni was making him even more cranky.

'Because, my fine nervous stud, I'm going to make damned sure there is.'

Ossie glared at her.

'From here on, everything's so simple, it makes me want to cry me an orgasmic river.' She put on her blouse and stepped into her skirt. 'We're all going to take us a trip on Friday night. I don't know about the rest of you, but I feel in the need of a little religion.' She turned to Giveadamn. 'You need some religion, Giveadamn?'

'I got me enough religion.'

'This is going to be down-home religion. Now I'll tell you what this religion is because I want you all to get a little of it, starting now. It's simple belief. You got to believe.'

'In what?' Ossie said.

'In me, beautiful. Believe in me. How about you, Toni?' she said.

'I believe,' Toni said.

'Ossie?'

Ossie grunted. 'I got to.'

'Giveadamn, you . . . do you believe?'

He did not hesitate. 'Yes.'

'Then, get dressed,' she said. 'I want you and Ossie to drive down to Chinatown. On your way you can stop off long enough to buy a truck.'

'A truck?'

'Why not?' Connie said. 'It's got to be a big flatbed.'

'And where do we keep a truck until Friday night? You think we can park it in front of this apartment house? And what about license plates?'

'You're a smart boy, Giveadamn. You and Ossie just put your heads together and come up with answers.'

Giveadamn sighed and got up. When he was dressed, he went to find Ossie.

* * *

Friday morning, Giveadamn and Connie spent an hour or so co-ordinating the plans.

'You got to handle this alone until I get there,' she said.

'No problem.'

There were little jobs to take care of, preparations to make. Ossie headed over to New Jersey to where, he said, there were a lot of migrant workers. Connie took herself off to a shooting gallery to get a hypodermic. Giveadamn went off to the old garage in the Bronx where he had the big flatbed truck parked. He carried, in two satchels, dynamite, wires and dynamite caps. He worked slowly and carefully, packing the dynamite in under the truck as carefully as he'd designed the machine that rested on top of the flatbed, under canvas, strapped with thick ropes.

When he'd finished, he carried the empty satchels back to Harry's limousine, threw them inside and checked around again to be sure he hadn't been followed – then moved off leisurely to pay one more visit to Harry.

At Harry's bedside he sat in silence for about twenty minutes, his head bowed slightly, his eyes closed as if in prayer. Harry lay in front of him like a corpse, and except for the little rise and fall of his chest, he was a corpse. Then just to see if he could get some response, any response at all, he leaned close to Harry's ear and whispered, 'Fuck you, Harry.'

It was a little like damning God. Giveadamn waited for a thunderbolt. Nothing happened. Harry never stirred. Giveadamn sighed and stood up.

24

They stood in the library dressing. Ossie put on a pair of dirty white overalls that were too big in the butt and too tight across his chest. But he had found among the clothes in the old panel truck a baseball cap with a broken bill that fit. He had it on. Backwards.

Nobody's clothes fit.

Ossie turned Connie around to inspect the ash-blond wig she was wearing. She'd made her face look vacuous to go with her role, and Giveadamn thought she looked like an albino crow who was not very good at sitting on the fence of a corn-field. She was no longer the preoccupied hawk. Giveadamn, at first amused, felt sad. He did not like seeing Connie's royal Egyptian beauty transformed into poor white trash.

It had taken Ossie hours to get those clothes and the other things. He had driven over a lot of New Jersey to find a migrant-worker family who'd sell them to him. They were up from Georgia – a man, his wife and two mostly grown daughters. Their panel truck had been converted into a camper. Ossie'd peeled off two thousand dollars for the truck and added another two thousand for everything in it.

'Put a dress on over those denims,' Giveadamn said to Toni.

'A dress?'

'That's the way farm women wear slacks for real.'

'I get it. I get it,' cried Connie. 'Gimme a dress there, Ossie. Only dumb country women wear dresses and slacks at the same time.'

'Can we change later?'

'Now, Toni,' Connie said, 'there'll be no time later.'

'We don't have a lot of time right now,' Ossie said, looking at his wristwatch.

When Connie had the dress pulled over her head, she picked

up the hypodermic, the biggest Giveadamn had ever seen . . . a needle on it as long as a pen. 'Now the next thing we need is blood. You first, Ossie. Get up on the library table and make a fist.'

'Will it make him weak?' Toni asked.

'How much you taking?' Giveadamn wanted to know.

'I could use a couple of gallons, but a little here and there from all of us will do. Or would any of you rather bleed from cuts?'

After the blood drawing, they moved through three rooms methodically, and upon each they wreaked their devious havoc.

Giveadamn could not bear to smash up the library. They picked Ossie's room, Connie's and the big lounge. They threw Connie's blood in her room, and in the lounge Giveadamn and Toni left some of themselves behind among the broken lamps, glasses and up-ended furniture. Then they were ready.

On their way out through the big double kitchen doors, Ossie slipped a silencer on his gun and shot the locks off the doors.

They rang for the freight elevator.

Connie adjusted the old battered fedora Giveadamn was wearing and patted him on the back.

'I believe,' Giveadamn said, but he couldn't grin.

The cars – Connie's sports car, the flatbed truck and the old panel wagon – were parked in the street behind Harry's apartment house. The flatbed bore the heroin machine – or, as Giveadamn had named it, the Golden Fleece. They'd needed a hoist to get it up on the flatbed. It rested there dimly under canvas and rope.

The street in front of Harry's building dead-ended above the East River Drive. The buildings across the river couldn't be seen. Too dark over that way now. Just some lights showed there were buildings.

Ossie and Toni got into the cab of the truck and Giveadamn put his hand on the cab window ledge and said, 'Take it mighty easy as you go, Ossie, and you'll be all right.'

'Giveadamn, that Golden Fleece of yours is so secure a fast turn wouldn't budge it.'

'I ain't the least bit worried about the Golden Fleece, Ossie. It's the dynamite.'

'I'll be careful,' Ossie said.

There was no signal. They moved out at once: Connie, in the little Toyota, Giveadamn in the panel job, Ossie and Toni in the big long open truck.

The air was crisp and clear. There were even stars in the sky. It was Friday the thirteenth, Black Friday on 112th Street.

Giveadamn made it over to Madison Avenue, then drove north to 112th Street. On 112th, he stopped the truck a little past the corner and stepped out to unlock the rear door. He reached in and got hold of a heavy iron bar. Attached to the bar was a huge roll of nylon tubing. He dropped the bar to the ground, then got back in the truck and drove slowly the distance of the block, stopping almost at the corner of Park Avenue.

He got out again. The black nylon tubing had been unrolled as he drove, held down by the iron bar. He finished pulling out the silken tubing and tossed it on the pavement. The street was still deserted. Nobody around.

At the time Giveadamn was laying the silken tube that looked like a windsock, Sonny Roberts, in his apartment, was facing the suspicious faces of his seven most trusted lieutenants.

They were thinking: fun and games is all right for whiteys, but not for us. Every whitey on earth is stupid in the clutch, and it was this fact that had made these seven men rich, happy, fat cats. But at the moment it seemed Sonny Roberts was not satisfied with just looking like a whitey. Sonny evidently wanted to *be* whitey, too. A fool could get killed for wanting less than he did. Like the whiteys had their Appalachia when no black boy was big enough, except maybe Harry Brown, to get himself invited. Or maybe Harry did get invited, but was too smart to go.

Anyhow, the white boys got rounded up. Great! It also was a lesson for the black boys to remember when they did come to power. Two smart black boys is company. Three is conspiracy.

Right here in this room there were enough felons to make the law come down with something a hell of a lot worse than that raid up in Appalachia. Sonny was getting dumb.

So the seven were letting themselves wonder who among them was going to take over Sonny Roberts' share of the heroin racket. They were uncomfortable and at the same time measuring the job for themselves.

Sonny got to his feet and left the room. He felt good. He got a golden incense burner out of a desk drawer and carried it back to the seven. They nodded appreciatively but did not smile. Only Watermelon Niggers smile. And not a single Watermelon Nigger had ever been in the business or ever would be.

They helped themselves, each in his particular style. Some had golden cocaine spoons. Two had a favorite thousand-dollar bill. One had a custom-made platinum razor blade.

No man took more than a minute quantity. Even so, they relaxed a little.

Sonny nodded absent-mindedly, but with grave and conspicuous politeness. You never let these men forget they were beneath you. One hell of a lot beneath you. If you allowed them to think they were your peers, they would start thinking they were too good for an occasional bust.

These seven men were called dealers by the daily papers, because white reporters never knew exactly what was happening. And maybe you could call them half-assed dealers. They were, after all, into narcotics. But that is all the dummies could be accused of. They masterminded nothing.

Dudes like Sonny allowed killers like these to have drugs on consignment. They went out and dealt off the stuff for cash or on credit again. The same rope ran out a little way from them.

Anyhow, the stupid asses brought back every cent of the bread they owed for the drugs so dealers like Sonny could turn over the bread for more narco for them to sell at their own risk. These men often had to kill to get their bread. It was their handiwork that made the whitey headlines.

A big dealer never gets busted. These seven were not dealers – buffers between the fuzz and the dealers, but never dealers.

What these men were were killers. That's all they were. They were skilled at thinking murder before they were weaned from the bottle. And since men like these were born murderers, they often made wonderful policemen. Cops without portfolio is what Sonny liked to call them.

And the seven would laugh when he called them that. They had no better sense. Sometimes one of them would get so big he thought he really was a dealer. It was then others of his breed cut him down to size – to fit a coffin.

Tonight Sonny was going for broke. Some of these men were more than likely going to get wasted before morning. They were the things going to get broken. This was doing it the hard way, but if he wanted to fly to Hollywood, he told himself, he had to buy the ticket first.

'Tonight the formula Harry Brown is known to have for converting the sorriest heroin into pure dynamite is going to get sold. Along with the formula is the whole works you got to have to convert the shit. Do I make myself clear?'

The seven nodded at Sonny.

'In other words, each of you can expect to be making exactly two times as much bread as you are making right now. Does that kind of deal satisfy you?'

Someone snorted a sound of disgust, disbelief. Sonny acted as if he had not heard the derision, but he stopped talking. The room was silent for a long time. Then Sonny said to the scoffer, 'What you want?'

'I'm with you, Sonny,' said the man.

Sonny nodded as if the words were an apology. He went on. 'This thing we are going to do tonight is psychological. We don't make no enemies.' He shrugged elaborately. 'Of course, we got to make some dead men to get Harry's still. That's what they call this vat thing for making this dynamite shit, a still. It's up for auction. It's up for auction to me, Jimmy Adams and Doll Baby. Top bidder gets Harry Brown's empire and everybody's goodwill. Brown's boy and his crowd gets the eight million the bidders have kicked in, minus two million put up by top bidder. Connie Dubois is auctioneer. There's thirty keys of heroin goes with the deal. Five low-grade keys get fed into the machine and five comes out, see . . . only it's worth thirty low grade.

'Now I'm already in for two million goodwill bread. Everybody wants everybody's goodwill, eh? Now we're going to get that still, with goodwill. At some point. If we have to, we take it by force, but we pay for it once we get our hands on it. We pay for it right there in the middle of the street, you might say. I don't have to explain more than that.'

The eyes of the seven glittered. Sonny was going to be the new Harry Brown in Harlem, and each and every one of them was going to be damned near an equal partner of Sonny's.

'You got all the bread you need to swing the deal, Sonny?' one of them asked. They all bobbed their heads to let Sonny know that every cent they owned was his to use tonight.

He coolly said, 'This machine has to be operated by a boss engineer or chemist. Giveadamn Brown knows how it works and he passes its instructions along to whoever gets the machine. Now if there's any shooting, just see that Giveadamn Brown don't get nicked.'

In a few moments the men left to go with Sonny to the apartment in one of the project buildings on 112th Street in Manhattan where the bidding would be held.

The Doll had called an 'open meeting.' These meetings were never held in what some of the boys facetiously called the 'Throne Room.' In the Throne Room the Doll sat on a high-backed and ornate chair and issued orders. Irrevocable orders.

But when the Doll wanted suggestions, even good ones he never intended to use, he had his men assemble in his boudoir, a magnificent dressing room with a smaller room beside it. The smaller room was nine by nine feet square, and the walls from floor to ceiling were covered with pigeonholes four inches wide and high. The pigeonholes on one side of the room held fifty-dollar bills. Those on the opposite side were stuffed with hundred-dollar bills. The fourth wall contained important papers. Deeds, promissory notes, legal and usurious, last wills and testaments of both the living and the dead; dead, mostly by Doll's hand.

There were hundreds of insurance policies. The Doll believed in insurance. But not banks. As an overgrown child, he had mowed the lawn of the richest banker in South Carolina and the Doll swore all bankers were crooks. Even black ones.

The boudoir was something else again. It was a beauty shop as well as a dressing room. It contained all the Doll's female accouterments.

There were sinks and washbasins, hair dryers and massage gadgets of all kinds ... a sauna, a Roman bath pool with customized Jacuzzi, even a huge bidet. There was a beauty table with three mirrors that could be adjusted every which way. It was before this table the Doll would sit and do his face while he held his open meetings. It made everything so very informal that way.

The Doll now sat at his table, head bandaged, and applied colorless lipstick. He could never be called a gaudy 'ho'.

With lips in a stiff pout, he said in an absently delicate way, 'I got the word that this here magic formula of Harry Brown's is gonna git sold tonight.' He paused. 'Well?' he bellowed.

The smallest of his young lovers in a tiny voice ended the silence that followed. 'That formula is yours, Doll Baby. You deserve to own it. By rights it's your property.'

'It's mines!' the Doll shrieked. He jumped up from the dressing table and strode around, jerking his thick arms. The sheer shortie nightie he wore was soaked with sweat and clung to him stickily. He glared at the biggest of his men, 'It ain't nothing in writing!' he screamed. 'It ain't nothing like that at all!'

'Then, what is it?' the small one asked. His name was Joe.

'It's a machine,' Doll said. Tears began to form.

'No kidding?' Joe said heavily. 'No kidding. Well, what you know about that?'

'I'm gonna kill him just the same,' Doll said stubbornly.

'Him? Who's him?' Joe said. 'You mean the son that's been making waves lately?'

'What waves?' Arnold, the prettiest, wanted to know.

'Who you think been making Doll Baby so unhappy lately?' Joe said to him.

'Oh. That one.' Lately, Arnold had been acting more and more like a girl than a man.

'No, Doll,' Joe said. 'This thing calls for finesse. We kidnap the machine and we kidnap the man Harry got to run the machine. Right?'

'Right,' Doll said. 'But as soon as I get my hands on that Ossie Winbush, I'm gonna kill him. He's black. He's blacker than I am. I'm white compared to that black-assed Ossie, but do he act like it?'

'Of course, you got one thing to think about, Doll,' Joe said slowly. 'Now that you got this government connection, how you think it's gonna be if all of a sudden you can take, say, Mexican Gold and turn it into white? And ten or twelve times as powerful? I mean your purchases are gonna drop. How you think the government's gonna like that?'

'Cunts-In-Action!' Doll snorted. 'They's dumber than me. All whiteys go crazy when they got more than a million dollars.' He stopped to glare individually around the room. 'What the hell makes it possible for me to make more and more bread each and every day? Huh? What you think makes *me* the greatest? What the hell makes you think I don't make more fucking bread in a day than Muhammad Ali?'

'My whole point,' Joe said in the same voice as before, 'is that if we don't take charge of this gizmo for making dynamite out of low-grade shit, you won't be tops no more if somebody else gets hands on it.'

'Go get me ten thousand dollars!' the Doll snapped. 'I'm gonna go pray.'

'Ten thousand? For what, Doll Baby?'

'You just get the bread and get the guns and get the cars. I have to do all the thinking from now on,' Doll said.

Tears flowed over the Doll's face. 'Go, go.' He waved his arms wearily. His shoulders sagged with all the weight he had to bear to keep his tiny flock together. 'Go,' he repeated hoarsely this time. 'Let me dress in privacy. And then we shall depart.' He'd heard those lines on TV.

After they had waved a goodbye to Giveadamn and Connie, Ossie and Toni moved the flatbed and its cargo north on First Avenue with the night traffic. In the upper nineties, they pulled into a bus stop, the only parking place they could find, to sit awhile and wait. Ossie switched off the truck lights. A street lamp was shining on the windshield. They lit up cigarettes.

Right on time Giveadamn's voice came in over the truck's radio receiver. 'When is Black Friday?'

'It's been Black Friday all day long,' Ossie said loud and clear.

'Roger,' he heard Giveadamn say. Then no more.

Ossie started up the truck and worked their gift-wrapped cargo over to Madison, then up Madison to 112th, and turned into the one-way block. He shifted down and moved forward slowly until they were beside Giveadamn. The block was dark and quiet.

Giveadamn had his old hat pulled down over his forehead, and when he raised his head he looked frightened. Toni rolled down the window on her side.

'I don't want to upset you two, but you're parked right on top of the fireworks.' He pointed to the ground. Ossie pulled on down the block, over to his right, and parked by the curb.

When they got out, Giveadamn said, 'I need some help unloading the rest of the stuff from my truck. I sure been missing Boots.'

Ossie pointed at the canvas-covered machine behind the cab. 'I'll get that unwrapped. You help Giveadamn, Toni.'

'Roger,' Toni said crisply. She was riding nice and high, a little junkie commando.

Some of the cartons had gallon cans of alcohol. Giveadamn and Toni took the cans from the cartons, opened them and sprinkled the street and the long black tubing that lay on the pavement. Farther back in the truck were cases of cherry bombs, pinwheels, roman candles, sparklers, and fountains. They got them all out and scattered them at random down the tubing the whole length of the block. Then back for the gallon cans of heavy oil. By that time Ossie had joined them. When they'd finished, they went back to the panel truck and got inside to wait.

'When's Connie going to get here?' Toni said.

'She'll turn up with what she calls the diversion,' Giveadamn said, 'and that won't be until all the dealers are here.'

'How will she know?'

'I got us a signal.'

'What we got to count on,' Ossie mumbled pretty much to himself, 'is them dealers fucking each other over on sight, and you can't count on them for nothing.'

The subway train jolted into the Fiftieth Street station and three girls got off carrying colorful suitcases. College students apparently. Black. The suitcases seemed heavy. The girls set them down and stood for a moment chatting. Jimmy got off at the other end of the car, and when the girls picked up the suitcases and moved on, Jimmy followed them leisurely up the same stairway.

In the street, the girls walked to a theater on Forty-seventh Street, but instead of going in they got into a Rolls-Royce sedan parked just past the theater entrance. The chauffeur put the suitcases in the trunk. Jimmy kept on walking.

Jimmy went to Eighth Avenue and turned left. He had gone only a short distance when a limo with four black men in it swept to the curb. The two men jumped out and seemed to roughly usher Jimmy into the car. That was cautious Jimmy all over again: if this car was stopped, Jimmy would claim he had been forced into a car of armed men against his will.

The car picked up speed and was shortly behind the taillights of the limo with the three girls. They stuck behind the Rolls until it pulled to a stop at the corner of 112th Street. Ossie dragged the wooden horse across the entrance to the street.

Jimmy pulled up ahead, the headlights of his car on Ossie. He put his head out the window. 'I thought it might be a good idea to get here a little early.'

Ossie smiled, then pulled the barrier away. Jimmy and his

men went through. The other Rolls followed behind them. Ossie hauled the barrier back and went up to Jimmy's side of the car. He said, 'This is fast and tight. Connie will be here in a minute. Stay cool. Just pull both cars up a little farther.'

When Ossie got back to Giveadamn, he was grinning. 'I don't know where he got those society bitches from, but a dollar to your doughnut they got his cash. All Jimmy's men got is guns.'

Giveadamn nodded solemnly. He was not feeling too good. He was getting weak. Too much threat of killing, he guessed, but a sickle-cell crisis was edging in on him.

A Mercedes luxury sedan wheeled past 116th Street and kept on toward 112th. The nine-passenger car was loaded with ten men: Doll Baby and nine of his pretty centurions. There were also nine high-powered rifles in the car and two handguns. The boys were going hunting.

The small youth, Joe, said, 'Chief, the whole deal is too corny to be not real. I wish we'd brought some bread along. I would've if I'd had that kind of bread.'

Joe was driving. Doll Baby sat beside him. All the rest were in the rear seats.

Doll Baby shook his bulk in petulance. 'I knows what I'm doing.' He wore a soft chinchilla hat that covered his head bandage.

'I grant you that, Doll Baby. But there's this angle I don't like. And that is the fact that those people got the formula and we don't.'

'We will when we get down there and talks to 'em.'

'That's just it, Chief. I mean, you got to realize that nobody wants you to have that formula.'

'What?'

'Suppose they got it fixed so that when you don't show to buy that formula, there's Jimmy Adams sitting right there, ready for you to renege so he can buy? Or Sonny Roberts? And maybe somebody doing Studs Thompson's dealings now. Sure, she's dead, but somebody could be dealing in her place. You know that, Chief.'

'I wanta know who's dealing just like Studs!' the Doll bellowed. Tears came to his eyes and he pulled out a handkerchief.

'It don't matter. It don't matter, Doll,' the youth beside him consoled. 'I'm looking into that little matter right this minute practically. I never have let you down yet, have I?'

'You is a dear,' Doll sobbed. 'But all the rest of these mother-fuckers is against me.' He turned in the seat and glared into the back compartment. 'All youse is against me!' he screamed. Then he lunged.

He came halfway over the seatback to grab for one of the rifles a youth had lying across his lap. Joe, the driver, began to talk softly, hypnotically.

'It ain't the right thing to do, Doll Baby. It's not right, Doll Baby,' he cajoled. 'Everybody is jealous of you because you are the greatest. They don't like you because you got twice as much bread stashed away as Harry Brown. But your men love you. They *can't* get jealous of you, Doll Baby, because they all love you . . .'

Joe kept talking. His voice got lower, softer. Finally Doll Baby relaxed and gave a huge mournful sigh and let go of the rifle. He turned around so he could look out the window. Here they were – 112th street.

They had been waiting maybe thirty minutes – Giveadamn, Ossie and Toni in the panel truck, Jimmy and his men inside two cars down the street. Once in a while, inside one of the cars, a cigarette or a cigar got lighted, but nobody got out. Giveadamn was getting nervous.

The street was dark. Now and then someone appeared on the sidewalk, but nobody so far had discovered the elaborate fireworks display laid in the street. Jimmy himself might walk over to talk to them and pick up a pinwheel along the way and want an explanation. Giveadamn had one ready just in case.

Ossie suddenly said, 'The Golden Fleece.'

'It's all set to operate,' Giveadamn said.

'I only got the ropes off. I got to unwrap it. So they see it.' He opened the door and got out.

Ossie was working gently with the canvas and had it off when Toni gasped and said to Giveadamn, 'He's alive. It's him.'

'Him who?' He stared at where she was looking. The massive bulk of Doll Baby had reached the front of the truck. A cluster of men was moving along beside Doll, and they all had rifles. The men paused by the truck to talk to Ossie, then two of the figures gave Doll Baby a boost and rolled him up on the flatbed. One by one, the others, the nine of them, climbed up to join the Doll and Ossie. By now Ossie was trying to jump off the truck, but three of Doll's men had him.

'Aw, shit,' Giveadamn said. He turned to Toni. 'Why didn't I think of that?'

'What the hell you talking about? We got to do something.'

'They were supposed to steal the still and the truck. I thought of that, but I didn't think any of us would be on it.'

Toni was already gone.

Giveadamn set out after her, but by the time he got to the truck, the action was over. Doll and his men had Ossie down on the flatbed and one of his men was about to step up inside the cab. He had just raised his left foot when Toni cut his throat.

Giveadamn came up short. The truck pulled away with Toni at the wheel. Neither the Doll nor any of his men saw what happened. The men on the flatbed were all busy with Ossie or looking at Giveadamn when the truck started.

'Hold up,' yelled the Doll pointing at Giveadamn. 'Him, too.' But the truck wasn't waiting.

Giveadamn turned and ran for the panel wagon, got in, and took off after the flatbed. The flatbed was already onto Park Avenue and headed uptown. Giveadamn swept into Park and saw the taillights of the truck turning into 115th Street. Then he watched in horror as little Toni began to swerve the truck from side to side as if she meant to topple it over. The machine, now all lit up on its internal batteries, was sliding around with Doll and all his men hanging on, Ossie too.

The Doll was screaming. He had climbed to the top of the Golden Fleece and had it wrapped in his arms. His fur hat had flown off and his big black head looked helmeted in white. 'Oh mercy, Gawd,' he was screaming. 'Don't let my fortune slide off. Strike that crazy fucker dead at the wheel.'

Toni turned into Madison Avenue, going against traffic. And she kept swerving the truck, her mind in a whirl. She could hear Doll screaming and the men beginning to shoot now – but not at her. They were afraid to shoot her with the truck moving the way it was. There was nothing to do but keep the truck moving and jerking. She couldn't believe, riding high on her last fix, she'd hurt her Ossie. Ossie was her man. How could a loving girl like her possibly break her man's loving neck?

The truck shot back into 112th Street with Giveadamn coming along behind, but not too close. He was expecting to see the whole truck and everybody and everything on it go sky high any minute. He had packed that truck with dynamite from cab to parking lights, and the caps he'd packed in with it were kind of delicate, no matter how carefully he'd cushioned them.

He began to curse Toni and Connie, too. He realized she meant to keep that truck moving until Connie got back. Once on 112th Street, she hit the brakes on the flatbed, threw it into reverse, hit the brakes again and started forward.

Light the fires, was all he could think. And here the goddamn flatbed, with the Doll still riding the Golden Fleece, came raring back at him. He thought he and the panel van were done for, but she hit the brakes and stopped so close he found himself looking straight into Doll's eyes. Then she started forward again and someone came across the top of the van, bounced up over the windshield, sort of flying, scrambling, slid over the roof, and dropped to the pavement behind. It wasn't the Doll; though Doll and his men, all clinging to the machine, trying to save it and themselves, slid to the edge of the rear of the truck and tottered there.

Why, that was Ossie she'd just delivered.

Light the fires.

At ten minutes to ten, Connie sat in her sports car on 115th Street a couple of avenues over. In the middle of the block, where she'd thought she'd find them, were the motorcyclists.

It was a dirty and commonplace side street in Harlem where every apartment had doors bolted with Fox police locks. Some of the motorcyclists were sitting on their bikes. The rest were leaning against stoops or walking around arrogantly, a can of beer in one hand, laughing. They wore leather jackets and blue jeans and hats with tiny glittering visors. Most of them had dark glasses over their eyes on a street already so dark it was hard to see to walk it from end to end. In any other part of New York, the cops would have rounded them up or moved them on for creating a disturbance. But this was safe turf for anything they felt like doing, and, watching them, Connie figured they were getting in the mood for a little fun and trouble.

She had both windows rolled down and she was listening as well as watching and waiting. Then she heard what she'd been waiting for – a lot of rapid fire off in the distance. It sounded a little too rapid, with too many kinds of explosions, for automatic rifle fire. She did not wait for the sky to light up. She opened the door of the car, got out and walked around the corner to the telephone booth. She'd checked out the phone earlier. This phone was working. She dialed 911, the police emergency number.

When a voice answered, she brought her voice up high as if in terror. 'For God's sake, man, there's a maniac running back and forth over a police officer on 112th Street. Right off Park. It's a motorcycle gang at it.'

'Where, lady, where?'

'112th, I said. Between Madison and Park.' Then she screamed and hung up. By now all those thousand dollars' worth of Chinatown fireworks were coming in so clear she thought the cop might have heard them over the phone.

Connie walked slowly back to her car, giving the cops a little time to react. She got in, watched the motorcyclists until she heard the first of the sirens, then drove down the block slowly toward the motorcycle gang as if she were looking for a number on one of the old tenements that lined the street.

When she came up beside the Coke Club members . . . she knew them by sight at least . . . she stopped. She got out. In the glow of the street lights, she knew she looked white. She'd removed the dress so they could see her shape in her jeans. One of the kids grabbed his crotch and yelled, 'Hey, babee – I got everything a blond bitch like you comes to Harlem looking for.'

He was just two steps from her, and she took the two steps slowly, swatted him up across his chops before he knew what was coming, and as he stood there staring, she yelled, 'You nigger shit, you.'

She was back in her car before anyone had moved. When they did move, it was for their bikes – because the hawk was going, going, gone. She slowed down around the corner for the first of them to catch up, then took off again. They had never seen a car go like hers. Was she a woman, driving like that? Once they thought they had her, but she was gone again, tires screaming.

They were coked up and rolling fast. Connie and the cyclists came careening down Eighth Avenue where police cars were flashing by with lights swirling and sirens wide open. The hawk took the red light at Lenox Avenue doing fifty, the motorbikes right behind her.

She put the accelerator down. A couple of the C.C. Riders were shooting now. Wild shots, as if they didn't care whether they hit her or not. Too coked up to care. Or like maybe she was a president's daughter. Right on, man. Whoo—ee.

At 112th Connie took the corner at top speed, hit the brakes and took the car in a graceful slide right up beside Giveadamn's panel van. She seemed to step out of the car at the exact end of the skid. An oil drum with a blinking red light on top of it tipped over.

She looked around. The whole block looked like a gangway to hell. The C.C. Riders arrived, skidding into a barrage of bullets the police laid down across their path. The cops were shooting at anything in leather jackets, and the cyclists still in the saddle rode right into them, shooting back.

As soon as Sonny Roberts parked the car, he heard the sirens. He grinned. He let out a sigh. 'Sounds like we're late,' he said, 'but I like that.'

'Like what?' one of his men asked.

'Being stylishly late. Keep people waiting and it gives you a real entrance.'

'Them's cops' sirens, Sonny.'

'I likes to deal right under the nose of the law. Shee-it! What you think? I pays and I pays good. If I'm buying, I want some law right behind me to make sure I don't get robbed. Only thing is . . .' he stopped grinning. '. . . This thing we gonna steal tonight is too big for a white boy's imagination. We don't want no hungry law running around tonight.'

It was at this moment the sky ahead of the men exploded into bright patches of streaming light, fiery tentacles reaching out everywhere across the sky; further bursts of fire and light popped loose at the tips of the tentacles. Ka-bam. Ka-bam. Whoosh. Bam.

Sonny and all his men stopped to marvel.

'That crazy Giveadamn,' Sonny said. He shook his head. 'Best be cautious now. Get out your pieces and walk behind me the way I'm going. Don't catch up. Walk slow. Four on this side of the street and four over there.'

Connie and Giveadamn crouched beside the stoop between the panel truck and Jimmy's limousine. Toni had got the flatbed stopped and was running toward them. The street was blazing, fireworks popping. The farm woman's dress flapped around her legs. If any guns were firing, it was hard to tell, and if anyone was shooting at Toni, she didn't care.

Doll's men weren't shooting. They stood on the back of the flatbed gazing around them, big-eyed and half-paralyzed, their rifles gone, lost on the wild ride. Doll Baby himself still clung to the top of the machine. He was crying and bellowing, his eyes squeezed shut with the mightiness of the misery and the abuse he was suffering. The machine's light illuminated him in its unholy glow.

'Connie?' Toni said heavily, panting. 'I thought you'd never get here. Where'd all those motorcycles come from?' Then she saw Ossie. He lay on the sidewalk where they'd pulled and carried him. His head was bloody. He was still only half-conscious. She grabbed his limp hand and looked at him, not just worried now, but scared. She started to cry, 'Oh, Ossie, Ossie . . .'

Connie said, 'What the hell you put in those goddamn oil drums? You've damn near set all creation on fire.' Her wig lost, she looked more like her stern self.

'It's just alcohol,' Giveadamn said. 'Won't burn much.'

'The hell it won't.'

Another busload of police drove right up to the barrier and began firing into the flames like stoned idiots.

Two fire trucks had wheeled up down at the far end of the block, and they were throwing water that made the fires burn brighter. At the other end of the block, Connie thought she could spot Freddy Morris with a walkie-talkie in one hand.

Connie laughed. 'A whole lot of people could get killed in this shit.'

And then the big flatbed truck with Giveadamn's contraption still riding on back, all its colored tubing aglow, began to move again. Doll Baby rode the top of the machine, his arms wrapped around it as if he'd married it. The rest of his men huddled below, hanging on. Little Joe was at the wheel.

Toni started to move. Giveadamn grabbed her arm. 'Let him have it.' He got up and moved in a crouch over to the open door of the panel van, got in and grabbed for the green box on the dashboard. He let Doll and the flatbed get down near the corner where it was picking up speed to shoot between the fire trucks. He clicked the switch.

About forty yards from the corner, the truck, the Golden Fleece on its concrete base, Doll, all Doll's men, everything, went up in the air with the biggest boom of the night. It was an eye-splitting sight to behold. The big truck bucked backwards, end over end, and the machine, Doll still astride it, all its lights blazing, rose some seventeen feet in the air, and when it all came down, the night sky was spraying men.

The machine turned end over end a couple of times and came down in a long arc like a minicomet smack on top of the panel truck where Giveadamn sat. Smashed it flat, but held the Golden Fleece intact. The van showered glass along with Doll Baby's final cry of rage. Then stillness.

Every gun on the street grew silent, cops and black killers alike. It was like an armistice called in awe before a holy sight.

Just before the truck blew ... the truck, the Golden Fleece, Doll Baby and his men, and every Harlem junkie's dream ... Jimmy Adams sat watching the street from a first-floor window. When things began to get hot, he and his men had commandeered an apartment. Its legal occupants were huddled on the floor back in the kitchen. Jimmy sat in a wingback chair in his lamb's-wool-collared coat. He had carefully drawn up the knees of his trousers to protect their crease. He looked worried. But he was mostly worried about his limousine. The whitey chauffeur had either fainted or run for it, because flames were heading toward the car and nobody was moving it. Hadn't even started the motor. Didn't the girls have enough sense to move the car? They knew what he was carrying in the trunk.

So he didn't see Toni scoot from the flatbed over to Connie and Giveadamn, but he heard the flatbed blow sky high and turned his head in time to watch it in flight.

He groaned.

He saw the heroin still, the Doll atop, his bandaged head like some kind of saintly halo, rise, rise, rise, and turn, as if Doll were riding a tiny star all his own. He watched in horror as it fell. Down it dropped on the roof of the panel van.

Once more Jimmy groaned and put his head in his hands. He had felt that crash as if the machine had come down on his own head. He'd have felt no worse if it had. When he looked again, he saw the machine was spitting forth little cellophane sacks. They were popping out from what seemed the Doll's thick legs, as if in death he was having the biggest, longest orgasm of his life.

He could only look back at his limousine when he sensed it starting up. It took an effort. He saw Ossie was up on his feet. Toni was helping him into the back seat. He had not seen

Giveadamn climb out unscratched through the popped windshield of the panel van and climb into the limousine beside Connie. He could see Connie, not his chauffeur, sitting at the wheel. His first thought was, 'Smart girl. She'll move it.'

What he saw next was Sonny Roberts and Sonny's men blocking Connie's way.

'We got no place to run,' Toni said. She hugged closer to Ossie. He was beginning to come around.

'I think we can run right over those dudes,' Ossie said. 'They belong to Sonny Roberts. He's not out here to waste anybody.' They were squeezed in the back with Jimmy's three girls.

Then Connie saw Sonny. He was just up ahead. 'Let's see what he's got to say anyway,' she said. 'Looks like we'll have to.'

Sonny was walking, but then he stopped walking and did a little jig – and that made sense because a lot of bullets were hitting him in rapid order. Then his six men started a dance of their own that ended when they hit the ground where some of them went on dancing.

'Jimmy Adams,' Connie said calmly. She turned to look into the back of the car and snapped at the girls, 'All your bags are in the trunk, right?'

The terrified girls nodded.

'Toni,' Connie said, 'kick one of those whores outa here. Now.'

Toni grabbed the nearest girl and got her out, but it wasn't easy. The girl kicked and fought. Connie went over the seat to help. Ossie was weak, but his bulk alone did some good.

Then Connie was back behind the wheel, had the car in gear and the clutch out. Behind her, one of the two girls was sobbing, 'I'm Jimmy's niece.'

Connie took the turn at the end of the block and snorted, 'Hah. Shee-it.'

Beside her, staring gloomily ahead, Giveadamn said, 'I blew everything. I blew it. I lit up the fires too soon.'

'You did just fine, Giveadamn.'

'Naw, I messed us all up.' He had not said a word until

now, not since he'd climbed out of the smashed van and got into the Rolls. Mostly he was hurting too much to speak. Crisis was getting nearer. At first he'd thought he was shot all apart, but he'd come out of that van without a mark on him. There were just bits of broken glass in his hair and down the back of his collar. 'I really messed us all up good,' he said and felt around for bits of glass.

He glanced at the speedometer. Connie was driving an even fifty . . . then she kicked the accelerator. The car spurted toward a street light that was just changing. They went skidding around onto 115th Street, then shot west until they came to Fifth Avenue. She turned left and dropped the Rolls back to sixty. Parked cars and entrances to apartments were wheeling past on each side.

The pain hit Giveadamn again, got a grip on his guts and twisted, twisted so hard he wished the machine hadn't missed him. Why had he been spared? For what? To die going sixty miles an hour through the streets of Harlem? Maybe she could let him out till he felt better. Pick him up later.

Giveadamn turned and looked back, through the clustered shoulders and heads.

'Anybody on our tail now?' Connie asked.

There were so many headlights behind them, Giveadamn guessed he could say anybody and everybody's brother was back there. It looked like at least six sets of headlights, all racing each other. 'Sure is,' he said.

Connie hunched lower over the wheel and took the red light at the corner of Fifth Avenue and 110th Street. Again she hit the floor with the gas pedal. They lurched on and in a minute or so Toni reported only one car following them. Connie took about four fast turns, but the car hung behind. She turned into Central Park, ripped up some meadow grass, came out a far entrance, and the car was still behind her. Who in hell could it be? Back toward Harlem she went.

It was Jimmy Adams – close on their tail – just sticking with her at first, now tailing her in earnest. He was in one of his pseudo-gypsy cabs. They could pass anything. And his best driver sat behind the wheel.

Jimmy was scowling. He was scowling murderously. That bitch Connie was gambling. And with his dice. What the fuck did she think she was up to?

Jimmy leaned forward. 'I got me an idea the dame got no place special to go. At least as long as we're on her tail, she ain't going nowhere but round and round. I betcha on that.'

The driver laughed. He was big and young. 'Looks like she knows all these streets. We might try herding her away from Harlem.'

'Try it.'

The gypsy cab cut down the distance between it and the Rolls. It was harder to do than the driver expected. The Rolls was souped up too.

Near Eighty-fifth Street the cab was neck and neck with the limo. Then the cab started pulling to the right, crumbling the Rolls's left fender.

Jimmy reached under his jacket and got out a 45 automatic, but he put it back again. 'Careful,' he said, 'that car's carrying cash and thirty keys of heroin. I want it all intact.'

'You'd think we'd have picked up some squad cars by now!'

'They either recognize this cab or everyone's over on 112th Street. Take it easy, I said.'

Connie swung back into Central Park. The police were on her mind, too. Back out of the park on 110th Street – still no police had seen her and the flying Rolls. The gypsy was still behind. She took the light. She had to. The gypsy took the light too, but it glanced off a passing bus. Stopped for a moment. Backed up and started after them again. By that time Connie had turned off Lenox onto a side street. She had a one-block lead on the gypsy. She thought. Jimmy Adams had picked up a mike in the back seat and was calling the twin of his gypsy cab.

'I blew everything,' Giveadamn said.

'Giveadamn, will you just shut up?' Connie gave the wheel a tug and turned into 116th Street. They almost went over on their side, but she gave the Rolls more gas and the car straightened. The light turned green as they hit Park Avenue and Connie floored the pedal again. Behind them, the back seat was quiet. Nobody had anything to say.

'Can you get away?' Giveadamn asked.

'I can ... I think,' Connie said. Her voice was low, pleasant, a little reflective. 'Are you holding up?'

'Not good,' he said. 'I'm feeling real bad.'

At eighty, Connie knew, a car could make all the lights on 116th Street. She seemed more relaxed as the Rolls headed crosstown. They passed Eighth Avenue, still doing eighty, but she was easing up; then to Giveadamn's as well as Jimmy's surprise, she took a wide turn into Manhattan Avenue, the wrong way. At a leisurely fifty-five, she took a left at the next two intersections.

She was back on 116th Street, but turning again to head down Eighth Avenue. Giveadamn had the feeling, speeding along that wide avenue, that everything he was seeing, addicts, gun-carrying studs, was all on film and the end of the film was coming up fast. After the end, no more.

'Connie, I'm not going to make the bus trip.'

'I been watching you,' she said. 'But Giveadamn, if I let you out now, you're finished. I got a good idea Jimmy don't want to shoot this car up, but on the street any of us he finds is finished.'

The gypsy cab had picked them up again. Connie slewed into 116th Street and raced over to Lexington Avenue. The cab hung behind, but its headlights were wavering eerily.

Ossie said, 'When they hit that bus, I think they knocked the front end out of line. If they did, that driver can't keep it on the road if, say, we get up to eighty again.'

Connie sped on. The Devil in Hell had his foot in the gas tank. She glanced in the mirror. Two cars were in the chase now. It figured. She didn't know how Jimmy did it, but that other car had been called in and found them. She glanced at the clock again and said, 'I got an idea.' She was back to 116th and Park. The cab was still half a block behind. Where had the second cab gone? Lost? Cracked up? No, here it came again. Good.

She roared up Park doing seventy-five. The two cabs were following side by side, as if it were a point of pride with both not to let the other get the lead. She held steady and knew the Rolls, a heavier car than theirs, was taking the bumps better. She smiled. She let them come up behind her, then made one of her daring swoops to the left, holding onto the wheel in a grip that never shook or wavered. Again she twisted the wheel, this time to the right, and the car skidded in an almost perfect line up a narrow alley between two dark buildings. The two cabs came behind her, side by side, swinging into the alley on special torsion bars. They slammed into each other and bounced off the brick sides of the buildings. Tires screamed. Metal crunched. One of the cabs had piled up, but the other was still coming, but not for real; rubber smoking from the right-front wheel and a bent fender said it all.

At the end of the alley, Connie turned the corner. Nothing was behind any more. Connie stopped. 'Okay, girls – out. Fast.' And they moved fast, scrambling over each other to get out.

'How you feeling now, Ossie?' Connie said.

'Coming around.'

'Can you do some climbing?'

'If I need to. Why?'

'We got to ditch this car. Jimmy could be on his cab radio right now.'

She drove about fifteen blocks, pulled into another alley and stopped. Giveadamn sat slumped against his door, holding his gut. His eyes were shut and his lips were pulled back so tight from the pain, his upper and lower teeth were gleaming. Connie switched off the car lights. She heard Ossie and Toni stirring in the back seat. She nudged Giveadamn. He grunted but never opened his eyes.

'Let's move,' Connie said. 'I think you'd all rather be killed softly, gently, than get it the hard way with this car-stealing bitch at the wheel.'

Ossie opened the door on his side but didn't move.

Giveadamn was sitting up now, blinking. Then he got out. He looked steady. He seemed all right. Connie got out and came around beside him.

'You're a block and a half from cab traffic, Giveadamn,' she pointed up the alley. 'Think you can make it?'

He nodded.

'You're going to be all right, Giveadamn. You're a tougher sonofabitch than I ever gave you credit for. If any of us are going to make it, you are.'

He grinned, but he was still hurting too much to say anything.

'You got four million safe in your name, and we ought to have us that much in the trunk of the car, but where we're going I ain't going to try to get in touch with you. That would be dumb.' She put her hand on his arm. 'Just one day, I'm going to turn up. Understand?'

He nodded.

'Now I mean it. So you keep up that habit of yours, taking one more breath and one more breath, till I get back. Meanwhile, don't try to put that goddamn machine together again. I don't think anybody's left alive to buy it who'd want it.'

Giveadamn mumbled something.

'What? The CIA?' Connie laughed. 'They'd be just dumb enough. Another time, Giveadamn.' She kissed him quickly.

Giveadamn started up the alley, and when she could barely see him moving in the darkness, she went back to the car and helped Ossie out. Toni pushed from behind. Ossie was unsteady on his feet.

Connie and Toni walked back to the trunk. 'Let's try these keys,' Connie said. The third key unlocked it. 'Six suitcases in all,' Connie said. 'See what they got.' She tried to examine each as they lifted them out, but they were locked. 'Okay, Ossie. How you doing?'

He nodded.

'Everybody take two,' Connie said.

They trudged up the alley the way Giveadamn had gone. There was no sight or sound of him ahead. Connie, in the lead, called back, 'You okay, Ossie?'

Ossie seemed not to hear, but the two women were thinking the same way: as long as Ossie followed, he was all right.

'Hear that?' Connie said. From the distance came the sounds of a down-home hallelujah-shouting congregation having a soul-revival hymn sing. 'We're close now.' She grunted. 'Seems like they should be singing *One More River to Cross.*'

Coming out of the alley, Giveadamn was staggering. A taxi had just pulled up at a bar down the street. He got there in time to open the door for the girl in back. She got out wrapped in white fur, looking him over nervously. He knew she thought he was drunk. So did the driver, but he got in and fell back on the seat.

At St Luke's he handed the driver a twenty, waved off the change, and made it to the hospital door before he stumbled. The driver was leaning over him. 'Hey, buddy, hey. Here, let me get you.'

The two of them made it inside.

Toni pulled off her dress and wrapped it around her neck like a scarf, the way Connie told her to.

They waded through the rubble, broken glass and garbage to a tall wire fence. Connie dropped her bags and climbed to the top, just below the barbed-wire topping.

She called down, 'Toni, see if Ossie still got that wirecutter.'

Toni frisked Ossie like a pickpocket in a hurry. She found the cutters and handed them up to Connie who was leaning down dangerously.

Toni gaped up in wide-eyed awe. Connie was doing in the dark of night, practically blindfolded, what the boys at school emptily bragged about.

'Okay,' Connie called. 'Hand me the bags.'

When the first suitcase was handed up, Connie tried to open it. The bag was locked.

She hung the bag by its handle on a metal rod that had supported the barbed wire. Then she leaned down even more precariously than before.

'Toni!' she said. 'Give me your shiv.'

Connie leaned over, one arm extended, while Toni took a kind of jump shot toward her with the hilt of the knife up.

226 | Robert Deane Pharr

Connie got it. Using the knife and the wirecutters, Connie opened the first bag. It held clear plastic bags of pure heroin.

Connie tossed them from her.

It was only when the bags took so long hitting the ground that Toni realized that on the other side of the fence was an excavation. She reached for Ossie's hand and began to pray.

All the suitcases were handed up. The ones with heroin Connie opened, slit, and tossed into the pit. The ones with money were another thing altogether.

The fence on the far side had a narrow footing between it and the hole in the ground. Connie had to take each bag, lower herself as near the ground as possible, then gently drop the bag of money so it rested securely on the ledge of the pit.

It was time for Ossie and Toni to climb the fence. Ossie was last, so the two girls could help with one hand if Ossie began to tumble. Ossie made it, but doing it, Connie saw it was Ossie's ankle, not his head, that was his problem. His head and his face were wet with blood, his hair clotted.

Now the girls went single file once more, along a narrow strip of ground, each toting a heavy bag. Ossie managed better now without a bag. He was, they knew, in real pain. Connie also knew the least bit of commiseration might make him give up and tell them to go ahead without him.

At the end of the fence, Connie turned, carefully placed her bag down, and once more climbed the fence. Again she went through the business of cutting barbed wire.

It was hard to see, but she stood teetering almost on the very top iron bar of the fence. Then she leaped and caught the ledge of the gutter that ran along the edges of the roof of the next building. It was a cinderblock building, approximately one and a half stories high. It had been many things in its day. Now it was a warehouse, packed and jammed with stolen booty, the property of Doll Baby's estate. The warehouse might remain closed for fifty years until someone in the tax office realized that no one had claimed ownership.

The moment Connie jumped for the gutter, a trio of dogs began to snarl and growl at the foot of the fence. Connie yelled down for Toni to take a position on the top of the fence to catch the bags as Ossie tossed them up, then relay them to her. Both girls wondered if he could make it. He did.

Pleasant memories of long ago. Connie had done this as a kid, and she wondered if she had aged as much as she sometimes felt. It had been fifteen years since she and Boots had negotiated this trail with the cops on their butts. A ghetto childhood has its values.

Ossie had made it up the fence, but he seemed befuddled by the height still ahead of him.

There was an iron pipe imbedded in the roof. It was somebody's excuse for an exhaust pipe for his whiskey still. It could be rotted through by now. But Connie remembered.

She told Toni to lie down with both arms hugging the pipe. Then Connie lay on her back and grasped Toni's ankles. Her legs dangled about two feet over the edge of the roof.

Ossie saw Connie's feet come over the ledge.

'You got to jump and catch my legs, Ossie. You can do that, can't you?'

He jumped. He caught Connie's ankles, but he was so sore and weak and dizzy that he could hardly hold on. The dogs waited below for his body to drop.

'Put your feet against the building and walk up,' Connie urged. 'Climb.'

He did. He made it.

On the roof he gazed at Connie.

'We ain't so old, after all,' he said roughly.

Connie punched his arm, then turned. She walked lightly, confidently, swinging her hips.

On the other side of the building was a tenement. It was only a two-foot drop from the roof to the second-floor fire-escape landing. They went up the fire escape to the roof and crossed over to come down the fire escape on the other side. The singing of the revival meeting was clearer now. Then it stopped and a lone voice was raised to God.

The song and the shouted words of the jackleg preacher formed a fitting background for all this crap, Connie decided.

When they got on the ground, they went to the back of the

church and huddled there in the darkness. Toni put her dress back on.

Connie looked at her wristwatch. It was almost eleven-thirty. She looked at Ossie, 'What you got on underneath?'

It took him a moment to realize she was talking about his coveralls. 'Nothing,' he said. 'Just my underwear.'

Connie shrugged. 'I don't think Jimmy can figure this one out anyhow,' she said. 'But if he does, it's you he's going to see first. Next time we do this, don't wear white.'

She went to the alley that ran alongside the church. The building had a false front that made the alley a dead end. It did not faze Connie. There were stairs built like a stile that led up to a side door. They followed her up the stairs. The door was unlocked. They walked into the empty church, Ossie limping. They found a bathroom and waited while Ossie washed the blood off his face, then they went down the aisle to the front door. Outside, carrying the suitcases they inched into a throng composed mostly of women and children. Everyone was dressed in farm clothes like Connie, Ossie and Toni. Grandmothers and grandchildren it seemed. Young mothers were there and only a few men.

The four of them could hardly get through the crowd, but the same crowd was no problem for the minister. He was young, dapper in a snow-white gabardine suit. He was preaching, preaching and praying in turn. As he appealed to God, he would dart full speed in one direction only to spin on his toes and run in another. Every time he darted hither and yon, a river of space in the throng opened miraculously for him.

The sisters were punctuating his prayers and his exhortations. The holy man was telling his congregation the Lord would provide. *The Lord had promised!*

Then he lifted his head and talked to the Lord, reminding Him of his promise.

Connie got through the throng. Ossie and Toni followed. There were three Greyhound buses parked at the curb. Connie went to the first. All three drivers were sitting inside, waiting. They were used to lateness when it came to black church excursions.

Connie rapped on the glass in the door. A driver opened it. She looked a hell of a lot saner to the driver than this screaming congregation.

By then Giveadamn was in Harry's room. He was shooting the rapids of his pain and staring in amazement at Harry's open eyes. As he had stepped into the room, he had seen Harry's gaze upon him and Harry had watched him, actually watched him, half-walk and stagger to the chair beside the bed.

Little Miss Howard, who came into the room a few minutes later, wasn't at all surprised to see Giveadamn. The hospital had been in an uproar all day, doctors going in and out of the room. The patient had spoken his first words. Young Mr Brown must have come straight from work, because he was in overalls, and she had never before seen him in overalls.

Harry's eyes were still open. His fingers were moving. She stepped into the room. Giveadamn turned in his chair to look at her. He seemed to be shaking.

'Mr Brown, are you all right?'

'He spoke . . . he just spoke.'

And from the bed Harry said again, clearly, 'Fuck you too.'

Payback Press

s an independent imprint within Canongate Books focussing on black
culture and black writing. The list features some of the most neglected but
mportant voices to come out of urban America this century. Below is the
full list of Payback titles currently in print.

Fiction

BLACK
> Clarence Cooper Jnr. — isbn 0 86241 689 2 — £6.99 pbk

THE FARM
> Clarence Cooper Jnr. — isbn 0 86241 600 0 — £5.99 pbk

THE SCENE
> Clarence Cooper Jnr. — isbn 0 86241 634 5 — £6.99 pbk

THE HARLEM CYCLE VOLUME 1
> Chester Himes — isbn 0 86241 596 9 — £7.99 pbk

THE HARLEM CYCLE VOLUME 2
> Chester Himes — isbn 0 86241 631 0 — £7.99 pbk

THE HARLEM CYCLE VOLUME 3
> Chester Himes — isbn 0 86241 692 2 — £7.99 pbk

PORTRAIT OF A YOUNG MAN DROWNING
> Charles Perry — isbn 0 86241 602 7 — £5.99 pbk

GIVEADAMN BROWN
> Robert Deane Pharr — isbn 0 86241 691 4 — £6.99 pbk

THE NIGGER FACTORY
> Gil Scott–Heron — isbn 0 86241 527 6 — £5.99 pbk

THE VULTURE
> Gil Scott–Heron — isbn 0 86241 528 4 — £5.99 pbk

CORNER BOY
> Herbert Simmons — isbn 0 86241 601 9 — £5.99 pbk

MAN WALKING ON EGGSHELLS
> Herbert Simmons — isbn 0 86241 635 3 — £6.99 pbk

AIRTIGHT WILLIE AND ME
> Iceberg Slim — isbn 0 86241 696 5 — £5.99 pbk

LONG WHITE CON
> Iceberg Slim — isbn 0 86241 694 9 — £5.99 pbk

MAMA BLACK WIDOW
> Iceberg Slim — isbn 0 86241 632 9 — £5.99 pbk

TRICK BABY
> Iceberg Slim — isbn 0 86241 594 2 — £5.99 pbk

PANTHER
> Melvin Van Peebles — isbn 0 86241 574 8 — £7.99 pbk

ONE FOR NEW YORK
> John A. Williams — isbn 0 86241 648 5 — £6.99 pbk

SPOOKS, SPIES AND PRIVATE EYES
> Paula L. Woods (editor) — isbn 0 86241 607 8 — £7.99 pbk

Not-Fiction

THE NEW BEATS
   S. H. Fernando Jr. — 0 86241 524 4 — £9.99 pbk

BORN FI' DEAD
   Laurie Gunst — 0 86241 547 0 — £9.99 pbk

BLUES PEOPLE
   LeRoi Jones — 0 86241 529 2 — £7.99 pbk

BENEATH THE UNDERDOG
   Charles Mingus — 0 86241 545 4 — £8.99 pbk

BLACK FIRE
   Nelson Peery — 0 86241 546 2 — £9.99 pbk

BLACK TALK
   Ben Sidran — 0 86241 537 3 — £8.99 pbk

PIMP
   Iceberg Slim — isbn 0 86241 593 4 — £5.99 pbk

THE NAKED SOUL OF ICEBERG SLIM
   Iceberg Slim — isbn 0 86241 633 7 — £5.99 pbk

SWEET SWEETBACK'S BAADASSSSS SONG
   Melvin Van Peebles — 0 86241 653 1 — £14.99 hbk (includes CD)

Call us for a free **Payback Sampler** which gives you more information on all the the above titles. The sampler also contains extracts from our most recent publications together with information about the authors. It is a great little booklet that fits in your pocket and gives you a broader taste of what we publish. Check it out!

Alternatively, if you are hooked up to the internet, look for the Payback Press website where you will find all the latest publication details, extracts from the books and author biographies.

Our books are available from all good stores or can be ordered directly from us:

PAYBACK PRESS
14 HIGH STREET
EDINBURGH EH1 1TE
tel # 0131 557 5111
fax # 0131 557 5211
EMAIL canongate@post.almac.co.uk
WEBSITE http://www.canongate.co.uk

All forms of payment are accepted and p&p is free to any address in the UK.